Praise for
The Bangalore Detectives Club

"Told with real warmth and wit, in *The Bangalore Detectives Club*, Harini Nagendra has created an intricate and fiendish mystery with a wonderful duo of amateur sleuths Kaveri and Ramu at its heart, and capturing the atmosphere and intensity of Bangalore in the roaring twenties. I can't wait for the next instalment. A perfect read for fans of Alexander McCall Smith and Vaseem Khan."

—Abir Mukherjee, London *Times* bestselling author of *Smoke and Ashes* and the Wyndham and Banerjee series

"From page one we plunge into the exuberant cacophony of 1920s Bangalore, right there beside Kaveri Murthy in her adopted city: the drawing-rooms and dirt lanes, the gardens and brothels, the temples and jails. Nagendra's depiction of an awkward but tender new marriage is a delight, and who couldn't help but cheer for Kaveri as she swims in her sari, studies in secret, and commits herself to the pursuit of justice?"

—Catriona McPherson, author of *The Mirror Dance*

"A classic whodunnit with the added appeal of a female sleuth in colonial India. For the Western reader, a fascinating glimpse into customs and a mindset very different from our own."

—Rhys Bowen, *New York Times* bestselling author

"I absolutely adored *The Bangalore Detectives Club*, a beautifully painted picture of a woman's life in 1920s India. Kaveri is a compelling character, headstrong, clever and dogged, and not at all deterred by the constraints of her position and gender. A fantastic book."

—M. W. Craven, award-winning author of *The Curator*

"This lush mystery will transport you to heady 1920s Bangalore, where new bride Kaveri stumbles into sleuthing—while dragging her doctor-husband into the fray. Mouth-watering fashion and food set against simmering colonial intrigue in this delicious whodunit can be devoured in one sitting."

—**Sumi Hahn, author of** *The Mermaid from Jeju*

"I loved *The Bangalore Detectives Club* mostly because I love Kaveri and Ramu and exploring 1920s Bangalore through their eyes. Kaveri especially is charming and practical and despite her age and inexperience, she uses her position—as a doctor's wife and as a woman who can speak to women who wouldn't speak to a man—to clear an innocent and expose a murderer."

—**Ovidia Yu, author of** *The Cannonball Tree Mystery*

"Set against the turbulent backdrop of 1920s India, *The Bangalore Detectives Club*, Harini Nagendra's absolutely charming debut mystery, features amateur sleuth Kaveri, a young doctor's wife with a head for solving puzzles. The richness of the setting, the finely woven plot, fascinating characters, and lots of period details add up to a series opener that will keep readers wanting more. This one is a winner!"

—**Connie Berry,** *USA Today* **bestselling and Agatha-nominated author of The Kate Hamilton Mysteries**

"*The Bangalore Detectives Club* is the latest entry into the recent flowering of India-based crime fiction. Nagendra's novel introduces us to Raj-era 1920s Bangalore and her calculus-loving amateur sleuth Kaveri Murthy. A cozy mystery that warmly illuminates a time and place not often examined in fiction."

—**Vaseem Khan, author of the Malabar House series and the Baby Ganesh Agency series and CWA Historical Dagger winner 2021**

THE
BANGALORE
DETECTIVES
CLUB

ALSO BY HARINI NAGENDRA

Nature in the City: Bengaluru in the Past,
Present and Future

Cities and Canopies: Trees in Indian Cities
(*co-written with Seema Mundoli*)

So Many Leaves
(*co-written with Seema Mundoli*)

THE
BANGALORE
DETECTIVES
CLUB

HARINI NAGENDRA

PEGASUS CRIME
NEW YORK LONDON

THE BANGALORE DETECTIVES CLUB

Pegasus Crime is an imprint of
Pegasus Books, Ltd.
148 West 37th Street, 13th Floor
New York, NY 10018

First Pegasus Books cloth edition May 2022

ISBN: 978-1-63936-159-5

10 9 8 7 6 5 4 3 2 1

Printed in the United States of America
Distributed by Simon & Schuster
www.pegasusbooks.com

For Venkatachalam Suri and
Dhwani Nagendra Suri, always

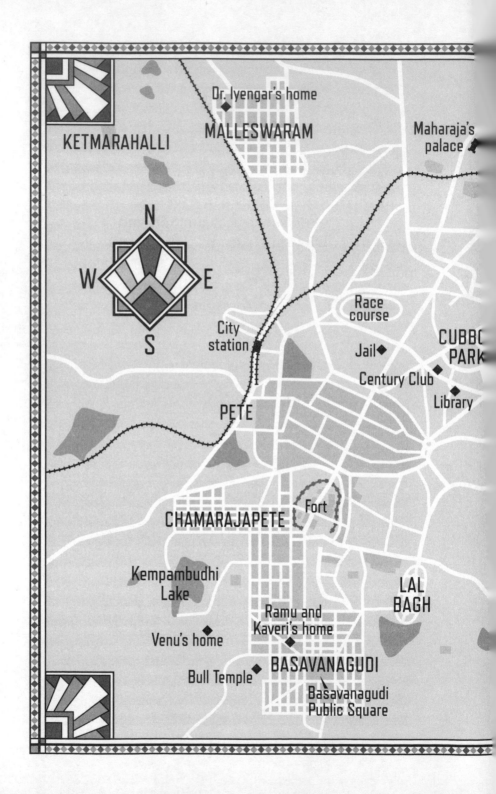

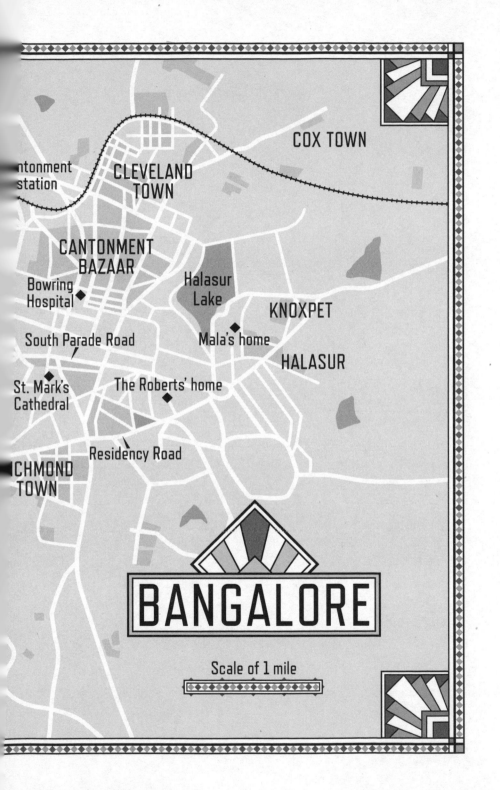

COX TOWN

ntonment
station

CLEVELAND
TOWN

CANTONMENT
BAZAAR

Bowring
Hospital

Halasur
Lake

KNOXPET

South Parade Road

Mala's home

HALASUR

St. Mark's
Cathedral

The Roberts' home

Residency Road

CHMOND
TOWN

BANGALORE

Scale of 1 mile

This story takes place in 1920s Bangalore, so a few of the words may be unfamiliar.

If you don't know them, **Kaveri's Dictionary** on page 272 will tell you what they mean and how to pronounce them. It also explains a bit about the geography and history behind this book.

And read onto **Kaveri's Adventures in the Kitchen** on page 274 for some delicious Indian recipes, adapted to modern times and inspired by the food in *The Bangalore Detectives Club*.

'Instinct is a marvellous thing. It can neither be explained nor ignored.'

—Agatha Christie, *The Mysterious Affair at Styles*

Prologue

Bangalore, August 1921

The stranger was from Majjigepura, the village of butter-milk. He had rented a car and planned to make it to Bangalore by noon, but a punctured tyre had left him stranded on the highway for hours. The vastness and chaos of the city frightened him, and the rapidly sinking sun made matters worse. Only the scrap of paper which he held with an address and a woman's name on it – *MRS KAVERI MURTHY*, Mathematician and Lady Detective – gave him the motivation he needed to abandon the car at the crossroads, proceeding on foot into dark and unfamiliar Bangalore.

All he knew about the detective was that she was a doctor's wife and, praise be to God, she was living in Basavanagudi. Lying just outside the sprawling maze of Bangalore, it was an extension of the city built to solve its overcrowding problem. Its perfect roads were the first thing he noticed, the street signs in Kannada as well as English.

Earlier that day, the man at the Mysore teashop had given him directions on finding his way to Albert Victor Road – the address on the scrap of paper – saying to look out for a statue of the Mysore Maharaja. The stranger had fobbed him off with a cute story about a reunion with a long-lost cousin, and had been sent on his way with a free cup of chai and a smile.

But it was a week after Amavasya – the date of the new moon – and the dull light from the galaxy was barely sufficient to pick his way through the high streets, let alone find an ancient landmark.

Was that it? He could vaguely make out a dark shape in the distance, too tall to be a human being and too short and narrow to be a house.

He hurried towards it and then, amazingly, the moon came out from behind the clouds. Calling out a quick thanks to the gods, he walked towards the statue of a man on a horse, whose features he vaguely recognised as those of the famed ruler of Mysore. He paid him a quick gesture of respect then took the road to the right of the statue, as the teashop man had instructed.

A large house, white, with a neem tree outside, a red compound wall, a large arch covered with scented jasmine creepers, a yard full of fruit trees. Nailed to one of the gateposts was the name plate he was seeking – **Rama Murthy, MBBS**.

The lights were on inside the house, and peering through the open windows he could see bright lamps, cups of coffee being poured, plates of fried snacks passed around. The lady detective seemed to be hosting friends. Of course! He hit his forehead with his palm. It was a Sunday.

He looked to the left, and saw a small shed adjoining the compound wall near the back of the house. From a distance it looked like a storehouse, the old-fashioned kind used to shelve mangoes, coconuts and other large fruit. He crept towards the shed. Perhaps he could shelter there till the guests left.

On closer inspection, he saw that the shed was nothing like the dingy, traditional village storehouse he had been imagining. It was spotlessly white – freshly painted, he realised, as he touched his finger to the still-sticky surface. The wooden door had a large board above it, with English capital letters spelling out a four letter sign –

THE BANGALORE DETECTIVES CLUB

The man carefully pulled open the latch and entered, wincing as it creaked a bit.

He fumbled for a match to light the oil lamp that hung by the entrance, waiting for his eyes to adjust while a yellow glow slowly filled the room.

The shed was stacked to the roof with books. Mostly mathematical. Volumes of arithmetic, trigonometry and calculus dominated two entire shelves. A third shelf, more interestingly, was filled with detective novels. A wooden desk stood in one corner, next to a chair – for visitors like him, he supposed.

A notebook lay on the desktop, neatly bound. The cover was embellished with creepers along all four corners, inked in indigo-blue. On it was written, in neat copperplate handwriting, *The Bangalore Detectives Club: The First Case*. Forgetting his nerves, the stranger from the village of buttermilk settled down in the chair and opened the notebook. The date in the margin read *April, 1921*.

1

Swimming in a Sari

Bangalore, April 1921

Mrs Kaveri Murthy pulled out her oldest sari, nine yards of checked cotton in dark brown. She felt so excited that she wanted to scream, but that would not do, so she resorted to her usual method for calming herself down, which was to make a mental list of all the objective facts at hand. Which were, at this very moment:

She was about to go swimming.

She had not gone swimming in three years.

Back at the Maharani Girls' School, she used to swim all the time, doing laps of the shaded marble pool in the courtyard. That had all stopped once she was married. Her mother had refused to let her entertain the notion, saying it would not do for the wife of a respected doctor to be seen in a wet clinging sari. Kaveri began to realise there were a lot of things that a good married woman did not do.

But she was in a new city now, her mother miles away in Mysore. She remembered herself three months back, an anxiety-ridden bride, travelling north to Bangalore to begin life with her new husband. She had bitten her nails in the carriage and worried that he would find her too tall. Their formal marriage ceremony had taken place three years earlier – a loud explosion of a ceremony with drums and gongs which had left her with tinnitus – but this would be the first time she could call him 'husband' in the true sense of the word. To be able to pad barefoot into the kitchen, still wearing her housecoat, and say, 'Good morning, husband!' Her husband, Doctor Rama Murthy, Ramu to his friends and family.

Her first day in Bangalore she had been unable to rest and did not fancy sitting in silence with her new mother-in-law, nervously drinking cardamom tea and praying she wouldn't accidentally let out a burp or say the wrong thing. Leaving her unpacked bags at the house, she had visited the hospital where Ramu worked and encountered kind, ample-bosomed Mrs Reddy – the wife of another doctor – who had taken her under her wing and told her about the swimming pool at the Century Club.

They had been standing in the shaded verandah of the hospital, fanning themselves.

'What I would give for a dip in a pool!' Kaveri had sighed.

'Do you swim?' Mrs Reddy had turned towards Kaveri, her pencilled eyebrows raised.

'Oh, I used to! My home—' she paused, 'my *parents'* home, in Mysore, used to have a large open well. My father gave us swimming lessons in it. He used to say that I must have been a water-sprite in an earlier life. I used to float in the well for hours when I was a little girl.'

'My dear! I also swam when I was young. Our male servants kept guard around the pond when we went for a swim, keeping their backs to us. Brandishing large bamboo *lathis*, they would swat away anyone who came too close!'

5

'At the Maharani Girls' School, the Maharani – the Queen – gave us access to the palace swimming pool. She strongly believed in the importance of exercise for young women.' Kaveri's face lit up as she remembered those days when she swam and studied and did whatever she pleased, unhindered by rules about married women knowing their 'proper place'.

That seemed to give Mrs Reddy an idea. 'My daughter goes for a swim each Sunday at the Century Club, with the Iyengar girls,' she said. The Iyengar girls were the daughters of another well-respected doctor in town. 'In the mornings, from seven to eight, the pool is reserved exclusively for the use of women.'

'Really?' This all sounded very modern and avant-garde to Kaveri – who was only nineteen, and the daughter of a conservative family.

'Of course,' Mrs Reddy said. 'You're in cosmopolitan Bangalore now, and we're in the 1920s, not some provincial backwater of centuries past. You must ask your husband to bring you next Sunday, and join us.'

'Next Sunday' was here, and Kaveri was humming – albeit under her breath – as she removed her bangles, earrings and chain and carefully deposited them in a golden silk pouch. She took hold of her long, black, braided hair and fastened it in a knot on her head.

Then, grabbing the delicate pleats of fabric in each hand, she hiked her sari up past her ankles, tucking the ends between her legs and tying them into a knot under her petticoat. Catching sight of herself in the long mirror, she giggled. This style reminded her of the advertisement for 'Oriental Harem Pants' she had seen in a glossy English magazine called *Vogue,* one of the souvenirs Ramu had brought home from London after his medical studies.

She normally wore an eight-yard sari in the modern fashion – wound around her lower body, pleats fanning out from her waist – but that would never do for swimming.

She gave herself one last look in the mirror and left the room.

Outside the house, Ramu, waiting for his wife, was also humming to himself. '*Cooo . . . coooo . . .*' he sang, imitating the koel bird that perched on the tamarind tree outside their home, a feathery prediction that heavy rain was on its way. He stood on the steps, hands in his pockets, gazing with pride at the car parked in the portico. The garage had finally returned the beloved Ford, and his servant had set to cleaning it last night, buffing its exterior until it gleamed in the moonlight.

Ramu, who had fallen in love with cars when he was studying in London four years ago, had imported the Model T Ford to Madras then driven it from there to Bangalore in a giddy daze. So when his wife had said she needed to go into town for a most important excursion – which when pressed further she'd admitted was to visit the swimming pool – he was already itching to take his new car for a spin, and eagerly offered to drive her.

The only thing that could drag his eyes away from the shiny Ford was Kaveri, who emerged from the house practically bouncing with excitement, and wearing a costume that looked suspiciously like harem pants.

After seating his wife in the car, Ramu felt a simple pleasure wash over him as he took to the wheel. Most of his friends employed chauffeurs to do this job, but he loved the sensation of driving, the thrill of feeling the magnificent machine moving under his hands, and could not imagine giving it up.

'You didn't tell me you swam,' he said, giving his wife a sideways glance.

'You never asked,' she responded quickly, her lips twitching with a smile that he was starting to become familiar with.

The conversation turned to nostalgia and pleasant reminiscences on their childhood. As she chatted, Kaveri often gazed out of the rolled-down window to take in a sight – the elegant stone balustrades of the Empire Theatre, or a procession of women returned from a *puja* at the temple, the telling sign of a basket with coconuts and flowers in their hands. She had only been in the city for three months and felt as if she would never tire of sightseeing.

Ramu stalled the car at the turning into Cubbon Park. A haven of green, flowering foliage and white statues, it seemed to radiate calm in contrast to the bustling city. He looked at Kaveri with a boyish grin. 'Shall we take a little detour? We have time. It's only just turned six-thirty.'

Kaveri enthusiastically agreed and Ramu began a luxurious long circuit along the park's wide boulevards, skimming massive rain trees and tall statues. They passed an aloof-looking white building, which Ramu explained was the Bowring Institute – home to an elite club which only admitted Europeans.

Kaveri's smooth forehead wrinkled and Ramu couldn't quite tell whether this was from squinting against the sun or a frown. 'But the Century Club – the club we're driving to, with the swimming pool – that's a different sort of place, isn't it? Your father told me about it in one of his letters,' she said.

'Yes, my *appa* was one of the founding members, along with the Dewan of Mysore. It was the first place where Indians could come together to talk, dance, dine. It was a different sort of club, one that would admit everyone.'

Ramu swallowed the lump that was beginning to form in his throat. His father had passed away recently, and he still found it difficult to speak about him. Kaveri patted his hand in tacit support and swiftly changed the subject by pointing to the beautiful St Mark's Cathedral on their left. 'How lovely,' she said, admiring the building, which had been modelled on St Paul's Cathedral in London, with its regal dome and arches.

They drove past the large granite building that housed Blighty's Tea Rooms, famous for its ice cream. 'I have never eaten "iced creams",' Kaveri admitted wistfully. 'Take me some day.'

Ramu grinned, for Kaveri had begun to hum under her breath. She hummed when she was excited, completely unaware that she was doing so. She sounded just like a bee – a tall, happy bee, he thought, then reminded himself to keep his eyes on the road as he drove.

A minute before seven, Ramu dropped Kaveri off at the Century Club. The guard swung open the gate for her and she made for the swimming pool, moving purposefully towards the ladies' changing room.

Inside, she found two young girls giggling on a bench in the corner, their heads close together. They looked up when she entered, then quickly stood up. 'Welcome, Kaveri *akka*,' they chorused, using the respectful *akka*, older sister, to address her. Kaveri was suddenly reminded of the gulf in experience between her and these children, though she was only a few years older.

Lalita Iyengar was about twelve, with thick black eyebrows and a long plait that fell below her knees.

The older child was Poornima Reddy. A girl of about fourteen, her movements were awkward and ungainly as though she was still trying to make peace with her long, coltish limbs. A recent spurt of growth, Kaveri guessed. She herself was quite tall for an Indian woman – five feet and five inches – and her parents had gone to pains to find a husband who would be taller than her. Poornima would also have some difficulty in this department, Kaveri thought, studying her covertly as they took their bags and went into the private changing stalls. You could tell a lot about a woman from her height.

But there was another reason she was staring at the girls. They were fitted with figure-hugging costumes of silk, exposing much more flesh than Kaveri had ever seen on a stranger.

'You should try wearing a swimsuit, Kaveri *akka*,' Poornima suggested, noticing Kaveri's curiosity. 'Swimming in a sari must be uncomfortable. We got these costumes stitched by the Anglo-Indian lady who runs Greens Store. Try it out and see. You'll be able to swim so much faster.'

Kaveri felt her breath catch in her throat at the exciting prospect of wearing something so revealing. Poornima held her hand and dragged her towards the pool.

'It's okay, Kaveri *akka*,' she said reassuringly. 'No men are allowed anywhere near the pool at this time. We can wear what we want, and no strangers will see us.'

Perhaps I should give it a try, Kaveri thought, as she watched the younger girls dive into the water and swim like fish to the other side, racing each other as they darted from the shallows to the deep end.

The girls swam for over an hour. Kaveri was the first one to tire, slowed down by her wet, heavy sari, its cold pleats moving around her uncomfortably and dragging her down as she swam. She changed into dry clothes, tied her damp tresses into a loose plait, and went to explore the gardens, stopping when she found herself confronted by a boundary wall which kept the pool away from the prying eyes of visitors. Kaveri looked around, and spotted an untidy pile of bricks. She dragged them over and made a neat pile of steps, using it to stand and peer over the wall.

Two women, towels tied around their heads to screen themselves from the overhead sun, were squatting in the grass, picking out weeds. A gardener deadheaded roses a few yards away. They were chatting in the Kannada tongue.

'Did you hear the Congress's call to join the strike?' the gardener called out to them. Kaveri had read in this morning's newspaper, the *Daily Post*, that volunteers of the Congress – a political party fighting for India's independence from the British Empire – had called for a mass strike amongst workers next week. Would doctors strike too? Probably not. She knew Ramu was as sympathetic to the Congress's cause as she was, but he worried about the impact on patients if doctors went on strike.

'Hush,' one of the women chided, looking around to see if anyone was listening. Kaveri ducked behind the wall, just in time. 'If anyone hears you, we'll be sacked.'

Kaveri heard the man curse. 'You're as jumpy as a pack of mosquitoes. Not a rice grain of courage in the lot of you. If we want the British to leave India, we have to go on strike. *We* outnumber *them*. If we refuse to work till they agree to our conditions, then we'll get rid of them much faster. But not if we behave like sheep.'

'It's all right for you to say, Ramappa,' the second woman shot back, in a hoarse voice. 'You have no one depending on you. Your children are grown. We have to work, not just to fill our bellies, but those of our children. Our husbands are drunken sots. We have only ourselves to depend on.'

Behind the wall, Kaveri considered this quietly. Large, unruly cities like Bangalore were dangerous places for lone women. But they were equally dangerous for women at the mercy of an abuser – whether husband, parent or lover.

'Besides,' added the first woman, 'we're in Bangalore, not Calcutta. The Maharaja takes care of us, not the *firangi*, the white people.'

Kaveri peeked over the wall again as Ramappa replied. 'The whites rule everything – the Maharaja is just another of their toys,' he said, sweat glittering on his forehead. He flapped a hand at the roses. 'Look at these foreign weeds. Why am I forced to spend my day tending to their flowers, instead of our beautiful jasmine trees? Because there is a party next week, and some white *memsahibs* are coming, that's why. They asked for roses. In *glass vases.*'

He plucked a white blossom that had been growing up a crack in the wall and inspected it with both hands. Kaveri immediately spotted that it was a datura flower – pale, trumpet-shaped, and just about as poisonous as deadly nightshade. 'Why not put *these* in a vase instead. Or better yet, cook them up and serve them to the English women. Let's see how strong their stomachs are.'

The women turned their backs to him, ignoring his passionate talk of poison and murder. Kaveri stared at his back. There was a steel-sharp edge to his voice that made her fear he was not just spinning tall tales to agitate the women. Yet inciting violence at a gathering for the British Raj was tantamount to painful death, or a lifetime in a mouldering cell in Bangalore Central Jail.

She climbed back down, made to leave, then remembered the pile of bricks. *Too obvious,* she decided, and quickly dissembled them in the pile of construction debris in the corner. Rounding the corner to the pool, she saw that she was just in time. Poornima and Lalita had climbed out of the water and were looking around for her, dripping a trail of water along the spotless white stone grounds, their wet hair piled inside white towel turbans.

Once the younger girls had changed clothes and plaited their hair, the three of them made their way to the Century Club dining hall – the swim had left them famished. Their antics in the changing room had melted away any lingering social awkwardness between Kaveri and the girls, and they chatted like old friends as they walked to the club lawns, holding hands affectionately and swinging interlocked palms. Kaveri felt wistful as she remembered early morning walks with her friends to the Girls' School in Mysore, trading stories and jokes, lingering on the way for a snack of roasted peanuts wrapped in a twist of paper from a street vendor or to gaze at a colourful wedding procession. Marriage was nice enough and being married to a husband like Ramu – a promising young doctor from a wealthy and prominent family, chatty and sweet and kind – was especially wonderful. But it wasn't all sweetness and light. She missed mathematics lessons and swimming classes. She hated being lectured about social restrictions, feeling pressure to perfect her lemon rice recipe so she could delight Ramu with hot, delicious plates of ochre tinted rice when he came home from the hospital.

'Ah, there you are!' Mrs Reddy and Mrs Iyengar said, as they made their way to the dining hall. 'We knew you would all be hungry. I placed an order for *dosas*. They are on their way.'

The waiter appeared with a huge plate piled high with the crispy golden pancakes, and Kaveri – now nearly faint with hunger after the swim – had to stop herself from diving into the plate headfirst. Trying to restrain herself in front of Mrs Reddy and Mrs Iyengar – she did not want to run the risk of embarrassing Ramu with tales of his greedy wife circuiting the neighbourhood – she dug into a plate of the dosas, then a steaming bowl of *sambhar*, topping it off with two teaspoons of silky green coriander chutney. The girls gobbled their food down, talking nineteen-to-a-dozen, as the two older women looked on indulgently.

Mrs Reddy, a beautiful sari in a rare shade of elephant grey wrapped carelessly around her ample form, was chattering loudly. Mrs Iyengar was much quieter. She had a prominent dimple in the middle of her sharp chin, which became visible when she gave one of her rare smiles. Though she looked intimidating in her expensive sari, with diamonds sparkling at her ears and throat, Kaveri had liked her on sight. She liked her even more now, as her quiet features lit up at their conversation, Mrs Reddy arguing for the importance of promoting sports to young women, the need for them to be able to dress however they liked, without the restrictions on modesty that 'proper' society imposed.

Full of dosas, and pleasurably exhausted, they all flopped back in their wicker seats. Mrs Reddy's spectacles had slipped down the bridge of her nose during their lively conversation; she rearranged them as she called for more water. The girls ordered banana milkshakes, and Kaveri opted for coffee.

She waited until the waiter had served the drinks and returned to the kitchen before asking, hesitantly, 'Where do you think I could get myself a swimsuit?'

The question had been playing on her mind all afternoon and it was a relief to let it out. After having watched the girls swim with ease while she struggled in her wet cotton sari, which felt like it weighed a ton, she coveted one of those costumes dearly.

Mrs Reddy clapped her hands delightedly. 'I'll take you shopping,' she offered breathlessly. 'I love that Greens store. They have the most beautiful silks in every colour of the rainbow – a bit of a burden on the money pouch, but oh, so superior! I want to pick up a few things for my daughter as well. Come visit us any day next week, I'll be happy to take you.'

Kaveri accepted this offer gratefully, although she was already starting to feel slightly nervous about the prospect of broaching this subject with Ramu's mother. What would her mother-in-law think if she saw her wearing a slinky costume that clung so tightly to her bosom, and left her neck and arms bare for everyone to see? Would she object? The Iyengar girls moved through the water, and through life, so much more freely than she did.

Did Lalita and Poornima have dreams of their own, she wondered, that they hid from their mothers beneath their girlish boisterousness and laughter? And what would happen to those dreams once they satisfied their mothers' nightly prayers and secured themselves wealthy, highly esteemed husbands?

While the group sipped their drinks and chattered peacefully, her thoughts wandered to darker matters. Just yesterday, she had read a horrific story on the front page of the *Daily Post*. A young man, an up and coming lawyer in Bombay, had hacked his wife to pieces, suspecting her of an affair with an older painter. It turned out that she had only wanted to learn to paint so that she could surprise her husband with a portrait of him on their anniversary. Women's dreams were only as big as their husbands' egos would permit them to be.

2

A Boy in Need of Rescue

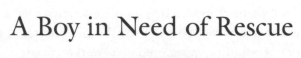

For English people, as Ramu had once told Kaveri, early May is a mild month of shy sunshine and gentle breezes. In Bangalore, it is the middle of the fearsomely hot summer. So it was only to be expected that on this particular afternoon in early May, Kaveri was baking as she made her way through the corridors of the main house, the polished red oxide floor a cool reprieve on the soles of her feet.

Swinging open the heavy front door, Kaveri ran outside to the storehouse. The mud floor had absorbed the heat and she winced as her bare feet touched the searing surface. Dragging the wooden ladder that stood stacked against the wall, she tucked up the folds of her sari into her petticoat, and climbed the rickety contraption into the loft.

When she emerged a few moments later, she was a peculiar sight indeed. She had an exercise book in her mouth, which she was gripping tightly between her teeth as she clambered down the bamboo rungs of the ladder.

It was her mother-in-law's nap time, i.e. the perfect time for Kaveri to take an algebra lesson.

* * *

Ten minutes later, she was deep in thought and frowning over a question at the kitchen table.

If 9 lbs of rice cost as much as 4 lbs of sugar, and 14 lbs of sugar are worth as much as ½ lb of tea, and 2 lbs of tea are worth as much as 5 lbs of coffee, what is the cost of 11 lbs of coffee if 2 ½ lbs of rice cost 6 ¼ d?

She hummed as she worked. All those hours of leaning against her father's knee as he marked his students' calculus papers had certainly paid off, Kaveri thought smugly. She had been as good as any boy in class – in fact, why be modest, *better* – and it was not for nothing that she topped the exam in her school every year. But now she was a married woman, there were no more term-times, no more calculus papers and no more matriculation. If she wanted to study, she would have to do so on stolen time.

She wished her mother-in-law was more supportive of her passion for mathematics, so she would not have to study in secret like this, furtively, like a criminal. Perhaps in time, she could convince Ramu to step in and support her, but she was nervous about telling him – what if he stepped in and forbade her from pursuing the whole business altogether, found it unbecoming for a doctor's wife to spend her afternoons squinting over a dusty book of sums? For now, the algebra books would have to stay hidden in the loft, so that Ramu would not see them when he came home in the evening and be offended.

The sun was low in the sky. As Kaveri carried her exercise book back to the storehouse, she fretted about how slowly she was making progress. At this rate, she would be nowhere *near* proficient by October – which was when she planned to go home for the Dussehra festival and secretly sit the university entrance exam for a BSc in mathematics.

It was eerily quiet in the house today. Their gardener and driver had taken off for three days, to join the Congress call for a mass strike. Ramu had given them his discreet encouragement, and paid them a bit extra, knowing that many other employers, less sympathetic to the cause, had cut salaries to make up for lost manpower. Subramaniam Swamy, the lawyer who owned the large white bungalow at the end of their road, had sacked his gardener, cook and driver en masse when they announced their intention to go on strike. 'Grovelling toady,' Kaveri muttered to herself as she glimpsed his building through the trees.

Their maid Rajamma had smuggled in a parcel of mushroom curry for Kaveri this morning. Kaveri had never eaten mushrooms before – for her family they were forbidden food, for religious reasons. Kaveri looked at her mother-in-law's bedroom window. *Still shut – she's asleep then*. She opened the parcel and ate the curry, mixed with rice, standing behind the large jackfruit tree, making sure she was hidden from sight. She licked the empty leaf after she was done, savouring the unfamiliar, rich flavour. Then grinned as she threw the empty leaf into the compost pit at the back of their garden. There. No one would get upset about what they didn't know, she thought, as she washed her hands and moved back through the garden to the gate.

Manju, their milkman, was late again today – as he had been every other day this week – but he was not on strike. Kaveri knew this because he had a day job at the hospital. Nobody who worked at the hospital could afford to strike, Ramu had said, because their patients needed them.

Kaveri's sharp ears had picked up the sound of cow bells at the far end of the road. Was that Manju? She hoped so. She badly wanted her afternoon coffee and their pantry was out of milk. Kaveri hurried back down the steps to the circular portico that framed the entrance of their house and looked out onto the road, a slim figure draped in mustard silk. Standing just within the gate, framed by a creeper thick with jasmine, she leaned her forehead against the wrought iron rails, waiting for Manju.

But it was not Manju who appeared at the end of the road. It was a young boy – and Kaveri could see even from this distance that he was severely underfed. He wore a grimy piece of cloth wrapped around his waist and an equally grimy vest, but a spotlessly clean towel was slung over his shoulder.

The cow was Manju's. White, with wickedly curved horns and a vicious kick, Gauri was a good milker but did not take kindly to strangers. Kaveri realised that the small boy was Manju's younger brother.

She hurried towards him as he led the large white animal towards the house. 'Venu, what happened? How come you're bringing Gauri – and why so late? What happened to Manju?'

'I don't know, Kaveri *akka*,' Venu said in an odd, flat voice. 'My brother went out in the early morning, saying he had a job to take care of. We waited for him – but now it's four in the evening, and he has not yet returned. Gauri is heavy with milk. My sister-in-law asked me to take her out.'

As he spoke, Venu took Gauri to her accustomed spot near the mango tree, and tied her rope loosely to its trunk. Using the stream of water from the outside tap, he squatted down and cleaned her udders, then efficiently milked her into the clay pot that Kaveri held out to him. As Venu wiped his hands on his loincloth, readying to leave, Kaveri stopped him.

'It's late,' she said, 'stay and have a plate of lemon rice.'

The boy's sad eyes lit up. He jumped to his feet with a small smile, patting the cow's flank as she snorted in confusion.

Back in the kitchen, Kaveri brought out the pot of leftover rice and hesitated over which bowl she should serve it in, her wooden spoon poised in mid-air. Back at her mother's home in Mysore, they had followed rigid caste restrictions. As milkmen were of a lower caste and deemed untouchable, all food was supposed to be served to them in a clay vessel, separate from the banana leaves reserved for upper caste people that Kaveri and Ramu ate their curries and chapattis off. Kaveri had been thrilled to find that her late father-in-law had not believed in hierarchies of caste, forbidding such practices in his house when he was alive. From what she could tell, Ramu agreed – he ate lunch with a mixed group of fellow doctors in the Bowring Hospital, including people from diverse castes and religions. Her mother-in-law Bhargavi's prejudices were a different matter, but she did not dare say much when her son was around.

The dish piled high with lemon rice and ghee, Kaveri went back out to the porch, where she could see the skinny child seated cross-legged in the grass. His ribs were prominent, his eyes enormous as they fixed on the plate. Kaveri felt a pit of anger building in her stomach at the injustice of this situation but she tried to keep her mind on practicalities, plucking a banana leaf from one of the trees to plate up his meal.

Venu waited politely until Kaveri was in a comfortable position on the ground, then began to shovel mounds of rice into his mouth at tremendous pace. The food seemed to stick in his throat, and he struggled with the effort to swallow.

Kaveri settled down opposite him, on the ground. 'Take your time,' she said. Her tone was gentle, but she was impatient. She could not help but notice things in the world sometimes – patterns and abnormalities. They multiplied and repeated in all directions, like random coordinates on a map, begging somebody – begging *her* – to make sense of them. For example, when Manju was late on Monday, and then late again on Tuesday, and then late again on all the following days, she had felt a small knot of curiosity begin to form at the base of her spine. His absence today was making that small knot tingle.

Meanwhile, the meal was bringing a bit of life back to Venu. 'Food is good, thank you, *akka*.' He winked at her cheekily. 'A bit salty though!'

Though she knew he was joking, it hit a nerve. Kaveri was new to running a household and anxious not to disappoint her husband by underperforming in the kitchen. Seeing her face fall, the boy added: 'First time cooking? Don't worry. My sister-in-law – my *athige* – also cooked like this when she first came to our house. Now she is an excellent cook. Even better than my mother.' He flashed Kaveri a quick grin. 'Don't tell my mother though. She still likes to criticise *athige*'s cooking.'

Kaveri rolled her eyes, thinking of her own mother-in-law, who seemed to wait with bated breath for her to do something wrong. She went back into the kitchen for some yoghurt and added it to the rice on Venu's banana leaf to make it easier to eat. He took one bite and gave her the thumbs up before wolfing down the rest.

He rubbed his hands on his dirty vest. Kaveri pointed him to the pail of water near the *tulasi* pot, but he hesitated. Her mother would have been furious at the thought of allowing a milk boy to eat off a banana leaf in the verandah of their house, and apoplectic at the idea of allowing him to touch the pail of water that went into the well, claiming that this amounted to defiling the purity of the well itself. Such nonsense, thought Kaveri, getting fired up all over again.

Kaveri could barely wait until the boy was seated on the ground again before asking, 'Did you not get lunch at home?'

'No, Kaveri *akka*,' Venu said, his eyes firmly on the empty plate. 'We have very little rice at home. My mother and sister-in-law had to eat, so I pretended I was not hungry, and ran out of the house.'

He suddenly raised his head and held her gaze firmly with large brown watery eyes.

'Kaveri *akka*, do you know anyone who can give me a job?'

'Why do you want a job, Venu?'

He rubbed at his eyes fiercely. 'It's for my mother and sister-in-law. I can go without food, but they can't.'

'Your brother has a good job at the hospital, I thought?' Kaveri said, her forehead creasing with concern.

'Yes, things were so good for two years, after Doctor Ramu got him the job, but these days, my brother . . .' His voice trailed off.

'These days, your brother . . .?' Kaveri prompted gently.

His unhappy eyes stared at her out of a gaunt face.

'He doesn't bring much money home. And if we say we are hungry, he . . .' Venu shrugged, and his towel slipped from his shoulder.

Kaveri gasped as she saw the large purpling bruise now exposed on his left arm. Venu flinched at her gentle hand.

She stilled. What could she do for this poor boy? If only she could find Manju now – she would take a broom and beat him around the shoulders until he begged for mercy, she thought grimly. Ramu had muttered something only yesterday about Manju becoming too big for his boots. Wearing expensive shirts and shoes, using perfume, displaying an annoying attitude with patients . . .

As she sat, thinking furiously, Venu licked every last morsel of rice from his leaf.

She gave Venu a reassuring pat, and poured out water for him to wash his hands. After he'd washed up, she sent him around the side of the house to the backyard, to drop the leaf-plate onto the pile of compost in the corner.

'Come back here after you finish your milk round,' she told him when he re-emerged. 'I'll give you a bunch of bananas and some papayas from our back garden. You can take them with you, for your mother and sister-in-law.'

Venu's eyes widened with excitement.

Kaveri watched him as he left, his thin, raggedy frame straining to open the large iron gate, leading Gauri behind him.

Bangalore was a strange city. Large, bustling, seemingly full of opportunity, but caste, job and family status kept people from progressing on merit alone. Of course Mysore's famous Dewan, Visvesvaraya was an exception – a man who'd risen from a life of poverty to become the Prime Minister of Mysore – but he had the advantage of being from a high-caste family, with access to education. How many young cowherds like Venu existed across the city, taking the burdens of their families on their young shoulders while they went hungry? She would ask Ramu to help Venu, she decided. He would know how. And when she found that villain, Manju – she picked up a thorny stick and stabbed it into a banana leaf, slicing it into ribbons as she plotted how she could shake some sense into him.

3

An Invitation to Dinner

Venu's bruised, skinny frame was on Kaveri's mind the rest
of the afternoon. She began to tell Ramu about Manju as
soon as he returned from the hospital but the moment she said
'Manju was late again,' Ramu looked annoyed and said,
'Again? I'll speak to him at dinner this evening.'

'This evening?'

'Yes, the doctor's association is hosting a reception at the
Century Club. Both British and Indian doctors will be there,
along with their spouses.' He smiled affectionately at her.
'Manju will be serving. He wanted some extra money.'

The prospect of a dinner with white men and women at
the club made Kaveri blanch – she had never met them
at such close quarters before. But here was a chance to bring
Manju to justice! She ran into her bedroom to change into
an appropriate sari, not even bothering to close the door
behind her, obsessing over what she would say when she
cornered that brute.

She selected a sari in a delicate leaf green shade, with a red
border, from her wedding collection, and fastened an ornate

ruby necklace – a gift from her mother-in-law, with its Gandabairunda, two headed bird pendant – around her slim throat. Kaveri winced as she felt the sharp hook of the necklace catch in her hair, and put her hand back to release it from her thick plait before placing the hook in the clasp.

'Oh, did the hook catch in your hair?'

Bhagarvi smiled at Kaveri, displaying her large teeth, slightly crooked in front, as she entered the bedroom and closed it behind her. She rearranged Kaveri's necklace so the pendant sat like a medal directly between her clavicles. She fussed with the sari pleats, draping the heavy Kanjeevaram silk around her daughter-in-law's shapely hips. Kaveri stiffened again, as she felt the sari being pulled just a trifle too tight.

'Ouch!' Kaveri said, then remembered herself and smiled between gritted teeth. 'Thank you, *amma*.'

'If I don't make it tight then how will you show off your beautiful figure?' Bhargavi gave her sari one final tug and glided back out of the room. Kaveri breathed a sigh of relief. She surreptitiously tugged at her petticoat, loosening the string just a trifle. Ah, that was so much better. She sighed in relief.

'Kaveri!' Ramu called up loudly from the living room. 'Ready yet? The carriage is here, the driver is waiting.'

'In a minute!'

Their maid Rajamma, who had practically adopted Kaveri once she moved in, looked fondly at her as she came out of the room. A fresh garland of jasmine flowers lay on the side table, wrapped in a banana leaf, sprinkled with water to keep it from wilting in the heat. Rajamma had plucked them from their garden, deftly weaving them onto a length of twine. Now, she helped pin the fragrant strands of white jasmine, glistening with drops of water, to Kaveri's thick plait where it swung gracefully below her hips.

'As beautiful as a bride.' Rajamma cracked her knuckles against the sides of her forehead to ward off bad luck. 'The white ladies will be struck dumb by your beauty.'

Kaveri shook her head and laughed, thinking of the mushroom curry she had pleasurably devoured in the garden, more a grazing animal than a lady.

Bhagarvi, who had reappeared in the doorway like a presiding black crow, looked at her sourly. 'Half the time, I don't know what you're laughing about.'

She followed Kaveri to the staircase, muttering in her wake.

'It must be all that education you had. Too much studying is bad for women, it makes their brain go soft. That's why I never let my girls study too much.'

Kaveri felt she couldn't let this pass without comment. But as she turned back to protest, Ramu called again. 'Kaveri!'

She picked up her sari and ran down the long corridor of the house, past the bay windows with the rays of the setting sun casting long shadows on the ground and down the stairs.

Ramu was placing his timepiece in his coat pocket as she neared, muttering impatiently under his breath as it caught on a thread. When he looked up and saw her, his expression changed. He gazed at his wife, a shapely sprite in soft pastel green silk, with threads of gold and ruby red woven through her sari, ruby bangles at her wrists, and a ruby chain at her neck.

'Will I do?' asked Kaveri, giving him a mischievous smile.

Ramu nodded, his heart in his eyes, as he held out his arm for his wife.

The sun continued setting as Ramu helped Kaveri climb into the ornate Victoria carriage, pulled by two large glossy white Arabian horses, which he had rented for the day. That morning, he had driven their car to the Ormerod garage on

South Parade Road for servicing, instructing them to return the car, once ready, to their Basavanagudi bungalow. The car had been making a strange knocking noise lately, and Ramu thought it safest to get it checked out. He now regretted that decision bitterly. How perfect it would have been if they'd been able to glide into the Club in their car!

Still, he supposed, the carriage would do. After all, none of the other Indian doctors had a car yet.

Kaveri cast sidelong glances at Ramu as she settled into the cart, admiring how handsome her husband looked in his formal three-piece suit and ornate Mysore turban, his classic timepiece with gold fob and chain dangling from his coat pocket. Ramu took it out and squinted at it in the fading light. 'Just in time,' he said with a sigh of relief. 'It won't do to be late. After all, I am one of the main organisers.'

As they settled back in their seats, Ramu adjusted the pile of cushions that Rajamma had placed into the carriage earlier that evening, helping Kaveri to settle herself comfortably against the backrest.

'So, how was your day?' they asked each other simultaneously.

'You go first,' insisted Ramu, his eyes warmly dancing over her face as the horse cart trundled past the wide roads of Basavanagudi, trailed by the smoke from evening meals being cooked on the woodfires by the street vendors at the side of the road, and the satisfied lowing of cattle tied to thick bamboo poles, feeding greedily on piles of grass. Calls of 'Soppuuuu . . . soppppuuuu' and 'KadleeeKAYI! KadleeeKAYI!' filled the air, as vendors of fresh greens and peanuts hawked their wares on carts.

As they were jolted along, Kaveri told Ramu about Venu's visit. 'Why does Manju beat the poor boy?' she asked, her voice rising as she spoke, the memory of the purpling bruises on Venu's scrawny flesh fuelling her indignation.

Ramu sighed. His hospital was teeming with abused women and children. Men beat their wives, younger siblings, children – at times even their elderly parents – simply because they could. And the hospital saw the fallout. Bruised bodies they could heal, at least, but the emotional damage inflicted by these victims of unhappy men, he wasn't so sure about.

'Something strange has happened to Manju in the last month, Kaveri.' The carriage turned a sharp corner, flinging Kaveri against Ramu. He called out a warning to the carriage driver, who pulled on his reins to steady the horse.

He had been going to tell Kaveri about the baffling incident of the previous week, when Manju had approached him after work one evening, rather late, and asked him for a loan. Ramu had stayed late to attend to a patient with appendicitis, and had been mentally preparing himself to spend the night at the hospital if needed. His stomach had been rumbling violently. Stooped over his desk while flicking through the patient's paperwork, he had distractedly called for Manju and sent him out to fetch some bananas.

But as Ramu got up from his desk, he realised that Manju was still standing there, looking at him expectantly.

'Sir – I wanted to ask, sir . . .' Manju stuttered to a halt. He began again. 'I am in debt, sir.'

Ramu tried to keep his face impassive but he could not stop his eyes wandering over his employee, taking in his new clothes and shoes, his expensive watch . . .

Manju shuffled his feet. 'My wife's mother, in Kolar, is unwell. We spent a great detail of money on a treatment for her. I took out some loans from the moneylenders on Main Street in Doddapete, but they are now demanding it back – they sent some ruffians to my home last week and threatened Venu. They said they would beat up my brother and my wife.' His face looked pinched with worry.

'How much do you need?'

'One hundred rupees, sir.'

Ramu's eyebrows raised. Ten months' salary! Manju must be lying. If his mother-in-law in Kolar had indeed fallen sick, all he needed to do was bring her to Bangalore. The hospital would have treated her free of charge. No, the real reason Manju was in debt must be something he was ashamed of, Ramu surmised, most likely a gambling debt. He deserved a curt refusal and a slapped wrist. But what would happen to Manju's family then? Moneylenders had a reputation. They would beat up his brother, rough up his wife and mother, perhaps even kidnap his baby son.

Ramu's heart softened. 'Manju,' Ramu interrupted, pulling out twelve rupees – all the money he had on him – from his wallet. 'Here. I can't give you a hundred rupees but this should tide you over for a month at least.'

Ramu pulled himself back to the present. 'He used to be one of our most hard-working employees, Kaveri,' he told her. 'He worked his way up from an odd-jobs boy to a delivery assistant and eventually to a hospital attendant, learning how to read and write along the way, and picking up the skills needed to tend to patients. He was ecstatic when his son was born a few months back. But he has been slacking off at work. Dr Appia told him that we may have to fire him if this continues.'

'What is he doing at the Club?' Kaveri asked.

'They needed some help with serving the food. His wife Muniamma will also be there, helping to clean the dishes.'

Kaveri sat up straight. This could be the opportunity she was looking for. 'That's perfect!' she announced. 'I'm going to catch hold of him and give him an earful.'

'No, Kaveri,' Ramu cautioned. 'Venu confided in you because he trusted you. If you confront Manju, he will be angry with Venu for telling you. You will only make things worse for them. Leave it to me. I'll keep an eye on him.'

Kaveri didn't think 'keeping an eye' was going to help. But she didn't want to pick a fight with Ramu just before dinner either. She pursed her lips as she sat back in her seat, wishing she had another banana leaf to take out her anger on. *Just let me find that man. I'll take him to a quiet corner, and then ask him to give an account of himself.*

The sultry evening temperature dropped by several degrees as the carriage took a sharp right turn, entering the densely wooded grounds of the Cubbon Park. The hooves of the majestic Arabian horses clopped along the driveway of the Century Club, drawing up at the entrance of the Party Hall. They had arrived.

Kaveri wrapped a fine ruby-red silk shawl around her shoulders and smiled at Ramu as he helped her down from the Victoria. He squeezed her hand, bringing it to his lips. 'Ready?' he asked her. 'Time to socialise.'

'Mmm,' Kaveri agreed, holding his arm. But she was already scanning the grounds for a glimpse of Manju.

4

A Beautiful Stranger

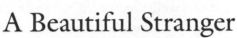

Kaveri's gaze took in every inch of her surroundings. The main hall of the Century Club glowed in the yellow light of the electric lamps, the sturdy furnishings of teak and rosewood offset by the delicate garlands of white jasmine, red roses and orange marigold draped around the pillars like serpents. The lamps were particularly impressive, mounted on tall iron pillars enhanced by ornate cornices and curls.

Outside, the gentle scritch-scritch of a broomstick announced the presence of a gardener, sweeping up the fallen leaves from the grassy lawn where dinner would later be laid out. A servant appeared silently on their left-hand side, bowing deferentially as he helped Ramu out of his coat. Ramu tipped the cart driver, telling him to have a good supper and to pick them up in a few hours. The carriage driver nodded cheerfully; his family lived nearby, and were expecting him home for dinner.

Aware that the gesture made her seem more like a bashful child than a distinguished wife, Kaveri could not help but cling to Ramu's side as they walked onwards into the club.

Animal heads were mounted like trophies along the wall, repulsing and intimidating her. A series of glassy-eyed deer with impressive antlers gazed mournfully down at them, and two large stuffed bison heads drooped their once-lethal horns towards the couple, defeated. Kaveri tried her best to walk around the snarling bearskin that adorned the floor, and as she caught sight of the two life-sized tiger skins mounted on parallel walls, Ramu felt her shudder. 'I told my father that we shouldn't install these awful, dead animals,' he said softly, so only she could hear.

'He didn't listen?' Kaveri whispered, averting her eyes from the glassy stare of the stuffed tiger in front of them. Its snarling face was vicious, and yet somehow deeply pitiable at the same time.

'No.' Ramu let out a sigh and Kaveri knew that he had suddenly become full of the old, heavy sadness she sometimes perceived in him, a sadness so deep she could not save him from it, and would only ever be able to console and listen. 'It's the British thing to do,' he continued. 'To go on a hunt – carefully protecting themselves from any real danger, of course, by flanking themselves with natives to watch out for the tigers and beat them a safe patch through the jungle. Then safely kill a few beasts and bring them back to the club as if they were trophies of bravery! This Club is supposed to be different – it allows the "natives" and the English to mingle socially. But it's not that different after all.'

His voice was bitter, hardening as he spoke. 'We pride ourselves on having the same things that the English do – if they have trophy animals and exclusive clubs, we must too. I have good friends, fellow doctors, who would love to join the Club – and I would love to sponsor them, but my hands are tied. They come from families without a supposed pedigree.'

Kaveri squeezed his hand in silent support. Her family, while wealthy, were certainly not socially prominent, and the last time she had felt this overawed had been her wedding ceremony. The hall had been full of distinguished guests, who she greeted in a daze. She had taken to her bed with a high fever the following day.

But she was not going to be nervous today. After all, she was an educated Indian wife, a rarity even in Bangalore's relatively advanced cosmopolitan circles. So what if Ramu's family was socially prominent? His older married sister had only studied until the eighth standard before being married off by her mother. She would no longer act like a silent chit of a girl from the countryside, she would behave like a budding mathematician, Kaveri decided, squaring her shoulders. And no matter how much the English men and women intimidated her, she would not be distracted from her mission to corner Manju at the party and give him a piece of her mind.

Ramu and Kaveri entered the hall and were instantly met by a hubbub of chatter. Charles Roberts, the Chief Medical Superintendent of Bangalore, and the man in charge of the Bowring Hospital, plodded over to them, warmly clasping Ramu's hands in his. 'Welcome, my dear boy, welcome. Such a pleasure to meet you. And a pleasure to meet your charming young wife. Welcome.'

'Daphne?' Roberts turned vaguely to his left. A beautiful woman wearing a gorgeous sleeveless gown in peacock blue, embroidered with peacock feathers, materialised at his side.

'My wife, Daphne,' Charles Roberts said.

'Oh, there you are, Charles,' she replied, and then: 'Rammy! *Dar*ling.' She seized Ramu's arm with an immaculately manicured hand. 'I met Rammy while I was visiting the Bowring one day to see Charles. Isn't he a darling?' She grinned at Kaveri. 'You must be so proud.'

Staring at the woman who was affectionately clutching at her husband yet could not pronounce his name, Kaveri dealt with the situation the only way she knew how: by posing herself a series of logical questions. Perhaps these British people had a habit of manhandling other people's husbands? She had heard that they tended to be quite forward, talking freely with other men and even flirting with them. Kaveri certainly admired the confidence with which Daphne wore her strange, strange dress. Coated with shimmering purple and silver beads, it was cut in a style that Kaveri had never seen before, with a hemline fringed with beads that scandalously skimmed her knobbly white knees, and a dropped waistline that would have looked matronly on Kaveri but only complemented Daphne's boyish figure.

Reluctantly taking her eyes away from Daphne's mesmerising outfit, Kaveri realised with horror that everyone was staring at her. Someone had clearly asked a question. *Silly goose – stop woolgathering!* she scolded herself mentally, and turned to Daphne. 'Thank you for inviting us, Mrs Roberts. It is a pleasure to be here.' It seemed to come out all right, as both Charles and Daphne smiled back at her before flitting off to meet other guests. Ramu rolled his eyes at Kaveri once their backs were turned, miming being sick, and she instantly relaxed back into the crook of his arm.

Leaving Ramu to talk with his colleagues, Kaveri joined a group of doctors' wives in the corner of the room, relieved to find Mrs Reddy among them. 'The Club is called the *Century* Club because we limit it to a select one hundred members,' Mrs Kantaraj Urs, a distant relative of the Mysore Maharaja and one of the Club's founding members, was telling them. Nodding away at Mrs Urs's monologue, Mrs Reddy carried an air of comfortable self-assurance that Kaveri found enchanting.

'We wanted to keep it exclusive, you see,' Mrs Urs continued.

'A capital idea!' proclaimed a red-faced Englishwoman who was passing by on the arm of her husband, and Mrs Urs smiled smugly. A tall, imperious lady dripping in diamonds and rubies, she was more like Kaveri's idea of the ruling British aristocracy than an Indian noblewoman. Mrs Urs had a sharp nose. She must spend her entire day looking down it at other people, Kaveri decided.

'You never know what kinds of riff-raff want to come in these days.'

Mrs Reddy looked at Mrs Urs steadily. 'Indeed?' She held her gaze until a scarlet flush appeared on Mrs Urs's fair cheeks and she turned away, embarrassed. Mrs Reddy caught Kaveri's eye and shook her head. She wore a gorgeous maroon sari, which, as always, was wrapped carelessly and most unbecomingly around her. But to Kaveri she looked like an avenging angel, like Lord Krishna in the *Bhagavad Gita*, appearing in human form to demolish snobs like Mrs Urs with a single devastating word.

A waiter silently glided up to them, a large silver platter in his hand. He held out a selection of vegetarian delicacies – grilled paneer, small cocktail samosas, bite-sized fried *vadas*, and pieces of grilled chilli-cheese toast. Ramu had reassured Kaveri that the menu was entirely vegetarian so she could eat anything she wanted. She selected a samosa and *vada*, and turned to ask the waiter for a napkin.

'Manju!' she exclaimed, her eyes opening wide. So there he was! Manju was already gliding away to the next group, the perfect invisible servant. Kaveri moved to go after him, but caught herself just in time – such a public venue was hardly the place to accost Manju. It was unfortunate – she so dearly wanted to give him a piece of her mind. How *dare* he attack his younger brother like that?

'My dear, the ruby bangles you are wearing are simply *superb*. Where did you get them?' Mrs Urs had accosted Mrs Iyengar, and was holding her wrist, which were covered in bangles. Kaveri's eyes widened. Surely a doctor at Bowring could not afford such expensive sets of jewellery for his wife? She remembered the diamonds Mrs Iyengar had been wearing when they had met in the Club recently.

The conversation around Kaveri burbled on.

'My youngest boy is so naughty – I have five, you know, all boys – they keep me on my toes.'

'The *vadas* are a bit soggy, don't you think? A bit of *rava* added to the batter would help them stay crisp. Maybe I should drop a hint to the cook . . .'

Kaveri tuned out the chatter, her eyes following Manju around the room. She could not spot him anywhere. Where had he gone? To refill the plate of snacks?

Through the open windows, she saw an indistinct flash of white moving stealthily around the corner, towards the back of the hall. Manju!

Kaveri muttered a hasty excuse about needing to go to the ladies' room, and escaped from the stuffy hall with its noisy chatter. From her previous visit, she knew the women's facilities were in a corridor that opened out to the back, from which, through a pair of conveniently positioned windows, the garden was visible. Just beyond the garden was a small room, the kitchen. She quickly made her way to the corridor, peering through the windows for Manju.

And then her jaw dropped.

Standing opposite Manju, like the statue of a celestial dancer Kaveri had once glimpsed outside a temple, was the most beautiful woman she had ever seen in her life.

5

Dinner on the Lawns

The woman wore a bright red chiffon sari, so thin that it was almost transparent, with a blouse so scanty that Kaveri's eyes almost popped out of their sockets. She wore her sari low on her hips. A delicate gold chain draped around her waist drew attention to its slimness, and a cascade of red and gold bangles adorned her wrists. Kaveri could not see her features clearly in the torchlight, but she looked like something out of a fantasy. But the fantasy woman now seemed to be saying something to Manju rather vehemently, holding out her palms as if to stop him from coming any closer.

Their discussion continued for some time. Manju raised his arms above his head violently, fists clenched. The beautiful stranger flinched and drew back. Kaveri could see Manju's face, illuminated by the lit torch next to him, contort in shock. He brought his hands down hastily, and moved after the woman, pleading. The woman shook her head, then as a cart laden with provisions clattered through the gate, held out her palms again to Manju, warning him to stop, and fled through an opening in the hedge.

Manju's face crumpled. He scrubbed at his face with the serving towel that he still held in one hand, whether wiping away tears or sweat Kaveri did not know. He walked back to the kitchen, moving in a daze. Kaveri had seen a man walk like that once before. Her neighbour had been hit by a falling branch from an overhead tree. He walked in shock until he reached home, then suddenly collapsed. Manju walked in the same way, almost too carefully, keeping one leg in front of the other, and moving each arm in sequence with fixed concentration. Kaveri's eyes followed him until he disappeared into the kitchen.

Who was the stranger? Should she follow Manju now and accost him?

As she struggled to decide, she saw another movement. A slender, almost emaciated figure stepped out from behind a tree. Kaveri recognised her as she moved closer, towards the light.

Manju's wife, Muniamma!

Ramu said she had been hired to work the dinner too.

The woman's thin shoulders shook and, her anger at Manju flaring, Kaveri realised that the woman could not have eaten in weeks. Only her swollen belly and the way she pressed her thumbs to her back, as if supporting an invisible burden, betrayed that she was with child.

Muniamma nervously knotted and unknotted the fringe of her sari, knelt to wash her face at the tap used for washing dishes, then rose quickly and walked up the gravel path to the kitchen, the same way that Manju had gone.

Dash it, thought Kaveri. Now that his frail, pregnant wife was in the kitchen, she had no way of storming in through the servant's doors and accosting Manju.

Thunder rumbled in the distance, a flash of lightning in the grove of trees far behind. Just before the light faded, Kaveri saw a figure in the grove. A large, dark man, wrapped in a white *lungi* which glimmered around him, making him look like a ghost.

How many people are hiding out in the garden today? Kaveri thought. It was almost as if they had a separate party going on out there – one at which the guests were unaware of each other's presence.

Lightning flashed again. This time she saw another figure standing beside the large man. It was the beautiful stranger who looked like an *apsara*. Kaveri strained on her toes, but it was too dark to see. Flash! Another crack of lightning. The large man had his hand around the woman's throat. He pushed her up against the trunk of a coconut tree.

The woman broke away and ran as though the devils of hell pursued her. The large man stood still, in the same spot, watching her go. Every line of his large body seemed suffused with menace. The horizon was dark again. *Should she call someone?*

'Mrs Murthy? What are you doing here?' a musical voice enquired. Kaveri jumped. Daphne, Mrs Roberts, was staring at her curiously. She took a step back, and peered out of the window. Everyone had gone – Manju, Muniamma, the large man, and the beautiful stranger. She hoped the beautiful woman had made it to safety.

Kaveri realised that Daphne was still waiting for a response. 'I was just admiring the view. The trees seem so beautiful at night.'

'Quite,' said Daphne, raising an eyebrow, still looking suspicious. 'We can go outside and enjoy the view if you like. Dinner is laid out on the lawn.'

Daphne led the way, and Kaveri followed. The hubbub and chatter had died down, and the large hall looked barren without the rich silks, shimmering jewels and glitter of the guests. Dinner would be held in a canvas tent on the lawn to protect them from any capricious outbursts of monsoon rain. The green grass, lush like a springy carpet under their feet, was bordered with a landscaped hedge of orange, white and blue flowers. Under the tent, round teak tables and high chairs formed a circle. The legs of the chairs were draped in garlands of marigold, and the tables were decorated with centrepieces: long crystal vases, each graced with a single, perfect red rose.

Kaveri gasped, thinking of the angry gardener at the Century Club. But Daphne seemed to have mistaken her dismay for awe, and was smiling at her reassuringly. Did she really look like that much of a gawking village simpleton to these English people?

'Come, my dear. Join us at our table,' signalled the tall, pale woman. 'Now, where is your husband?'

Kaveri looked for Ramu, finding him embedded in a cluster of doctors.

'Ah, darling, I was wondering where you had disappeared to.' Charles chuckled at his wife, and dug Ramu with his elbow meaningfully. 'The ladies have to prettify themselves before the meal begins, you know.' He looked fondly at his wife. 'I don't know why you do it though. You always look beautiful, even without any effort.'

Daphne reached up on tiptoe to give him an affectionate peck on the cheek. Kaveri's eyes widened. Exchanging a kiss in public! She had never seen anything like it. Trying not to show how startled she felt, she looked away.

'Let's get seated, darling,' Daphne urged her husband, linking one arm through his elbow and another through Kaveri's. 'I want Rammy and Kaveri to sit with us. She has just moved to Bangalore, I hear. We must get to know her better.'

They moved towards the largest table, at the edge of the lawn. Close by, a makeshift stage had been set up, covered with a white cloth embroidered with a rich velvet fringe.

On it, the performers of the evening were beginning to tune their instruments. Daphne turned to Kaveri as they sat down.

'A concert. How delightful,' she declared, clapping her hands. 'Tell me, Kaveri, do you know much about music?'

'Yes, of course, Kaveri is a musician herself. She plays the *veena*,' Ramu said proudly. Kaveri was too distracted to admonish him for speaking on her behalf, because Manju was back. He was the impassive waiter again, a clean towel over his arm, filling the cut crystal glasses on the table with water. Kaveri looked away from Manju to Daphne, who was waiting expectantly for a response from her as Manju moved around the table, avoiding eye contact, focused on the glasses. His eyes were still reddened, she'd noticed.

'The vina? What is that?' Daphne asked.

'*Veena*,' Kaveri corrected Daphne gently, thinking back to the conversation she had had with Ramu about the constitutional inability of the British to pronounce the simplest of Indian words. They mangled names wherever they went, changing Bengaluru to Bangalore, renaming Thiruvananthapuram to Trivandrum, and Visakhapattanam to Vizag, with casual arrogance. 'Veena, with a long "ee" sound. The veena is one of the oldest Indian instruments. It's stringed, and one plays it cross-legged, sitting down.'

'And you play it? How fascinating.' Daphne was evidently shocked by this revelation. 'How ever did you learn? Did you go to music school?'

Kaveri was beginning to feel like she was back in the schoolroom. She strove to keep her face impassive and was grateful for the waiter who, carrying in a plate of juicy cutlets with mint chutney, momentarily formed a barrier between her and the interrogation.

'In many South Indian families, the women learn Carnatic classical music from a young age,' she explained.

'We have three *veenas* at home, one for me, my mother and my sister.'

'Wow. A musical family.' Daphne turned to her husband, and tapped his hand imperatively. 'Did you hear this, darling? This young woman's family is quite something, it appears.'

'India has a long tradition in the arts.' Ramu leaned across the table, deliberately drawing Daphne's attention away from Kaveri. 'Most families make sure their children learn at least one – either the dance form of Bharatanatyam, or classical music.'

The talk about music continued, with Daphne telling them how she had been forced to go to piano classes, and Kaveri felt her knotted nerves beginning to relax. These *firangi* people were not as difficult to talk to as she had feared, after all.

'The mistress caned us on our knuckles each time we played a false note!' Daphne winced, with a strained laugh. 'And oh, my dears, I was the most terribly unmusical of children – so I got caned quite a bit. As you can probably understand, I acquired a great hatred of the instrument. I much prefer the violin. Charlie has ordered me one from London.' Daphne patted her husband's hand affectionately, as the waiters began to serve the soup course. 'There is a lot of similarity between our scales of music – *do re mi fa so la ti* – and your *sa ri ga*, correct?'

Kaveri nodded, glancing across the table at Ramu, who was now engrossed in a solemn discussion with Daphne's husband. 'Thymol solution does the trick every time. Much better than eucalyptus oil or cough powder,' Charles declared. Ramu nodded politely, looking dubious.

As the main course was served – vegetable pilao with raita, and a luscious cauliflower curry on the side, accompanied by naan – the conversation slowed down. Everyone focused on the food, which was delicious. Looking around, Kaveri noticed Daphne surreptitiously dabbing at the corners of her eyes and nose with a delicately embroidered handkerchief, and saw her nose turning pink, and realised with some shock that the food, mild for Kaveri's taste, was far too spicy for Daphne, although she seemed to be attacking it with enthusiasm.

As Daphne was returning her handkerchief to her reticule, it caught the edge of her spoon and cauliflower curry splattered everywhere.

'Oh no!' gasped Kaveri at the bright yellow stain blooming on the Englishwoman's dress. 'Your beautiful gown!'

Daphne stood up abruptly, refusing to look at her. 'Excuse me,' she muttered, setting her plate aside and making her way swiftly towards the ladies' room.

Kaveri looked after her uncertainly, wondering if she should follow and offer to help. Ramu gave her a slight shake of his head. These English people were strange, Kaveri thought, settling back into her chair. If it were another Indian woman, she would have welcomed some assistance to get herself cleaned up quickly.

They continued chatting with Charles Roberts. *What a nice man he seems to be*, Kaveri thought. He exhibited none of the oddities that Daphne did. He took a fobwatch out of his pocket, with a locket, and opened it out to show them miniature portraits of his young children. They had heard quite a bit about his two young girls, aged four and two, by the time Daphne returned. Her dress was damp in a few places, her hair was tousled, and she had high spots of colour on her cheeks.

'Dratted tap,' she grumbled, sitting down and picking up her spoon again. 'Leaks all over.'

Kaveri nodded. Turmeric stains were very hard to get rid of, unless one cleaned them immediately. The pair of women sat in silence for a while.

'Is this your first time at the Club?' Daphne asked finally, putting down her knife and fork and leaning back with a sigh of satisfaction which seemed out of place for a woman who had just flounced out of the room in disgust.

'We had our wedding reception here three years ago,' Kaveri said.

'Three years ago?' Daphne stared at her. 'You must have been a mere infant?'

Kaveri bit her lip. How judgemental these English people could be! 'In my community, we tend to marry early,' she explained. 'My sister was married when she was twelve. I wanted to stay in school for as long as I could. So I kicked and screamed, begged and pleaded, and even went on hunger strike to avoid marriage. My mother was aghast but my father is very fond of me, and permitted me to continue my studies.

'But my mother continued to worry that no one would marry me if I grew too old. So when news arrived of a well-known family from Bangalore,' Kaveri gestured at Ramu, lost in animated conversation about a difficult medical case with Charles Roberts, 'my mother jumped at the opportunity.

'My husband wanted to marry an educated girl, whom he could talk to about more than just rice and chapatti dough. He agreed to wait for me to pass my exams before taking me to his home.'

'Good for him!' Daphne declared with a flourish, thumping her arm on the table dangerously close to the water glass. 'But sixteen is still so young. And Rammy, how old was he?'

'He was twenty five. My grandmother insisted we get married quickly. It was just before the end of the war, and she was worried that my husband might be called up.'

Charles Roberts, who was listening in, nodded. 'It's the same in England. There was so much risk of people dying during the war that marriages happened quickly.'

'My father-in-law did not believe in child marriage,' Kaveri continued. 'So, while the marriage itself was conducted three years ago, we only became husband and wife in reality three months ago, when I completed my studies and moved to Bangalore.' She slowed to a halt. It was awkward to speak of such personal details with someone she had just met.

'I see. So *that's* why you two remind me so much of a honeymooning couple. Looking at each other so fondly and lovingly.' Daphne let out a surprisingly loud cackle of laughter. 'Your lovely wife tells me your wedding reception was held at the same venue,' she said to Ramu.

Ramu's eyes lit up. 'My father was one of the founding members. You see . . .' He stopped, looking embarrassed.

'There's a bunch of stuck-up snobby Brits that wanted Bangalore United Services Club to remain a whites-only club, my dear,' Dr Roberts took over, understanding Ramu's difficulty in saying anything that could cause offence to his boss. 'That's why they built the Century Club, with the idea that it would be open to all.'

Kaveri knew from Ramu that Roberts had recently moved to Bangalore from Amritsar, escaping the tense aftermath of the horrific Jallianwala Bagh incident, where hundreds of Indians had been massacred. Tensions between the British and Indians had been on the rise since then. Thankfully, Ramu said, Roberts was a different kind of Englishman. Interested in Indian customs, and quick to make friends, he had formed strong bonds with many of his Indian colleagues and subordinates.

'It is quite a curious name. Century Club. I suppose it's because it was established in 1900, at the turn of the century,' Daphne said.

'On the contrary, it's an aspirational name, referring to the elite and select membership of the Club,' Roberts explained.

'In fact, I only got in because I inherited my father's membership,' Ramu admitted somewhat sheepishly. Kaveri knew that this rankled with him.

'It's much the same in England, you know,' Daphne said. 'My husband has his club membership passed on from his father, and my brother uses my father's name to gain admittance to his club. I often think it's rather hard on those who don't have famous fathers to ease their way their way into these networks. Ah well, but that's the nature of society I suppose, whether in England, or here overseas.'

The dessert course was brought in – carrot *halwa*, glistening with slivers of almond, and garnished with flourishes of sweetened cream. The veena player took his place at the same time, accompanied by a violin to his left, and a percussionist playing the *ghatam* to his right. The conversation halted as the guests enjoyed the beautiful experience of the melodious music, to the accompaniment of crickets chittering in the night, and the soft moonlight casting a magical sheen on the grounds.

As the *ghatam* player reached the end of the performance, his tapping rose to a crescendo. The audience was transfixed. Kaveri had heard similar concerts many times before, but even she was impressed at the skill of the player. His fingers looked like they were flying through the air. The audience stood up and clapped as the hefty, middle-aged player threw the baked clay instrument up in the air, caught it in mid air, drummed on it and returned it to its resting place on his ample paunch, all without losing a beat.

As the percussion reached a crescendo and then dipped, a loud scream rang out. Alarmed voices sounded from the direction of the kitchen, and a woman's voice continued to scream, higher and higher in pitch, until there was the sound of a slap.

The screams stopped abruptly.

And it was then that the woman started to sob.

6

A Foul Attack

The room became a hum of conversation as everyone looked in the direction of the screams and the sobbing, trying to figure out what was going on. Roberts looked at Ramu, and both men started to get up. They stopped as they heard feet running down the corridor.

A liveried steward came into the tent, and swiftly made his way to Roberts. He bent down and spoke into his ear.

'What? Murdered?' Roberts exclaimed.

Kaveri started, as Daphne let out a scream.

'Murder? Who was murdered? How?' she asked, turning pale and beginning to rock back and forth, moaning softly. Roberts hurried to her.

'There there, my dear.' He turned to Ramu, all the while stroking his wife's hands consolingly. 'Be a good boy and see what's going on, Rama Murthy,' he rapped out in an impatient tone. 'I can't leave my wife in a state like this.'

Ramu's back was stiff. He carefully blanked out all expression from his face as he got up and followed the steward.

Roberts was crouched next to his wife, murmuring soothing noises into her ear. Kaveri hesitated, then offered him her chair, moving to exchange places and take Ramu's empty seat. *Strange*, she thought to herself. The woman had been so composed when her dress had been ruined, but had gone to pieces a few minutes later after hearing a scream. She wouldn't want to live with someone like her.

Murder, though! Who could it be? She hoped it wasn't the beautiful woman she'd seen in the garden earlier. Then a thought struck her. Could it be Manju? Or Muniamma? She hoped not. Roberts had his arm around his wife now, hugging her close and rubbing her shoulders. They seemed to have forgotten all about her. Kaveri shivered, looking longingly at the other tables, where everyone was engaged in conversation. She wished she felt confident enough to approach the others, but she had met them only a few hours ago. Perhaps she could go over to sit with Mrs Reddy or Mrs Iyengar?

As she was hesitating, the steward came in with a large flask of coffee, and stopped in the doorway. All conversation ceased, and everyone turned to stare at him.

'Madams, sirs.' The steward spoke steadily, although Kaveri could see a sheen of sweat on his face. And – was that blood on his trousers? She squinted, but the entrance was poorly lit.

'There has been an . . . an unfortunate event. A stranger was trying to enter the premises. He has been killed.'

'Killed?' there was an exclamation from one of the other tables. Kaveri recognised the nasal tone as Dr Iyengar's. 'Who was murdered? Surely not one of us?'

'Is anyone missing?' a woman asked.

'No, madam,' the steward responded swiftly. 'It seems to have been an intruder. Possibly a thief. We found the body outside, near the kitchen.'

'Oh, a thief!' Dr Iyengar sank back in his chair, looking relieved. 'Not one of us, then.' He waved a hand, dismissing the entire incident as irrelevant. 'Is that coffee?'

'Yes, sir.' The steward looked shell shocked, but his training took over. 'We must wait for the police. They have been summoned. In the meantime, we apologise for the inconvenience. Please have some coffee. The police will be here soon, and you can then leave.'

'Intolerable,' Kaveri heard Daphne mutter. 'Really, if the man was an outsider, what does it have to do with us?'

'But, darling,' Dr Roberts repostulated, 'I'm sure the police will need to take our statements.'

A stranger. So not Manju or Muniamma. But the steward had not said if it was a man or woman, even though most people, like Daphne, may have made that assumption. Kaveri couldn't bear it any longer. She slipped out of her chair and hurried out towards the corridor that led to the ladies' room. The steward noticed, and moved close to her.

'Madam, you must stay in your chair until the police get here.'

Kaveri drew herself up to her full height and stared at him down her nose, trying to channel what she had observed of Mrs Urs's aristocratic behaviour.

'I need to go to the ladies' room,' she said with cold hauteur. 'Am I to understand that I need to seek permission from the police before I can attend to the call of nature?'

The steward looked away, unable to face her direct stare, and moved back a couple of feet.

'Not at all, madam,' he said. 'But please —' he looked at her pleadingly '— please come back as soon as you can. And please don't go anywhere else.'

Kaveri was quite pleased at the effect she'd had on him. 'Naturally,' she responded in the iciest tone she could summon, and went forth. She hurried down the corridor, stopping before the windows looking across towards the kitchen.

Ramu was crouched in the garden, near the washing stone set out behind the kitchen area to wash dishes. Near him, the body of a man was sprawled on the grassy lawn. A woman – not Muniamma, presumably another of the servants brought to help with the washing – stood in a corner, weeping. Clearly no one had thought to bring her coffee. Another man, whom Kaveri did not recognise, stood over the body shining a torch.

Kaveri gasped out loud, then quickly put a hand over her mouth to muffle the sound. Fortunately, no one seemed to have heard her. The torch shone on a gash in the dead man's bloodstained chest. A surprisingly small amount of blood, surely, for an injury that had killed such a large man? The person holding the torch was now standing up, and the light illuminated the entire body. The man was indeed large, and powerful-looking, with a white shirt and a white *lungi*, now stained with red and ruched up between his legs. His eyes were wide open in an angry stare, and his face twisted into an ugly grimace. Even though he was dead, Kaveri felt afraid of him. She moved back, and let out a little cry: *The large man she had seen near the coconut tree, holding the beautiful woman by her throat.*

Ramu looked up, straight into the window. His eyebrows rose as he saw his wife peering out at the body. Kaveri stared at him for a long moment, not knowing what to say.

The sound of a car engine cut through the silence of the night. The police were here.

She saw Ramu give an unmistakeable jerk of his head, signalling that she should go back.

Kaveri made her way back down the corridor to the dining room, making it to the table and sitting down before the police entered the club. The steward shot her a look of relief and hurried over to pour her a cup of coffee.

'Where is Manju?' Kaveri asked him.

'He left about half an hour back. His wife fainted. He had to take her home.'

'I see.' Kaveri nodded as the steward left the table.

She could still feel her body shaking. She had never seen a dead person before. Except for her ill grandmother, whom she had nursed when she was bedridden for several months, helping to lay out her body for cremation. But that was very different. As she took sips of her coffee, she paused, and added two more generously heaped teaspoons of sugar. Almost gagging at the sugary taste, she forced herself to down the rest of the cup, and slowly felt the shivers ease. Her mind whirled with questions. Who *was* the murdered man? Not a thief, she decided. A thief would have waited for the party to end before he tried to enter. And why would a thief want to go to the washing area behind the kitchen? There was nothing of value there, only crockery and utensils.

They heard low murmurs from a distance. The police had made their way to the body. Kaveri could recognise Ramu's voice, pitched low, though she could not hear what he was saying. After a while, a young policeman came in to the dining area, followed by an older man. The second man, clearly the senior policeman in charge, had a gargantuan paunch and even more gargantuan flowing white beard. He introduced himself as Mr Ismail, the Deputy Inspector of the Wilson Gardens police station. Kaveri was taken aback by his size – she had never seen someone so large carry himself with such easy agility.

'My apologies for keeping you waiting,' Ismail said as he stood in the doorway. 'I'll not keep you for long. If I could just get some quick statements from you . . .'

'Appalling,' a loud authoritative voice rang out. Kaveri looked up. Yes of course, Mrs Urs.

'Surely you can't suspect us of anything. We have been inside all evening. And we need to get home soon.'

Ismail nodded. 'Of course, madam.' He looked at Mrs Urs as he spoke, meeting her eyes directly. So, not a subservient man, but one who knew how to smooth over unpleasantness before it started. Ismail reminded Kaveri of her uncle in Mysore, who was in the Railways. He had always displayed a peculiarly effective mix of respect and authority while dealing with influential people who believed they had only to clap their hands, for others to jump.

'We only wish to take your statements to understand if you heard or saw anything that might be helpful to us,' Ismail continued smoothly. 'It will just take a few minutes. We will be as fast as we can. And it would be really most helpful to us.' He smiled at Mrs Urs, who thawed visibly.

'Well, if we can help in any way, then of course we must,' she said, conceding the point, then sat back in her chair with a majestic sniff.

Ismail nodded. 'Now, whom shall we start with?' he said, looking around the room.

Roberts rose from his chair. 'I say, best to start with us. My wife is not feeling too well, you know. Her nerves, shattered by this news of murder.' Indeed, Daphne was still huddled against him, looking decidedly pale.

'Of course, sir.' Ismail led Roberts and Daphne to a table at the far end of the dining area, which the steward had brought in as they spoke, setting up a few chairs. The young policeman took out a notebook and began to take laborious notes. Ismail took a tiny pad from his short pocket and scrawled in it. In a couple of minutes, Dr and Mrs Roberts had left, and Mr and Mrs Urs made their way to Ismail.

Kaveri sat back and waited for Ramu. While the last couple, the Reddys, were speaking to Ismail, he came in, wiping his hands on a large white handkerchief. He made his way to her swiftly, putting his arm around her as he sat down.

'Are you okay?'

She only had time to give him a quick nod before the Reddys got up, and Ismail nodded to them.

'Dr Rama Murthy. I have spoken to you already. Thank you for your patience. I will come to your office tomorrow in case I have any further questions.'

Ramu rose up at the clear dismissal, and turned to Kaveri. He looked surprised as he saw that she was still sitting.

'I have something that might be useful for you,' Kaveri said, turning to Ismail. 'I saw the dead man a while before.'

Ramu sat down. Ismail looked at her steadily.

He saw a young woman. Slim of figure, but very attractive. Something about her confident style of speaking and the frank way in which she looked at him reminded him of his eldest daughter – his favourite, though wild horses would not have dragged the admission out of his mouth. 'Please go on,' he said.

'I was returning from the ladies' room when I heard a commotion.'

'When would that be?' Ismail interrupted her.

Kaveri turned to Ramu. 'I'm not sure. A few minutes before dinner was served.'

'Around eight thirty p.m.,' Ramu responded, still looking at her in some surprise.

Kaveri hesitated, wondering how much to share. Would she implicate Muniamma or Manju?

Ismail looked at her, his face grave. 'Mrs Rama Murthy. Any information you can provide would be most helpful. Please don't hesitate to tell us everything you saw. I can assure you, we won't rush to conclusions.'

The big solid man emanated an aura of reliability. He reminded Kaveri more of her uncle than ever. She decided to trust him.

'I saw Manju and Muniamma.'

'Who are they?' Ismail asked, making notes in his tiny paper pad.

'Our milkman and his wife.' Kaveri explained that Manju hadn't turned up that afternoon, and that Venu had said he hadn't been sending money home. She left out the part about Manju's physical abuse of his brother, not wanting to cast any more suspicion on him than she had already.

'Then I saw the man . . . the man who died.'

'How do you know who died?' Ismail interrupted her again, looking up at her sharply.

'I was curious,' Kaveri admitted. 'I didn't want it to be the beautiful lady who was killed. So I went to find out.'

Ramu grinned at Ismail. 'My wife came to the corridor that leads out from the ladies' room, and watched us examining the body.'

Ismail sat back and looked at Kaveri, a trace of a smile on his lips. 'And?' he asked.

'It was the same man who stood in a corner and watched Manju and the woman argue, and who later pushed the woman against a tree and put his hands on her throat. He frightened me,' she added, moving closer to Ramu.

'Ponnuswamy.' Ismail looked at her directly.

'Who?'

'The murdered man's name is Ponnuswamy. The woman – we can't be sure, but she must have been one of the several women whom he . . .' Ismail paused to clear his throat '. . . employed.'

'Employed?'

Ismail looked down at his hands. 'I apologise for saying this so bluntly, Mrs Murthy. But you seem like a sensible young woman. And you have provided us with most useful information. The steward seemed to have jumped to the conclusion that the dead man was a thief, surprised in the act of entering the kitchen. Perhaps one of his associates had killed him as they fled. But Ponnuswamy was a well-known local pimp. He supplied high class women to wealthy and influential men in the city. It is very unlikely that he would involve himself in petty theft.'

So the beautiful woman she had seen was a prostitute! Kaveri had heard of the 'ladies of the night' from eaves-dropping on whispered conversations between her mother and her friends. This was the first time she had seen one in person, though. Despite the horror of the evening's events, she felt strangely interested in finding out more about her. Respectable women from good families had very little chance of bumping into prostitutes – though respectable men from good families seemed to have a lot to do with them.

'Then what was Manju doing with her?' Kaveri couldn't figure this out.

'I'm not sure,' Ismail replied slowly. 'We need to pull him in for questioning.' He stood up. 'Thank you for your time. This has been most useful.' He turned to Ramu. 'Thank you as well, Dr Murthy. I'll come and see you tomorrow.'

'I could find out from Muniamma about the woman I saw,' Kaveri offered.

'No!' Ramu exclaimed, surprising Kaveri. 'This is danger-ous business, Kaveri. One man has already died. Leave the detecting to the police. We have already taken up enough of their time.' He took Kaveri by the elbow and almost pulled her out of the room. She stared at him in annoyance. Ismail stifled a grin as he watched Ramu leading her away.

She was *jolly well* going to speak to Muniamma, Kaveri decided. And if Ramu didn't like it, he could just lump it. In fact, Kaveri thought as she sat back in the carriage, what Ramu didn't know wouldn't hurt him. She gave him a sweet smile and snuggled against his shoulder, turning her face into his arm as she plotted what to do the next day.

7

In Time for Tiffin

The next morning, Ramu was getting ready to leave for work. Kaveri was sitting on the steps of their home, watching him as he put on his socks and laced his shoes.

'Will you be late today?' she enquired.

'Not too late. I don't think we have any seriously ill patients. With any luck, I should be home by five p.m. In time for *tiffin*. What do you have planned today?'

'Nothing much – cooking classes. Uma aunty from next door is going to teach me a new dish.'

'*Balekaayi bajji*?' Ramu asked hopefully. 'The banana tree at the back has got a bunch at the perfect stage – just beginning to ripen. Those are my favourites.'

'All right,' Kaveri promised recklessly. She was the worst of cooks – but her husband was a good eater, and she was keen to learn how to feed him well.

She watched him leave from the gate, and then skipped back into the house, doing a little dance of happiness. Her mother-in-law had gone to visit a sick aunt, and she was going to be alone all day. It was time for her to do some sleuthing.

She waited impatiently for Venu to come. She needed more information about Manju, Muniamma and the beautiful stranger. She climbed onto the lower bars of the gate, peering out onto the street. At last she saw Venu, kicking his feet in the mud disconsolately, trailing Gauri's rope behind him.

'Why so glum-faced?' Kaveri asked. To her horror, she saw tears trickle down Venu's face.

'What has your fool brother done this time?' she demanded fiercely.

'I don't know where he is, Kaveri *akka*. The police are looking for him everywhere. They came last night at around midnight, pounding on the door. They made such a noise they woke us all up, even the baby. They said . . .' He faltered, looking up at her. His eyes were large in his small face. 'They said there was a murder last night at the Century Club.'

Kaveri nodded. 'We were there. A man – Ponnuswamy – was murdered.'

Venu looked blank. Clearly the name meant nothing to him.

'They questioned Muniamma *athige* for a long time,' Venu continued, as he tied Gauri to the tree. 'The baby wailed so much that they went away. They have made a list of all the houses of Manju *anna*'s friends and our relatives, and said they would send teams to find him if he was in hiding there.'

Venu looked at her, his eyes full of fear.

'They also asked *athige* if she had any knives at home. They took away all our knives. They also borrowed a sharp meat knife from the neighbour's home and a piece of meat, and asked her to show them how she used it. I think they suspect her too.'

Kaveri gasped. This was so unfair. If anything, Manju was the fellow they should go after. Why pester a poor defenceless woman like Muniamma?

'Unfair!' she muttered under her breath. Should she go to Ismail and plead Muniamma's case?

'What?' Venu looked puzzled.

'Never mind, Venu. Give me the milk, quickly. I have to go out now. But I'll try and find some way to help you. Can you run down to the corner and call a horse cart for me? I need to go out for a bit.'

Kaveri took the milk from Venu and placed it indoors, then called out to Rajamma.

'Rajamma,' she said when she appeared. 'Look after the house for me. I'll be back by lunchtime.'

Rajamma looked startled. 'Are you going to see Ramu *anna*?' she asked.

Kaveri hesitated, then lied. 'Yes, he asked me to bring some letters to the hospital.'

She waited for Venu to bring the cart, plotting where to go. She had decided to head out on impulse. If she sat at home fretting about why the police were chasing Muniamma, she'd go mad. But what was the best plan?

'Venu!' she called out as he came running down the road, a horse cart slowly following him.

'What, Kaveri *akka*?' He looked up at her trustingly.

'Why were the police looking at knives in your house?'

Venu looked doubtful. 'They did not tell me. But I hid behind the wall, and overheard two of the men talking. They said the man who was killed yesterday was killed with a kitchen knife. I don't know how they could tell that, though.'

'Different kinds of knives leave different kinds of wounds in the body,' Kaveri explained, drawing the boy close. Ramu had attended to an emergency call last week where two ruffians had got into a fight and knifed each other. One had used the Rampuri *chaku*, a sharp knife used in street fights, while the other had deployed a simple kitchen knife. Both wounds, though very different, had caused severe damage.

She placed two rupees in Venu's hand. 'Buy some food and take it home, and buy a couple of knives too, to replace the ones the police took away,' she said, sending him out of the gate with a gentle push.

So the murder weapon had not been found yet. Where could it be? Whoever the murderer was, it seemed very unlikely that he would take the knife away with him – what if someone found him with the knife? He must have kept it hidden in a safe spot, close to where he stabbed Ponnuswamy.

It had been dark last night – could it be possible that the police had missed something? She looked at the horse cart driver, who was waiting patiently for her.

It would look strange – women from good homes did not step out alone. It simply wasn't done. If Rajamma had looked at her askance when she announced her intention of going out alone, there was every chance that the staff in the Club would too.

There was no help for it. She would just have to convince Ramu to accompany her. She hoped he was not too busy.

'Bowring Hospital,' she told the driver. But when she reached the crossroads that separated them from Cubbon Park, she had a burst of inspiration. Behind the kitchen, near the place where the body was kept, she had noticed a hedge of beautiful hibiscus plants. She would ask for a cutting for her garden, and make her way to the hedge to look around.

'Century Club!' she ordered the driver, who looked disgruntled as he turned the cart around, muttering under his breath about foolish women passengers who changed their minds as quickly as the wind changed direction. Kaveri decided to ignore him.

The cart drew up in front of the Club's gates, and the guard opened them, looking astonished. Kaveri ignored him too. She had decided to channel her inner Mrs Urs again.

She asked the driver to wait, and went into the dining area. The steward was missing, but a woman was on hands and knees, wiping the floor with a wet cloth. Kaveri sent her to call the steward, who came within minutes, holding a silver tray and polishing cloth in hand. He looked distinctly irritated, but as soon as he saw her, his expression changed to one of extreme surprise.

'Madam?' He moved towards her, setting the tray and cloth hastily down on a nearby table. 'Can I be of help?'

Kaveri turned her brightest smile on him. 'I saw the most delightful flowers on a hedge behind the kitchen yesterday. I thought I absolutely *must* have them for my home. I was going to the hospital, to meet my husband for lunch – and stopped in on an impulse. You will help me get a cutting, won't you?'

The steward looked distinctly astonished, but was too well trained to express any doubt.

'Indeed, madam, it would be our pleasure,' he said smoothly, gesturing to the sofa in the corner. 'If madam would be so good as to wait here, I can get you a cup of coffee, and send the gardener to dig out a couple of plants for you.'

'Oh dear, no, that will never do!' Kaveri exclaimed.

'Madam?'

'I mean . . .' she said, improvising hastily, 'I need to inspect the plants personally. I am a most keen gardener, and I want only the best cuttings for my garden. Please call the gardener, and I'll go along with him.'

The steward hesitated.

'The police have told me not to allow anyone there. It is a crime scene.'

Kaveri turned the full force of her charm on him. 'I assure you, I have no wish to tamper with a crime scene. The very idea. How ridiculous. I'll take a side path to the garden, and go only towards the hibiscus hedge. And besides, your gardener will be with me all the time.'

She stopped and tried to conjure her inner Mrs. Urs again, continuing in an icier tone. 'If you do not trust me, you can send a couple of men to accompany me. Or come with me yourself.'

He stepped back, babbling apologies, and sent for the gardener. A few minutes later, an ancient man with a wrinkled face, a cloth turban loosely tied around his head to protect him from the heat, stepped up. The steward gave him rapid instructions in Kannada, the local language, and sent him off with Kaveri, looking nervously at the two of them as they made their way around the side path to the garden, avoiding the kitchen area. Kaveri felt bad for the intimidated steward, but was distinctly pleased with herself.

She chatted with the dour gardener. 'How beautiful these flowers are,' she said.

He grunted 'Aiy.' Kaveri stopped and stared at him. Unless she was mistaken, this was the anti-British gardener whom she had overhead pressing the women to go on strike! She artlessly prattled on, wanting him to think her somewhat of an idiot, and an annoying one at that. 'My favourite colour is blue. And maybe orange. And also purple. What is yours?'

He stopped, looking at her incredulously. 'Colours are colours. I don't pay attention to foolish things like that. That's for women to think of.'

Time to change tack, Kaveri decided.

'I love marigold, jasmine, and hibiscus!' she said, baring her teeth in what she hoped was an amiable smile. The dour man grunted again, signalling for her to follow him. If ever a back could express emotions, this would be such a back, she decided, as she followed him. His expressed disgust, contempt and bitter resignation, all at once.

'But I hate roses,' she added brightly. The gardener stopped dead in his tracks. Kaveri rubbed her hands in satisfaction. She was right. This was the man she had overheard near the pool, who hated taking care of British roses.

She said slowly, deliberately, 'Oh, I'm so sorry. Perhaps I offended you. Maybe you like roses?'

'Can't stand them. Beastly things.' The gardener turned to look at her. His face had distinctly softened.

'Yes, I don't know why we can't plant more Indian flowers. We have such beautiful flowers which we use traditionally.' Kaveri rambled on. The gardener was nodding, and yes – most definitely – he was smiling at her. 'But we insist on aping the white people, and doing whatever they do.'

They had moved closer to the part of the garden which was visible from the corridor where she had spied on Manju. The events of the previous night seemed vivid and immediate, as though she had just experienced them. She closed her eyes and squinted, trying to recreate the scene in her mind. To her right, several feet away, was the coconut tree against which Ponnuswamy had pushed the unknown woman, hand on her throat. Just a few feet away from her, directly ahead, was the compound wall of the club, lined with hibiscus shrubs bearing flowers in riotous colours. In front of the wall was a large washing stone. That's where she had seen plates, serving spoons and knives piled up. *Could the killer have snatched a knife from this stone? That seemed likely*, Kaveri thought, stepping back to survey the area better. But if the killer had picked up the knife from the kitchen, surely the steward would have known it was missing when he'd counted up the crockery. She made a mental note to ask him.

She had to send the gardener away if she was to investigate properly. She turned eloquent eyes on him. 'I feel like such a fool. I noticed a lovely Parijata tree – that is Parijata, isn't it, near the entrance?' The guard was eating out of her hands by now. 'I wanted a cutting, to plant in my garden. Will it take root?' She looked at him hopefully.

'I'll make sure it does. I'll get out a pot, and select a good cutting for you, and plant it in a mix of the best red soil and manure.' The man was beaming with eagerness. Kaveri felt a pang of guilt at fooling him like this. But they could do with a Parijata tree in their garden, she comforted herself. And it was all for a good cause.

Kaveri thought back to Sherlock Holmes, her favourite detective. What else could she deduce from a survey of the evidence? If the killer had snatched up the knife from the washing stone, then the killing couldn't have been premeditated. If he had planned it, he would have carried the knife with him.

To her right was the kitchen entrance, where Muniamma had entered after washing her face at the tap next to the washing stone. In front of the stone, there was a patch of grass – still stained rust-brown. That was where Ponnuswamy's body had lain, where he had been attacked.

Kaveri looked around. The grounds were large, with an open grassy lawn. Sparrows were spread across the lawn, exploring for insects. It was almost impossible to hide a knife in such exposed surroundings. Had the killer replaced the knife in the kitchen? No – that was the first place the police would have checked. And Venu had said that they were still looking for the missing knife.

As soon as the gardener was out of sight, she ran to the hibiscus hedge. The area behind the hedge was bare. She had been so sure she would find the knife there. But that was probably the next place the police would have looked.

Where else could someone hide a knife?

She went over to the large jackfruit tree and peered behind it. No knives in sight. She inspected the trunk. Nothing there either.

She heard footsteps. The gardener was coming back up the path, clomping on the terracotta tiles in his heavy gum-boots. She ducked below a branch to avoid hitting her head, and moved hastily away from the jackfruit tree.

A flash of light caught her eye.

8

A Bloody Fingerprint

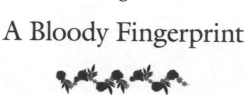

High up on a branch, where the tree touched the wall, was the hilt of a knife. Someone had taken the knife and embedded it in the gap between two branches, angling it upwards so that it was hidden from casual sight. It was only because Kaveri had bent to duck below the branch that she had chanced sight of it.

She reached up to pull it free, then stopped herself. This was information that needed to be shared with the police.

Kaveri marched up to the steward, the gardener trailing behind her carrying the pot with the Parijata cutting. As the gardener placed the pot in the cart carefully, Kaveri took the startled steward back to the tree, showing him the spot where the knife was embedded.

'Is this one of your knives? From the kitchen?'

The steward's face blanched, but he came obediently to the tree, inspecting the hilt from a distance. 'Yes, this is the meat knife that was missing. We had used it to cut a large jackfruit last night for the party. Muniamma had cleaned it and left it on the washing stone with the other vessels.

We couldn't find it afterwards. I told the policeman when he came. See —' He pointed to a crack in the hilt. 'It's been like that for a while. We've been planning to buy a new one, to replace it.'

'Keep someone on guard and make sure no one touches it,' Kaveri told him. 'I need to make a call.'

She saw the steward looking at her anxiously. 'To the police station, of course!'

Kaveri picked up the phone, hopping from one foot to another. Should she call Ismail? He had seemed like an intelligent man when she had met him last night. But maybe he would not take her seriously enough. She decided to call Ramu instead, looking at the clock. It was eleven – he would be in his room if she was lucky, having completed his rounds of the ward.

'You did what?' Ramu exclaimed.

'I found it almost by accident,' Kaveri explained defensively. Another long pause. Then she added, 'Well, I did think it might be there. But I also went to get hibiscus cuttings.'

Ramu burst out laughing. 'I should have realised yesterday that you had no intention of giving up the investigation.'

'Well,' argued Kaveri indignantly, 'I couldn't leave it alone, could I? The police had started questioning Muniamma. What if they took her away?'

'The knife you found could still have been wielded by Muniamma,' Ramu said gently.

Kaveri's shoulders slumped. 'I know,' she said with a sigh. 'But perhaps there's some clue on the knife. Something that exonerates her.'

Suddenly, she jumped. An idea had occurred to her. 'What about fingerprints?'

'Fingerprints?'

'Yes, fingerprints,' Kaveri responded tartly. 'We read about them in biology classes last year. Perhaps the fingerprints of the murderer are on the knife.'

Then she remembered why she had called Ramu.

'I've asked the steward to place a man to keep guard on the knife. Can you call Inspector Ismail and tell him what I've found?'

Ramu nodded, then realised she couldn't see him. 'Yes, Kaveri, I will. But you go home, all right? I don't want you to spend time waiting around there.'

Kaveri shook her head. 'No. I'm not going home. I found the knife, and I want to tell Inspector Ismail myself.' She added firmly, 'I'll be quite safe here. The gardeners are working on the lawn. I'll get them to set out a chair for me under the shade of a tree, and sit there with a cup of coffee.'

Ramu sighed. 'I'll hail a carriage, and come and join you.'

An hour later, Kaveri, Ramu and Ismail watched from a safe distance as the young stout policeman who had accompanied Ismail the previous day took a large cotton handkerchief and wrapped it around the hilt of the knife. He struggled to pull it out of the crevice between two branches where it was embedded, jiggling it back and forth. A trickle of sweat made its way down his face to his neck, as Ismail snapped, 'Gently, man. Don't break it.'

After a few minutes of unsuccessful jiggling, he stepped back. Ismail took over from him. In one quick tug of his powerful hands, he had the knife out.

They all gathered around to look at the knife. It was a long, slender knife, with a thick wooden hilt. Still holding it by the hilt with the kerchief wrapped around it, Ismail experimentally sliced a leaf on the jackfruit tree to shreds.

'Sharp,' he murmured, showing it to Ramu.

Ramu nodded. 'This explains why there was so little blood. The knife made a deep cut – till here.' He pointed to a line of dried blood, visible on the knife, close to the end of the blade.

'About eight inches deep,' rumbled Ismail. 'It matches the autopsy report which just came in.'

'A deep cut which must have punctured his lungs straightaway, avoiding the heart.' Ramu turned to Ismail. 'So the killer wouldn't have got much blood on himself either.'

'Most likely to have been a man,' Ismail agreed. 'A powerful thrust was required to get the knife in so deep – both into the dead man, and into this tree trunk.'

Kaveri let out a happy sigh. 'That clears Muniamma then,' she said brightly.

Ismail looked at her. 'Indeed it does, good lady. I take it all this sleuthing was in the noble cause of freeing Muniamma of suspicion?'

Kaveri was about to argue once again that she had come out to the hedge for the express purpose of getting hibiscus cuttings, but thought better of it. No one believed her anyway. She looked at Ismail directly.

'Venu told me the police had suspected Muniamma. They asked her to take a knife and show them how she would use it.'

Ismail shook his head. 'I told them yesterday that it was unlikely to be her. She's so small and thin.'

'Some small women are very fierce,' the young policeman added doubtfully. 'My grandmother was small and thin, and could cut and clean an entire goat in less than an hour.'

'You can check if the knife has fingerprints,' Kaveri interjected.

Ismail looked at Kaveri with an approving glance. 'How did you hear about fingerprints, madam?'

'In school. My biology teacher told us about it in some detail.'

Ismail's smile widened. He clapped Ramu on the shoulder. 'Your young wife is full of surprises.'

He angled the knife and showed the side to Kaveri and Ramu.

'This is a partial thumbprint in blood. We will wrap this up and send it to Chennai for fingerprinting, along with Muniamma's prints – and Manju's, once we find him. Then we can find out who did it.'

'I'm sure you'll find Muniamma's prints to be missing,' said Kaveri, more confidently than she felt.

Ismail nodded at her. 'I think you may be right. But it's better to have evidence to present before the court.'

Ramu took Kaveri by the arm.

'We should be getting home now,' he said firmly. 'It's about lunchtime.'

Kaveri's mind was still racing at all of the information she'd managed to get out of the steward while she'd been waiting for Ismail and Ramu to arrive at the Club. As they got into the horse cart, which was waiting patiently for them, Ramu looked at Kaveri. She gave him an unrepentant grin. Ramu shook his head ruefully.

'What am I to do with you, Kaveri?'

'Why, nothing.' She batted her eyelashes at him, as she had seen Daphne do to Roberts the previous evening. 'Just back me up whenever I ask you to!'

She dodged, laughing, as he tossed one of the pillows kept in the cart at her.

At home that evening, she told Ramu about the dour gardener. They sat together over dinner, reading the local newspaper, *Karnataka*, which carried responses to Gandhiji's calls for civil disobedience.

'So many letters to the editor,' said Kaveri, closing the paper. 'Many readers seem to agree with my gardener about the need for change. Do you think the British will ever leave our country?'

Ramu looked grave. 'I think they must, eventually. How long can they occupy the colonies? But I doubt we will see them leave in our lifetimes. At least, not without a major fight. It's that mayhem, and the deaths that will follow, that I'm most afraid of, Kaveri. We can't risk another massacre like Jallianwala Bagh.'

9

A Quest for Information

Kaveri was back in the loft, engrossed in working out another set of sums. With her mother-in-law away for the next few weeks to care for her aunt, there was little cooking to be done. Ramu had sent a note home telling her he'd be working long hours at the hospital that day, and might not return for dinner. She'd taken the note, gone into the bedroom and performed a little happy dance, then sent Rajamma home for the day. Alone at last, she'd settled down with a pile of school work next to her.

Time flew past as she worked her way through exercise after exercise. When she was solving sums, nothing else came to mind. But when she paused, to stretch her legs, or take a sip of water, she could not keep out the image of Ponnuswamy's contorted face with its wide open eyes, frozen forever in contorted, ugly violence. At last, coming to the end of a chapter, she set the book aside and turned to this other problem that was occupying her mind.

Who was it?

She looked down at the dusty floor where she had traced

the question with a wet finger, and wrinkled her nose. This was terribly unclear. There were too many ways in which to interpret her question. Not like mathematics at all, where questions were straightforward – what was 2 plus 3, for instance. You could not step up and ask the person who'd written the question, What did you mean? But *Who Was It?* could be understood in many different ways, each perfectly valid.

She took her maths notebook and turned it over, starting at the last page, and writing upside down. It was a trick they'd used in school often, when they forgot a notebook. You could use the last sheets of a book to work on something completely different, without dragging in the other topic.

What did she want to know?

Who killed Ponnuswamy? That was the first question. But to answer that question, she would need to know a few more things.

Who was the beautiful woman? What were she and Manju arguing about? She sucked on the end of her pen thought-fully, then wrote *What was she saying 'No' to Manju about?* Were they lovers? It certainly looked like she was rejecting him.

Why was Muniamma spying on them?

Why did Ponnuswamy put his hands around the woman's throat?

She lay down on the straw mat, on her stomach, placing her chin on her crossed hands for support, and stared at the paper. She must have dozed off, for the next thing she knew, she was walking in a dark forest. The canopies of the trees embraced each other like lovers, and below, the flowers bloomed in rich profusion. The ground was thick with rotting leaves, and she picked her way along the slimy, slippery path with great care. One slip, and she could twist her ankle. She heard a silvery laugh behind her. She grabbed a tree trunk for support, and looked around. She saw a flash of a colourful sari as someone moved behind a tree. The trunk that she was holding began to vibrate. She looked up. A woodpecker was tapping insistently on the tree. Tap tap tap . . . the sounds became louder and more persistent. A handle rattled once, and then again, more loudly.

A handle rattling in a forest? Most peculiar. Kaveri rubbed her eyes – then woke with a start. Someone was banging on the door and rattling the handle with great force now. She jumped up and ran to the open it.

Venu almost fell inside. His spiky hair was in disarray, and he looked flushed in the heat. 'Kaveri *akka*! Why did you take so long to answer? I went all around the house looking for you. I even climbed up and looked inside all the windows, but I couldn't see you. Then I thought of looking here. I peeped through the keyhole and I saw your feet. But you didn't answer. I thought . . . I thought . . .' He could not complete his sentence.

'Nothing happened to me, Venu. I just dozed off, that's all.' Kaveri ruffled his hair, and brought the boy inside, pouring him a glass of water.

She saw him looking at her notebook, and hastily closed it, before remembering that Venu could not read. *I must teach him*, she decided, wondering how she could make time for it.

'Has your brother returned?'

'No, Kaveri *akka*,' Venu muttered angrily. 'Now he's disappeared completely. The police keep coming around and looking for him. I don't think they believe us when we say we don't know where he is.'

He looked up at Kaveri hopefully. 'Can you do something? Help us find Manju *anna*? My mother and sister-in-law are very worried. That's what I came to ask.'

Kaveri opened her book, and surveyed the questions she had written down. Most of them required answers from Manju. Without him, what could she do?

'Where is Muniamma now?' she demanded.

'My *athige*? She will be at the white *memsahib*'s house.'

'Which *memsahib*?'

'You know, the one who is married to the doctor in the hospital where Ramu *anna* works. She goes there in the morning, and returns by late afternoon. She washes dishes, dusts the windows, mops the floor, and does other odd jobs.'

Kaveri looked at the clock. It was only 11 a.m. She could not wait until late afternoon for Muniamma to return to her home. And it would be impossible to question her in her house in any case, with Venu and his mother looking on.

'Well, then.' She got up, briskly rubbing her hands and stamping her feet to get the blood moving. 'Come on, let's go. No time to waste.'

'Where are we going?' asked Venu, obligingly trotting along beside her.

'To Daphne's house.' She looked at Venu's blank face. 'The white *memsahib*. I need to speak to Muniamma.'

Luck was on their side. When the horse cart drove up to the Roberts' home, with Venu pointing out the way, the guard told them that both Dr and Mrs Roberts were out.

'I'm looking for one of their maids – Muniamma. I'm one of the doctors' wives – it's all right, I just need to speak to her for a few minutes,' Kaveri assured the doubtful looking liveried guard at the gate. He closed the gate firmly, and went in to call Muniamma.

A couple of minutes later, a worried looking Muniamma came to the gate, and peeped out uncertainly. Her face cleared when she saw Venu.

'Did you find him? Has your brother returned?' she asked, grabbing the boy by his slim shoulders, almost shaking him in her eagerness.

Venu looked down, tracing a pattern in the dust with his bare feet. Muniamma's face crumpled.

'I need to ask you some questions,' Kaveri said firmly. 'If you can help me by answering them, I may be able to help find your husband. But you need to give me straight answers.'

She turned to Venu. 'Where can we sit and talk?'

Venu took them across the road to a stall heaped with fresh tender coconuts. She handed him a few coins and the vendor sliced open the tops of three coconuts for them. They sat down on the stone benches, sipping the fresh coconut water.

'Venu – I need to speak to Muniamma privately. Can you go sit in the cart?' Kaveri asked, placing a gentle hand on his shoulder. Muniamma's eyes flashed with fear, but she sat submissively, her face covered with her sari *pallu*. Manju had beaten the will out of her, Kaveri thought, bile surging in her throat. Once Venu left, she turned to Muniamma.

'I need you to answer some questions for me. Trust me,' she added, as she saw Muniamma hesitate. 'I saw some things happen at the party that night, but I could not understand it fully. I need to understand, so that I can try and figure out where Manju might have gone.'

She tried to pat Muniamma's hand, but the woman snatched her hand back, hiding it nervously in the folds of her sari. Her fingernails were blackened with soot and dirt, and her eyes were red-rimmed with hours of crying. Her belly was gently swollen, a sharp contrast to her skinny body.

'How many months along are you?' Kaveri asked gently.

'Five months,' Muniamma whispered, so softly that Kaveri could barely hear her.

Kaveri saw her look towards the gate. She needed to be quick – Muniamma could not stay out much longer without getting a scolding.

'I saw you that night,' she said quickly. 'I was standing in the corridor, looking out at the garden. I saw Manju standing and talking to another woman. Who is she?'

'Mala,' Muniamma whispered again. She sat cross-legged on the bench, twisting her toe rings back and forth with one hand.

'Who is Mala? Is she one of Ponnuswamy's women? Was Manju visiting her regularly?'

Muniamma nodded, but refused to look up. 'I need to go,' she whispered. 'Please. I need to go. Otherwise I might lose my job.'

Kaveri pressed her a couple of times. But she could get nothing out of her. She gave up. The woman did not trust her – and why should she, Kaveri rationalised. She was a perfect stranger as far as Muniamma was concerned, even though Venu knew her well. She walked across the road and stood near the cart, watching Muniamma go in.

Just then, a car pulled up to the gate. The guard snapped to attention, saluting briskly, and opened the gates wide. Kaveri saw a pair of astonished blue eyes looking at her through the back window.

'Kaveri? What a surprise!' Kaveri was pinned under a steely gaze. 'Won't you come in?'

It seemed like one of those invitations one could not refuse.

10

Native Servants
Can Be Renamed

Muniamma scurried in like a frightened mouse, tucking herself securely inside the folds of her sari, a ghost in a faded, raggedy blue shroud fading away into the house. *So this was how they treated their help.*

Kaveri thought of the contrast with Rajamma, who had spent several minutes this morning chiding Kaveri for keeping the milk in the sun, and not using up the ripe bananas before they spoilt.

Daphne was waiting for her beside the door. She wore a summery purple dress made of chiffon fringed with lace, dark brown with large purple orchids printed all over, standing several inches taller than Kaveri in matching high heels and a stylish purple cloche hat. She looked like an overgrown hothouse, with cloying perfume to match, overlaid with the pungent odour of fresh sweat. 'I don't know how you Indians bear the heat. Oh my goodness.' She raised a limp hand to her hair. 'But I guess you're used to it. Your skin probably doesn't burn in the heat like mine.'

She looked critically at Kaveri's flushed face. 'I think you could do with something cool to drink, though. So could I.'

She called out, and another maid came in. 'Yes, madam?'

'Bring me a tall glass of beer. And for you?'

Kaveri had never tasted alcohol before. Well brought up Indian women simply weren't permitted to. She itched to respond, with an airy wave of her hand, 'I'll have the same.' This probably wasn't the best time to get drunk, though. Not when she was scouting for information. Could she convince Ramu to give her a sip of his beer sometime later?

'Juice for me, please,' she smiled at the maid, who bobbed her head and scurried away. Daphne seemed to have forgotten her existence completely. No please and thank-yous wasted on the help in this house, Kaveri thought. Daphne had been perfectly pleasant towards her, but she was suddenly glad Ramu worked for Roberts, who was far nicer than his wife.

'You must think it perfect cheek of me to come up to your house and borrow your help.' Kaveri decided to take the bull by its horns, looking up directly at Daphne.

'Not at all.' Daphne gave her a tight-lipped smile. 'I'll confess to some curiosity, though it's very ill mannered of me to do so. What did you want with her?'

She placed her large handbag, made of crocodile leather, to the side, sipping her beer, and watching Kaveri. The maid proffered a glass of juice to her, bobbing her head again, vanishing as noiselessly as she had entered.

'Muniamma . . .' Kaveri began.

Daphne looked at her blankly. 'Who?'

'Your house help. Muniamma. The woman I was speaking to.'

Daphne waved a dismissive hand. 'I can't pronounce the complicated Indian names these native servants seem to go by. I call her Mary. We always give them Christian names. Our servants are used to it.'

Kaveri could feel her eyebrows rising. She hastily pulled them back down again. Daphne had not just changed Muniamma's name, she had also changed her religion. Muniamma was named after a sacred local goddess. How would Daphne feel if Kaveri started calling her Jayanti?

But she was a guest in this woman's house. Besides, Kaveri reminded herself practically, her husband was Ramu's boss.

'Her brother-in-law, Venu, works in our home,' Kaveri said, improvising fast. 'He wanted to speak to her urgently. That's the young boy I brought with me, in the horse cart. I knew the guard was unlikely to let her come out if he came alone, so I offered to accompany him.'

'Ever since the murder at the Club, Mary seems to have gone to pieces.' Daphne frowned, looking down at her empty glass. 'Her mind isn't on her work at all. I hear her crying all the time. It's most annoying.' Her thin lips pinched closed tightly.

Kaveri clenched her fists, hidden in the folds of her sari.

'She must be worried. The police have been in and out questioning them about the murder.'

'Why? Did she see anything?' Daphne looked at her intently.

Kaveri shrugged. 'I don't know. Venu said they came to their house looking for knives.'

'Aha. So the murder weapon might be in their home. Do you think she did it? I can't have a murderer in my home.' Daphne gave a large, affected shudder.

Kaveri bristled. 'It's very unlikely.'

'Why? They *are* cowherds. I'm sure they keep large, sharp meat knives in their home.'

'But they found the knife used to kill the dead man. It was in the garden, next to the place where the body was found.'

Kaveri stopped. In her urge to defend Muniamma, she had let out more information than she wanted to.

'Really? Where did they find it?' Daphne looked fascinated, swinging one well-shod foot against her knee as she sat back, settling in for a long gossipy chat with every appearance of enjoyment. Uneasily, Kaveri wondered if this was how she herself appeared to others, such as Ramu, or Ismail. Was she obsessed with the details of the murder in the same way?

No, she said to herself, pushing these uncomfortable thoughts aside. *I'm not obsessed with murder, and I don't find it thrilling to talk about it. I want to find out who did it, so that Venu – and Muniamma – can live in peace.*

'Well, actually, I found it,' Kaveri admitted. There was every chance that Ramu might have told Roberts, and she did not want to be caught out in a lie when he and his wife traded notes.

'You did?'

'Yes, completely by accident.' She decided to stick with the fake story she had given to the police – even though she knew Ismail had disbelieved every word. 'I saw some lovely hibiscus flowers, of the most delicate shades of orange. Orange is my favourite colour.'

She prattled on artlessly, feeling she was becoming quite good at this business of acting like a ditzy young woman without a brain in her head.

'I went to the hedge, and saw a flash of light reflected off the knife.'

'Where was it?' Daphne asked, with a catch in her breath, one hand pressed to her throat.

'The murderer had pushed the blade deep into a crevice of a tree.'

'Into a crevice?'

Kaveri nodded. 'Yes, he must have been quite strong to do so. It would have taken quite some force. That's why –' she leaned back and paused for dramatic effect '– that's why I'm sure it couldn't have been Muniamma. It had to have been a man. No woman would have been able to push it so deep. It took the police quite some time before they were able to tug it out.'

Daphne looked disappointed. 'I suppose so. Well, maybe it's her husband then.' She looked at Kaveri meaningfully. 'Did you get everything you needed from Mary?'

Kaveri took the hint. She didn't want to overstay her welcome. 'Yes, thank you. Venu needed to ask her where she had put the medicine the doctor prescribed for his mother. I should take him back home now, so he can give it to her before lunch.'

Daphne stood at the door, watching her intently as she climbed into the cart.

11

A Dastardly Attack

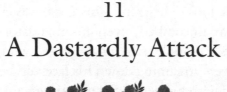

The next morning, Ramu and Kaveri were chatting in soft voices as Ramu was leaving for work. They looked up as they heard a noise. Venu was outside, struggling with the gate. Wrestling it open with difficulty, he burst into the compound, his dirty vest splattered with red stains. He held up his hands – they were red too.

Wild eyed, he raised his hands to the heavens and wailed, 'Kaveri *akka*! Ramu *anna*! Help me. My sister-in-law . . . my *athige* . . . murdered . . .'

'Muniamma?' Kaveri winced, thinking of the thin, desperately fragile-looking woman she had spoken to just the previous day.

But there was no response. Venu had fainted into Ramu's arms.

'Water!' Ramu demanded, and Kaveri ran to him with the bucket they kept next to the well. He threw some water on Venu's face and the boy choked and spluttered back to consciousness. He opened his mouth, and closed and then opened it again, but no sound came out.

Ramu propped Venu up against his shoulder. Kaveri brought a glass of water and slowly funnelled a trickle into Venu's open mouth.

The boy's tear-choked voice called out hesitantly. 'Ramu *anna*?'

Ramu gently combed back the boy's unkempt hair with his hands. He looked haggard – his *lungi* was crumpled and dirty, his hair uncombed, even his mandatory towel was missing from his shoulder. His eyes darted wildly across the road. Tears were streaming down his face and he vainly tried to stem them with his sleeve. 'Ramu *anna* – my *athige*! Can you save her? Will she die?' Venu choked out.

Ramu tried to calm the boy down as the torrent of words continued.

'Ramu *anna*. Please come. Where is Manju *anna*? What happened to him? I have been searching for him . . . He didn't come home last night. *Athige* was going out to deliver the milk . . .'

Venu grabbed Ramu by the sleeve, towing him outside the gate towards the back lanes that led to the quarters of the cowherds. He pointed to the lane beyond. 'There, *anna*. Please come. I can't bear to tell my mother. I don't know what is happening to *athige*.' Tear filled eyes looked up at Ramu pleadingly. 'Can you save *athige*? Will she die?'

'What happened to your sister-in-law?' Ramu forced out, through dry lips.

'Her head!' Venu dissolved into tears. 'Her head . . .'

Kaveri sat down heavily. Two attacks in a week – it was too much to take in.

'Can't find a cab anywhere,' Ramu said, his face set in grim lines. 'We'll have to make it there on foot. As fast as we can.' He sponged Venu's face with a wet cloth, and fed him a couple of lumps of jaggery sugar, watching the colour return to his face.

'Stay here,' he called out to Kaveri.

She shook her head firmly. 'I'm coming with you.'

Ramu gaped at her. 'Kaveri, there's going to be . . .' He stopped, and tried again. 'It's not going to be the kind of sight you're used to seeing.'

'I'm a doctor's wife. I need to get used to it.' Kaveri put on her bravest face for him, although she could feel her chin wobbling. 'You may need my help.'

Ramu caught Venu by the hand. 'I don't have the time to argue. Come if you must.'

They ran to Venu's home, following the boy as he moved sure-footedly through a maze of tiny congested lanes towards the cowherd colony.

Struggling to keep up, Kaveri hiked her sari high above her ankles, without a care for who saw her or what they might think. Navigating her way around the muddy paths and the ramshackle huts leaning precariously close to the road, she coughed as she breathed in the smoke from the wood-lit stoves cooking morning meals. Indistinct figures moved through the smoke-lit streets in the foggy morning, like ghosts drifting into the boundary between night and day. She ran faster, to keep Ramu and Venu in her sight, suddenly afraid as cold tendrils of fog caught at her arms and throat. They were getting farther and farther ahead of her. She didn't know where Venu's home was, and she wouldn't be able to find her way back if she lost sight of them. She breathed a shuddering sigh of relief when they finally drew up outside a small hut, shouldering their way in past a large group of women gathered around a small figure lying on the ground, wailing loudly.

Ramu cursed, shouting to the women to step aside and give the patient some air. A young woman lay on the mud-packed floor, a coarse grey sheet wrapped loosely around her. Blood pooled around her head, oozing from a head wound.

Venu ran to her, clutching at Ramu and babbling incoherently. Ramu took the trembling boy into his arms and hugged him hard, patting him on the back like a baby until he stopped shaking. While he held him with one arm, he went down on his knees and moved the blanket off the top of Muniamma's head, gently exposing the bloody wound.

Muniamma looked so vulnerable, her tiny form crumpled like a little rag doll someone had discarded on the rubbish heap. 'Where did you find her, Venu?' Ramu asked gently.

Venu hiccupped, sobbing. 'I found her in the cowshed, next to Gauri. She had gone to check on the cows in the morning, and give them fresh water. She was like this.'

'And who brought her in?' A babble of loud voices answered him, confessing that they had brought her in and laid her down while Venu had gone to fetch him. Ramu nodded absently, focused on the woman's injury. Kaveri couldn't tear her eyes away from the blood that was still seeping out of the wound, now bleeding into Ramu's trouser legs. She swallowed, and pinched herself hard. It would not do for her to faint now.

Ramu had spotted signs of breathing – the folds of Muniamma's sari gently lifting and settling back around the young woman's chest. They needed to get her to the hospital.

He scanned the room quickly. No sign of Manju. Venu's mother was clearly going to be of little help – she had joined the crowd of wailing women, and Venu had now gone over to try to console her.

'You,' he snapped, gesturing to a young boy who had moved towards them, staring at them curiously. 'Bring a bullock cart here. We need to get her to the hospital. Quickly! Run.' Then, as he looked around and saw Kaveri – 'Boil some water for me. And get me a clean sheet.'

Kaveri looked around helplessly. Where was the fire and where were the pots kept, in this strange house? Despite the crisis, she felt a strange pull of fascination. It was the first time she had been in the house of a cowherd. She saw a tiny space in a dimly lit room, with ramshackle walls built from poles of wood, plastered with lime. The mud floor was hard below her feet. Kaveri marvelled at how so many people fitted into such a tiny space. A few vessels were neatly stacked in a pile, near a small makeshift stove built of mud bricks. The fire was lit, and a mud water pot was bubbling over. Muniamma must have been heating water for their morning bath.

As Ramu checked Muniamma's pulse and examined her head wound, Kaveri rummaged in the corners of the dark room, and almost stumbled on a soft squishy pile. She recoiled in surprise. It was Muniamma's baby. Swaddled in a blanket, he lay in a corner of the room, peacefully asleep, unaware that his mother was battling death.

Hearing her squeal of surprise, Ramu glanced over at Kaveri. She held up her arms in a rocking motion. 'Baby,' she mouthed at him. 'Sleeping.' She mimed the action. Ramu's eyes widened in surprise. And sorrow.

Next to the baby, a faded, threadbare cotton sheet was neatly folded and stacked against the wall. Torn and stained, but it appeared clean enough. She handed the sheet to Ramu, who tore it into strips.

'Hot water?'

She brought the pot over, and looked around. The baby was still sleeping. Ramu was crouched over Muniamma's body, and Venu sat next to him, helping him to clean her wounds with hot water.

I'm not needed here, she thought.

She tiptoed around the side of the hut, trying to make as little noise as possible.

She approached the cowshed cautiously, squinting as she tried to emulate the characters in her favourite detective novels. What would Hercule Poirot do, or the intrepid Lady Molly from Scotland Yard? Look around for footprints, she supposed.

The packed mud was hard. She flinched when she saw the pool of drying blood. A large, metallic blue horsefly alighted on it, making a penetrating buzzing sound.

The sun went behind the clouds, taking much of the morning light with it. Kaveri suddenly felt very alone. Were those footsteps she heard? The thin branches of the drumstick tree, laden with fruit, hovered close to her head, brushing her cheek with what felt like tens of clammy fingers. She could hear her heart beating loudly, *dhud-dhud-dhud*.

Lady Molly would not be scared, she thought, mentally chiding herself. She stepped around the pool of blood to the vegetable patch, bounded by a pumpkin creeper on a bamboo trellis, separating Venu's hut from the mud lane behind. *That's a footprint*, she thought with excitement. Someone had climbed over the fence – here, where they had crushed the tomato plants.

She bent down and squinted at the footprint. It was large, and looked like it had been made by a man's heavy hobnailed boots. Imprints of the nails were lined up in neat rows, contrasting starkly with the debris of the wrecked kitchen garden. The acrid smell of crushed tomato and tulsi leaves filled her senses. She bent down to measure the size of the boot with her palm. It was two times as long as the span of her hand. Was there something else, glinting in the sun? There, behind the pumpkin. She reached over and pulled it out. A large brass safety pin, with a letter and some numbers on it – H35.

What was such an incongruous object doing in a cowherd's garden?

She stood up, brushing the mud off her sari as she heard the sounds of a bullock cart rattling along the bumpy lane at the front of the hut, then ran back to the front of the house.

Ramu cradled Muniamma's unconscious body in his arms as he stood.

He looked at the mass of women blocking the approach to the hut. Kaveri rushed over and asked them to clear the way. No one paid the slightest of attention to her. She took a deep breath. What could she do? Then she thought of her school maths teacher, Kamala Miss. Four feet ten inches, a tiny figure of a woman and a widow to boot, she commanded attention wherever she went. It was the formidable confidence that Kamala Miss exuded, Kaveri thought.

She opened her mouth and shouted, with a new-found sense of conviction, 'Make way.'

The women moved aside. Ramu had wrapped Muniamma's slight frame in the cotton sheet, hiding her wounds from the curious crowd. He placed her onto the cart, holding out a hand to pull Venu up.

'To Lady Curzon Hospital, driver. Gently.'

Only then remembering Kaveri, Ramu turned to look at her over his shoulder, as the cart was leaving the lane.

'Go home,' he shouted over the noise of the rattling cart and the heaving sobs of the women crowded behind it. 'I'll come later tonight.'

Kaveri waved back to him, and began to walk slowly down the road, clutching the safety pin in her hand. Of course she was not going to go home. She intended to head to the police station immediately, to hand over the safety pin to Ismail, and insist that he send someone over to take careful measurements of that footprint before it was obliterated by hoofmarks. Weary but determined, she trudged down the road, looking for a cart to take her to the police station.

12

A Fugitive Pays a Visit

On her way back from Ismail's office, Kaveri stopped by the hospital, heading straight to the infirmary in the General Ward section to check on Muniamma's condition. She was still unconscious – breathing shallowly, and running a high temperature. Venu sat next to her, holding her hand. Thimakka, the other hospital attendant, had just brought in lunch and was attempting to coax Venu to eat something, when Kaveri saw him shake his head. She waved Thimakka away and pulled Venu outside, leading him to a bench in the corner.

'You have to eat, Venu,' she told him firmly, smoothing his hair back from his forehead. She watched him swallow down a few morsels of food unwillingly, looking too tense to eat. The hospital was no place for a child.

Ramu was in the theatre, operating on another patient with a serious injury, so she left a scribbled note for him in his office: *Taking Venu home.*

But when Ramu had not returned by evening, she left Venu with Rajamma and went to the hospital again. Venu was still fretting about his sister-in-law, and so was Kaveri.

'There's been no change in her condition since the morning,' Ramu said when she peered into the room. His voice shook with fatigue. 'She's been lying motionless since we brought her here.'

Kaveri sat down heavily, feeling her legs tremble. On her way to the hospital, she had broken a coconut as an offering to Ganesha in the temple, praying for Muniamma's recovery.

Ramu reached out and patted her hand. 'How is Venu?' he asked softly. 'I'm glad you took him home.'

'I wanted him to stay with us for a few days. But he refused. He says he's going to his grandmother's home tonight. He's worried about her, and wants to be with her. Rajamma said she would take him there on her way back home.' She paused, then added, 'Can we go to your office? I need to tell you something in private.'

'What?'

'I found the place where the attacker must have entered Muniamma's hut,' she said as they reached Ramu's office, closing the door firmly behind them. She animatedly described how she'd discovered the footprint of a large hobnailed boot, and the numbered safety pin.

'I took it to Ismail,' she said.

Ramu groaned. 'Kaveri. You cannot keep bothering the police like this.'

'Bothering?' Every line of Kaveri's body quivered with indignation. 'You think the police would have found the knife if I hadn't shown it to them? Or the safety pin? The fingerprint?'

'They would have found it, Kaveri. They are experts after all,' Ramu tried to explain patiently. 'It's just that you found it first.'

'I'm not so sure. The murderer buried the knife in the crook of the tree to avoid notice. I'm sure he planned to return and retrieve the knife before the police found it. He would know how much it placed him at risk.

'And what if you were looking for the knife just when the murderer returned?' he asked softly. As the colour drained from her face, he reached across to hold her hands in his.

'Please. Give up this investigation. The man you are looking for has killed once, and attacked a second time, causing grievous damage. He's dangerous, and might do anything to save himself.'

Kaveri shivered. She opened her mouth to protest, out of habit, but closed it again. She knew Ramu was right.

'All right,' she said. 'I won't go sleuthing alone again. But I'll still try to find out what happened from a safe location.'

Ramu nodded. 'I guess there's no hope of convincing you otherwise.' His eyes were dead serious as they rested on her.

'Can I tell you now what Ismail told me?' Kaveri asked, somewhat crossly. She hated being reprimanded like this, even though she recognised the justice of what he was saying.

Ramu nodded.

'The safety pin is of the kind commonly issued to soldiers. They pin it to their laundry for easy identification.'

Ramu shook his head. 'The killer was a soldier? That doesn't sound likely. The cantonment, where the soldiers' barracks are, is far from Muniamma's home near Basavana-gudi, and their movement in the Indian parts of the city is heavily restricted.'

Kaveri nodded. 'It could be a *dhobi*, a washerman who took it from a pile of laundry, though. But why would a washerman be wearing hobnailed boots?' Like the cowherds, washermen usually went barefoot everywhere.

A thought suddenly occurred to her. 'What about Manju? Maybe he saw something. Did you find him yet?'

Ramu shook his head. 'No. He's been missing ever since the attack on Ponnuswamy. The police came to the hospital to check up on him. They've sent search teams to the homes of his extended family and friends, hoping to catch him.'

After Ramu had sent Kaveri home in a horse cart, he made his way back to his room. Dr Roberts caught him on the way, as he was climbing the steep staircase.

'Rama Murthy! Just the man I wanted. Come, come.' Roberts beckoned him into his office. He had just bought a new apparatus advertised in the *Daily Post* – an Aymard milk steriliser. As the doctors surrounded him and watched carefully, Roberts poured milk into the large inner compartment and water into the narrow outer compartment, then placed the contraption onto the fire. The water boiled, and the steam heated the milk inside, killing the germs. Seeing the look of fascination on Ramu's face, Roberts promptly offered to pack it for him to take home later that evening 'as a belated wedding present'.

As he jolted his way home in another hired cart, Ramu sorely missed his car, wondering with a frown when the infernal garage was planning to send it back. The Aymard steriliser dug into his stomach with each turn, and he had to readjust its position. The car must need a large repair job, he supposed, leaning back with a sigh.

Ramu jolted out of his memories to realise that the cart had turned into the North-East Diagonal Road that led into Basavanagudi. After a day spent in the confines of the hospital, he suddenly felt cramped. The afternoon heat still lingered in the air, and it was stuffy and smelly in the narrow cart, with its cane hooded covering. The stink of onions and turnips was strong within.

'Did you have a busy day?' Ramu called out to the cart driver.

'Yes, *Ayya*, how did you know?' the cart driver responded in surprise.

'Just a lucky guess,' Ramu murmured.

'Yes, I struck lucky today,' the driver went on. 'I went the whole of yesterday without a single customer. This morning, my wife told me to make a visit to the Daari Hanuman temple on Avenue Road. As I began to drive away, a man hailed me. He was setting up a new wholesale vegetable stall in Chamarajapete. I spent the whole day transporting vegetables from the large market in Chickpete to his stall. I gave him a special discount because of the large number of trips he took, of course.'

Ramu nodded absent-mindedly.

'And I was really in luck.' The driver looked over his shoulder and grinned at Ramu, giving him a glimpse of his deeply stained teeth. Then he hawked his wad of *paan*, and spat a torrent of red juice onto the road.

Ramu winced. 'Why in luck?' he asked.

'Because he gave me a sack full of discarded turnip greens and half-spoiled potatoes! I don't need to buy food for my precious one tonight,' he said as he gave his horse an affectionate pat on its neck.

'Most lucky for you,' said Ramu, reflecting that it was really past time he got his car back from the garage. He badly wanted some fresh air. 'Stop here!' he called out.

The cart stopped, the driver looking astonished. 'Any problem, sir?'

'No, no problem,' Ramu reassured him. 'I just feel like taking a walk. I was sitting in the hospital all day, and I need to stretch my legs.'

He paid the cart driver, adding a generous tip for him to buy his horse some fresh grass to supplement the half-spoiled potatoes, yet half suspecting that the driver would use the money to get himself a good meal of mutton kababs with a half quart of rum. Ahhh. It was good to be out in the fresh air. He clutched the bulky milk machine in his arms and began to walk home. He decided to take a long detour, walking past the central public square of Basavanagudi, with its landscaped gardens, and taking a turn towards Kempambudhi Lake.

As he strolled along enjoying the fresh air, he skirted the large wooded grounds of the Ramakrishna Ashram. Kempambudhi Lake was to his right, and as he crossed the wetlands below it, he heard the familiar musical call of the lapwings, 'Did-you-do-it? O-why-did-you-do-it?' He looked up. A V-shaped flock was flying home in the dusky evening sky, returning to their roosting sites in the wetlands. Egrets flew above him too, aggregations of white specks high in the sky. Ramu stood for a while at the lake, watching the sun slowly disappear behind the horizon as the fishermen retrieved nets full of fish from the water, and grazers began to hurry their cows home.

He sighed with relief as he reached the corner connecting to the North-West Diagonal Road. Not much farther now. He crossed a small raised platform that signalled the presence of the local *garadi mane*, a wrestling home used by local strongmen. To the back stood a small hut with a makeshift curtain of cloth rigged up to provide the wrestlers with privacy as they changed and bathed themselves. In front of the hut, a group of six strapping, muscled men, their bodies glistening with oil, performed their exercises in a pit filled with soft sand. They grunted with effort as they picked up huge cylindrical and wheel-shaped objects of granite, raising them above their heads and twirling them with a loud shout before throwing them back in the sand. To the side, their teacher squatted on a stone platform, in the shade of a peepal tree, occasionally shouting encouragement or insults.

'*Daakhtre*! *Namaskara*!' The teacher hailed him as he walked past. '*Tiffin ayitha?*'

Ramu waved back and nodded. 'Yes, I have eaten. And you?'

Pleasantries exchanged, he quickened his steps. Soon, he'd be home. He couldn't wait to kick off his shoes, exchange his stiff shirt and pants for a comfortable loose *lungi* that he could wrap around his waist, and relax with a steaming hot cup of coffee, sitting next to his wife.

But on the next stretch of road, the newly installed electric street lights had failed. It felt more like the roads of his childhood, walking in the dim light that came from a few torches of wood dipped in oil and stuck into crevices in the stone. They cast more shadows than light. He passed a large tamarind tree. Locals claimed the tree was over a century old. Bats hung from every branch: large, upside-down, ungainly, fascinating sights. Ramu quickened his steps. People claimed that it was bad luck to pass under the tamarind tree at dusk – the *pishachi*, the evil woman spirit that lived in the tree, had a specific fondness for young men in the prime of life, and would suck the life out of them, leaving a dried-up husk below the tree to be found the next day. In his rational mind, Ramu knew this was nonsense. But at this time of day, all he could remember was the voice of his grandmother, filling his ears with stories of unwary travellers duped by *pishachis* when he was a small child. He walked on fast.

13

Lessons for Elderly Ladies

The next day, Kaveri waited impatiently for Ramu to leave. She had promised him she wouldn't venture out alone again, but she planned to continue working on her project.

She placed her maths books in a neat pile and looked at them, pursing her lips, then set them aside. The murder more urgently claimed her attention. She took out a notebook and began writing down a list of suspects. Who were the people at the dinner that evening?

Manju and Muniamma, the mystery woman, and Ponnuswamy. She paused before writing, then decided to write down names in both pen and pencil. Pen for prime suspects, and pencil for unlikely ones – she could always erase those and move those names to the other column if she found out more. She wrote Manju's name in ink in the left column, and Muniamma and 'mystery woman' in the right column, in pencil. She wrote down Ponnuswamy's name too, in pen, and put a neat line through the middle, striking it out. After all, if he *were* alive, he would have been a prime suspect.

What about the steward, gardener and the other cleaners? She thought for a moment. Before Ismail and Ramu had reached the Century Club on the day she found the knife, she had managed to engage the steward in conversation. By then he had been quite in awe of her, and willing to tell her anything she asked. He had told her, and the woman cleaning the floor had agreed volubly, that they had been in sight of each other all the time.

The only other people at the site had been the two gardeners, but they had left by 7.30 p.m., well before dinner was served. The security guard at the gate, whom the steward had called over, confirmed this. The guard had not seen them return, and claimed he'd been standing at the gate for all of that time. He said the Urs's driver had been chatting with him, and could give him an alibi. Kaveri shook her head. Too many alibis to check – still, she was sure the police would look into all of that.

She added a third column, heading it 'Those with Alibis', listing beneath it the names of the steward, the woman cleaner, the security guard and the Urs's chauffeur. The Reddys had come by horse cart, as had the Iyengars. Mr and Mrs Sastry, also doctors at the hospital, had left early, before dinner. Mrs Sastry had apparently been feeling unwell. The other drivers had gone out for dinner, and returned only at 10 p.m., along with Ramu's cart driver. Once again, this had been confirmed by the security guard. And Dr and Mrs Roberts had driven themselves. She decided to leave out the gardeners, as well the cart drivers.

What about the doctors and their wives? She chewed the end of her pencil absent-mindedly. It was unlikely that any of them would have committed the murder. They may not even have known Ponnuswamy, let alone wanted to kill him. Still, perhaps she should write down their names too. In the column of 'Those with Alibis'? Perhaps not. After all, it was a party night and no one was closely observing their neighbours. Maybe Daphne had gone out and stabbed Ponnuswamy while pretending to clean her dress? Kaveri giggled. She could not imagine the proper looking Englishwoman, Daphne, who had collapsed into a moaning heap at the mention of murder, confronting a hulking brute like Ponnuswamy and killing him with one swift blow to his chest.

As Kaveri wrote down the last names on her list – Mr and Mrs Reddy – she stopped for a while, wondering whether she should add Ramu's and her names too, just for the sake of completeness. It really came down to the fingerprints in the end. She needed to brush up on her knowledge of fingerprinting science. If only she hadn't left her biology books behind in Mysore.

Absorbed in her list, Kaveri didn't see an elderly woman enter the yard carrying a small child on her hip, nor hear her name being called at first. She emerged suddenly from her trance when a voice enquired, 'Kaveri? My child? What are you doing . . .'

'Yeeaagh!' Kaveri leapt into the air, scattering notebook, pen, pencil and eraser across the floor of the room. She turned around. 'Uma aunty?' she said – calling the older woman aunty as a mark of respect – as her astonished neighbour backed slowly away from her.

'Kaveri, I am sorry if I disturbed you,' she said, her voice shaking as she eyed Kaveri uncertainly. 'I called you for several minutes, and there was no answer. Then I peeped inside and saw you sitting on the mat, with a pencil in your hand . . . *Kaveri* –' Uma's voice dropped to an awed whisper '– are you studying?'

'Shh,' Kaveri cautioned in a fierce whisper. 'I'm working for my mathematics test. Don't tell anyone, no one knows here. I don't know what they will think of me.'

Uma aunty nodded, but her eyes were questioning. 'How

did you learn how to do such big sums, my dear?' she asked, flipping through the pages of her maths notebook, which were covered with numbers written in Kaveri's neat handwriting. 'I can't even read my name.'

Kaveri asked Uma aunty to sit down in the kitchen and got her a cup of coffee. She gave Uma's young grandson Ravi a piece of paper and a pencil to keep him busy. As the boy scribbled away, she sat down facing Uma and said, 'Yes, aunty, I went to school in Mysore. There is a school for girls, the Maharani's school, where I studied till matriculation. Then . . .' Her voice faltered. 'I moved here. My husband is very supportive of all that I do,' she added hastily. 'But my mother-in-law told me early on that she doesn't approve of women going out to study, or work outside the house. I . . . I don't know if she will approve of my plans to study further. So I practise and revise when I get time, mostly when my mother-in-law is sleeping – and then I hide the books at night. So you can't tell anyone that you saw me reading.'

'Not even Ramu? He knows, doesn't he? An educated wife would be fitting for a doctor like him.'

Kaveri looked at Uma aunty in wonder. Uma aunty was so broad-minded, despite being so traditional in her observances. She wished her mother-in-law would think more like her. How wonderful life could be then.

'I haven't dared to ask him, aunty,' she said. 'My father always encouraged me to study, of course. My father is a high school mathematics teacher in Mysore, you know. He pushed me to study, against my mother's objections. My mother always said that my husband's family would think it shameful if I went to college and wanted to work outside the home in a regular job. They would say, "Such a wealthy family, can't they afford to keep her at home?" I really want to finish my BSc in mathematics and then become a teacher in a women's college.'

'But Kaveri,' said the ever-practical Uma, 'how will you do your BSc exams without telling Ramu?'

'I've worked it out with my father,' Kaveri said, moving closer to her. 'If nothing else works, he'll say he's missing me, and write to Ramu. I'll go home for a few days, sit the exams, and return.'

Uma nodded. 'My parents refused to send me to school.' She had a tight lipped ironic grimace on her face. 'They got me married and handed me over to my husband's home when I was eight. I asked my husband to let me go to school, but he refused. Where was the time? Cooking, cleaning, looking after my mother-in-law, bringing up four children . . .' Kaveri reached out a hand to squeeze Uma aunty's hand.

'Kaveri – will you teach me also to read?' Uma aunty asked hesitantly.

Kaveri jumped at a hissing noise. The milk, forgotten on the fire, had boiled over, and was now spreading across the kitchen floor. She jumped up and took a cloth, using it to carefully remove the pot of milk. When she turned back, Uma was tentatively touching her maths textbook's cover.

'Aunty? Do you want to learn? Or are you just playing with the idea?'

Uma aunty grabbed her hands, gripping them with desperate urgency. 'Kaveri, teach me, please. I promise to learn. I promise to practise. I promise to be serious. Please, my dear. I have always wanted to learn. First my father refused me, then my husband, then my son. I had been pinning my hopes on my darling boy Ravi.'

Hearing his name, her grandson looked up at her. He moved closer to Uma, digging his elbow into her hip as he continued to scribble on the paper.

'You can teach me easily,' Uma continued. 'I can come and visit you in the afternoons, when no one is at home.'

Kaveri cringed inwardly as she thought of the time that she would have to take out of her scarce afternoon study time to teach Uma aunty. But how could she resist such an earnest request?

'Do you know, my father wrote to me this morning,' she said. 'My cousin, Krishna, passed his MA degree examination in English with flying colours, securing a Distinction. My father is so pleased. I am even more pleased.' Her eyes were shining.

'Why?' Uma aunty was curious.

'Only three candidates passed the exam this year. And . . .' She paused dramatically.

'The other two were women.'

Uma aunty clapped her hands.

'The world is changing. These women, and their daughters, will make sure that all women like you, aunty, will learn how to read and write. So that they can face the world on an equal footing with men.'

14

A Visit to the Library

That evening, Ramu came home early. As he approached the gate, a voice hailed him. He stifled a groan. Uma aunty again. He liked their elderly neighbour – when his mother had been away, she had often handed him parcels of food – but he hoped she wouldn't make a habit of waylaying him on the road each evening.

'Ramu! Stop for a minute,' Uma demanded as she came up behind him, out of breath from having hurried. Her grandson was, as usual, attached to her hip. Ramu did not remember ever having seen that boy walk. He would become a spoiled child if she kept carrying him around like that all day, he thought idly.

'What was that large parcel you brought home last week?' Uma aunty demanded.

'What?' Ramu was confused. Then he remembered. 'Oh. The Aymard milk steriliser.'

'The what?'

'A new invention, Uma aunty. You place the milk in it, and it heats it safely to a high temperature without burning the milk. It disinfects the milk so that all the germs inside die, making it very safe to drink.'

Uma aunty stared at Ramu, perplexed. 'That's what you brought home for your wife? Not a sari? Or jewellery?'

'Kaveri liked it. She was so happy when we used it today.'

'Ramu,' Uma began, then stopped.

'Yes aunty?' Ramu encouraged her.

'I wanted to thank you. For your wife. For agreeing to teach letters.'

'Teaching? Teaching who?'

Uma aunty laughed. 'Teach me, Ramu. Kaveri. Your wife.'

'I don't need to teach her letters. She has already passed her matriculation,' spluttered Ramu, feeling increasingly confused.

Uma aunty only laughed harder.

I wish she would stop laughing and tell me whatever she wants to say clearly, he thought crossly.

'Silly boy. Kaveri is teaching me, see. She has been teaching me letters yesterday. I can now read – at least all the vowels. A, Aaa, E, Eee . . . I can also write two of the letters, Ramu,' she added with obvious pride.

She pointed to Ravi, leaning on her hip, sucking his thumb. 'I don't want my grandson to grow up like his father, grandfather and great grandfather – sneering at illiterate women,' she said vehemently as she turned to go back to her house.

Ramu continued home, his brain whirling with thoughts. His new bride was full of surprises. He knew that Kaveri had studied up to her matriculation degree, in the Maharani Girls' School in Mysore, of course. He vaguely remembered his mother saying that she had insisted that they stop sending her to school once she completed her matriculation, as she did not want her daughter-in-law, from a respectable family, going outside the house to talk to and be taught by strange men. Ramu now wondered, with some embarrassment, why he had not paid greater attention, overriding his mother's objections.

Kaveri's father had been very happy to have his younger daughter married to an educated doctor. He had put in a word to his son-in-law, Ramu remembered, asking him to consider enrolling her in college. Focused on his work at the hospital, Ramu had not given a thought to it. How selfish of him.

As he entered the house, he couldn't see Kaveri anywhere. He went in search of her. She was climbing a ladder in a corner of the outhouse, reaching out to the loft. When he came behind her and called her, she jumped, and the rickety ladder wobbled. He ran across the room just in time to steady it and catch his wife as she fell with a thud into his arms, scattering a pile of books on the floor.

'Ca-calculus?' he said, surprised.

Kaveri squared her shoulders and raised her chin. 'I want to study mathematics further. I am preparing for my degree examinations,' she announced, daring him with her eyes to respond.

Ramu surprised her, reaching forward to clasp her by the shoulders. 'That is excellent, Kaveri,' he said warmly. 'I am so proud. Shall we take you to Central College to register for a BSc once the college reopens after the summer break?'

'Your mother will not like it,' Kaveri warned, as she moved towards him.

'I'll explain to her,' Ramu said. 'We'll make her understand. If it's so important to you, we must support you.'

The radiant smile on Kaveri's face was answer enough.

'Can you take me to the library this evening?' she asked. 'I want to get a membership, and collect some books. Especially a book on fingerprinting. Can we?'

Thirty minutes later, their car parked by the side of a

majestic *ashwath katte*, a raised platform under the canopy of a sacred banyan tree, Ramu and Kaveri headed towards the majestic red brick and mortar building with gabled roofs that housed the Public Library. As they passed the tennis courts laid out to the side, they walked past the statue of Seshadri Iyer, the former Dewan of Mysore, and stopped to admire the rose garden that surrounded it. Kaveri breathed in the fragrance of the roses, looking at the large blooms in shades of red, pink, purple and white, lit with electric lamps.

'There is another Bangalore Club housed here,' Ramu mentioned, as they walked up the steps.

Kaveri looked at him. 'Really?'

'Yes. The building has various tenants. There is a museum, the Club rooms are over there –' he waved his hand '– along with a billiards table.'

'Two clubs in the same park?' Kaveri asked curiously.

'Well, this one is relatively exclusive. Sir M. Visvesvaraya and a few other select people constitute its only members.'

'That explains the tennis courts,' Kaveri said, as they reached the Library entrance. She looked up to admire the large impressive red building with its Italian-styled columns and gabled roof. With two front porches adorned with granite columns, multi-level tiled roofs, and tall glass windows, the building exuded an inviting air.

Kaveri was quivering with excitement. She missed her school's library, from which she used to borrow and devour the latest mystery fiction. These days, she only managed to read the local Kannada language newspaper, the *Karnataka*, from cover to cover.

She looked up in wonder at the tall ceiling which soared above them, stretching close to fifty feet above their heads. Soft evening light shone in from the two levels of windows above, and the wooden ceiling reflected the light of the electric lamps. The library was a cornucopia: thousands of books were neatly arranged in stacks of curved wooden bookshelves, extending in all directions.

A bored-looking clerk handed them a printed sheet of paper with membership guidelines. A Class membership could be accessed through a monthly subscription of Rs. 2, and entitled the subscriber to borrow four books at a time; B Class membership cost Rs. 1 per month and entitled you to two books; while C Class membership, at Rs 1-8-0 per month enabled access to one volume at a time. Kaveri looked at Ramu, startled. So expensive! She decided to take the C Class membership. Before she could speak, Ramu handed over two rupees from his wallet to enrol them as A class members. Perhaps he also needed books for his work, she surmised. She decided to select two books, and leave two for him.

Ramu showed no signs of selecting a book for himself. He ambled along with Kaveri, watching her as she eagerly moved, first to the science section, where she selected a book on mathematics and one on fingerprinting. She then moved on to the history and English literature sections. She picked up two detective novels, then returned them to the shelf with obvious reluctance.

'Don't you want them?' Ramu asked her, surprised.

'No . . .' Her voice trailed off. 'I'll pick them up next time.' She turned to Ramu. 'Have you ever read this? It's a favourite of mine. By Baroness Orczy – can you believe, a Baroness who writes detective fiction?'

'Who's the detective?' asked Ramu, leaning against one of the bookcases.

'It's a policewoman, also titled. Lady Molly heads the female section of Scotland Yard,' Kaveri continued chattering to Ramu as they walked to the checkout desk, telling him excitedly about the different mysteries in the book.

'Where are your books?' she asked him.

'Here they are.' He handed Kaveri the two books she'd returned to the shelf so reluctantly just a few minutes ago. *Lady Molly of Scotland Yard* and *The Sign of the Four*, Arthur Conan Doyle's Sherlock Holmes masterpiece.

'I barely have any time to read, Kaveri,' he added. 'I got the subscription for you.'

As they left the library, Kaveri floating down the steps, books clutched tightly in her arms, Ramu looked at his watch.

'Seven p.m. Time to go home,' he said with regret. 'I wanted to take you to the Brothers bakery, but we'll have to leave that for another day. They close at seven.'

He glanced at her as they got into the car.

'You're very quiet. Tired?'

'Not really,' Kaveri said. 'Just . . . pleasantly exhausted.'

She turned to Ramu. 'Tell me about your work in the hospital.'

'What do you want to know? I've been busy all day looking at accounts. Boring stuff. You know, for the new upgrades we're planning to the hospital equipment.'

Kaveri nodded. She had read all about it in the newspapers – as had all of Bangalore. The hospital had received a large sum of money from the British government to purchase some modern equipment. The money was stored in a large safe in Roberts' room, and a constable was stationed outside the door at night to guard it from thieves.

'No medical work?' As Ramu turned to look at her, she said wistfully, 'I just wonder sometimes, what you are doing, when you are work all day. You know what I do.' She gestured dismissively at herself. 'Chopping vegetables, cooking, cleaning. Women's work. What do you do at the hospital all day?'

'Not all women, Kaveri. Had you come to the hospital to see me a few weeks previously, you could have met a lady doctor on our staff.'

'What? Who?' Kaveri sat bolt upright, looking at him incredulously.

'Yes. Miss A. G. Allen. She was the Assistant Surgeon here, but was recently posted to the town of Davanagere, to take charge of a new female dispensary.'

'It must be useful, having a female doctor,' Kaveri said.

'Yes, Miss Allen is an expert in treating women. In fact –' Ramu turned to Kaveri '– she recently ordered a Winternitz electric bath for Lady Curzon Hospital.'

'What's that?' Kaveri asked, fascinated.

'It's an electric light bath, Kaveri. The Winternitz baths were picking up in popularity when I was in London last year. They're a craze amongst the wealthy women of Europe and America, who believe the process reverses signs of ageing.'

'Really?' Kaveri badly wanted to meet this woman. How nice it would be, to get out of the house and get back into a college. Maybe she could become a teacher, or even a doctor, once she finished her Bachelors. She leaned back against the headrest and closed her eyes, plotting how to convince her family that she needed to get a job after completing college.

15

A Fingerprint Test

When Kaveri saw the crow cawing at her from the mango tree, she cringed. She had slept very badly that night. Her sleep had been plagued with dreams: of drowning in knee deep water while three evil looking snakes floated around her, sneering at her panic-stricken flailing attempts to keep herself afloat. When she got up and went to the garden, she saw a black cat on the road, sunning itself on the neighbour's wall. And now a crow. Bad omens all around. If her mother-in-law had known this, she would perhaps have banned her from touching anything.

At 6 a.m., the moon had finally tired of sentinel duty. The sun was taking its place, inching up the sky, painting the horizon with delicate shades of pink and mauve. Kaveri finished grinding the dosa batter, set the stone and pestle aside to clean later, and wiped her sweaty face with the *pallu* of her sari. The crow cawed at her derisively as she went outside to collect some of the jasmine blossoms that hung like white bells from the creeper that trailed over the compound wall. She plucked a handful of flowers, placed them in a bamboo basket, and took them inside to the prayer room.

She sat down with Ramu as they sipped the first coffee of the day, foaming at the brim. Kaveri admired the way Ramu drank his, steaming hot and well frothed with milk, pouring it straight from the tumbler down his throat. It had now become a treasured morning ritual for the two of them, this five minutes of togetherness before their separate days began, at hospital and home.

'The police came and collected Muniamma's fingerprints in the hospital,' Ramu said softly. 'She was unconscious through it all. The police daubed her fingers with ink, then pressed her fingers onto a blank piece of paper. She did not even move once.'

'Did the prints match?' Kaveri scarcely breathed, waiting for Ramu's response.

'Today is the day that the fingerprint reports on the *lathi* are expected back.'

'Will Ismail tell you what they've found?' Kaveri asked.

'I hope so.' Ramu sighed. 'We have not yet been able to trace Manju, to collect his fingerprints for testing.'

He put down his coffee cup, and got up decisively.

'Let me go and find out what is going on, Kaveri.'

At the gate, he turned back. Kaveri's slender figure was silhouetted in the doorway. She was watching him intently – even a little forlornly. His shoulders slumped. They had barely spent any time together in the past few weeks. The pleasurable drive they had taken a few days back seemed like years ago.

Today would be yet another long day.

'Don't wait for me for dinner, Kaveri. I may be late. If I'm not back before it gets dark, eat, and go to sleep.'

She nodded. Ramu knew it was futile – she would most likely wait up for him before she ate. With a last wave over his shoulder, Ramu got into the car and drove away. Kaveri gazed at his retreating figure with a lump in her throat. *Stuck at home again.* Then she squared her shoulders decisively.

Time to stop mooning and act like a sensible person.

Less than five minutes after Ramu had reached the hospital, a ponderous thump of heavy nailed boots announced the arrival of a visitor. When Ramu hurried down the stairs, he was greeted by the sight of – as he had half expected – Inspector Ismail. He waited to the side as Ismail unhurriedly took off his coat and hung it on one of the hooks on the wall near the entrance for the doctors to keep their sweaters, mufflers and shawls, wiped his feet on the mat, and took off his boots. Ismail nodded at him, as Ramu greeted him with a *namaste*.

With a quick 'Shall we go up?' Ramu led the way upstairs. Neither Appia nor Roberts had as yet come in. It was too early for them – Ramu was usually the first doctor to arrive, as the others had large families and other domestic responsibilities that prevented them from leaving home as early as he could. It was a habit he had developed as a bachelor – of leaving home as soon as he'd hurried through his morning ablutions and breakfast, and heading straight to the hospital. Ramu thought of Kaveri's forlorn wave to him as he'd driven away that morning, and wondered if he should change his timings, to come in a bit later and spend more time with his wife. He came back to earth after a pointed cough from Ismail, who was looking at him with an air of gentle enquiry.

Ramu flushed, wondering – not for the first time – what there was about this formidable giant of a man that flustered him.

'Please sit,' he said as he invited Ismail into his room. There was barely enough space; a large wooden desk, with a chair on either side – for doctor and visitor – took up most of the room. Ismail folded his bulk into the visitor's chair and sat down. The chair creaked, testing Ismail's bulk out, then stopped. Ramu let out the long breath he had no idea he'd been holding, and winced. He looked at Ismail sheepishly.

Ismail raised his eyebrows, silently teasing Ramu. 'The chair will not break. It looks like it has held, and weathered, better men than myself.'

He took out his notebook from a voluminous pocket. Today, he was wearing standard policeman-issue uniform. With this, strangely, he wore a large sleeveless woollen jacket, with massive side pockets. Ramu stared in fascination at the pockets.

'My wife knitted this,' Ismail said, following his gaze. 'Very useful for a policeman like me. I can carry all my stuff.' Ismail continued slowly flicking through the pages of his notebook until he found what he was looking for.

Ramu looked at the file he was holding. 'The fingerprint report?' So he wouldn't have to chase Ismail down to ask for it after all.

'Yes.' Ismail handed the folded sheet of paper to Ramu.

The report was short. At the business end of the knife, the bloodstains matched the common group O+. Ponnuswamy's blood group was O+, confirming that the knife was most likely the weapon used to kill him.

Additional evidence came from the fingerprint report. There was a smudged partial thumbprint in blood – which Ismail had shown them on the knife Kaveri had discovered in the Century Club gardens. The police had also found a complete fingerprint from an index finger, which had shown up when they had used fingerprinting powder. Ramu nodded. Kaveri had dived into the book on fingerprinting as soon as they'd reached home, and summarised the procedure excitedly for Ramu later that night, when they were in bed.

Ismail leaned close to him and said slowly, 'Muniamma's prints do not match the ones we found on the knife. We need to get Manju's prints. Ponnuswamy was an awful man, but justice, if it was to be served on him, should have been served by the law.'

Ramu nodded. 'My wife would agree with you.'

'Your young lady is a formidable woman. Let us just say that if I were a criminal, I would not like to come up on the wrong side of her.'

'How can we help?'

Ismail looked grave. 'I don't know how to ask. But perhaps the clue lies with Manju, and the woman he met that night. If we know who she is, we may be able to pursue the case further. At least, we need to find out who hit Muniamma on the head.'

'How do you know that it wasn't Manju?' Ramu interrupted.

'He took an awful lot of trouble to disguise himself in that case. If he just wanted to hit his wife on the head . . .' Ismail paused, looking at Ramu frankly . . . 'then he would have hit her at any time. In any case he had hit her on many previous occasions. Why would he wear hobnailed boots, climb over the wall, drop a brass safety pin in the tomato patch, then hit his wife on the head?'

Ramu nodded. It was most peculiar. Why would someone else want to hit Muniamma on the head though? Unless . . . A thought occurred to him.

'Did she see anything that night?'

Ismail stared at him for a few minutes before responding.

'A witness to Ponnuswamy's murder? Yes. I hadn't thought of that. It is certainly possible. But Manju was with her all the time. He may have seen something too.' He spoke urgently to Ramu. 'We must find Manju. How will we convince him to step out of hiding?'

16

An Excursion into Forbidden Quarters

Meanwhile, restless at home, Kaveri decided to visit Uma aunty for a change of scene. It would be nice to spend the morning with her, perhaps even learning a new recipe to try on Ramu. She had liked the surprised look on his face when she'd made *bisi bele hulianna* for dinner yesterday. Watching him lick the leaf clean of the hot spicy rice with lentils, then ask for a second helping had left her with a pleasing feeling of accomplishment that still warmed her belly.

As she left the house, she asked Rajamma to lock and bolt the door behind her, opening it only when she returned home.

'Uma aunty?' Kaveri called over the wall.

Her elderly neighbour came out, holding her hands above her eyes and squinting against the sun.

'Come in, Kaveri. Have a cup of coffee,' she invited.

Within a minute, Kaveri was in Uma aunty's house, sitting

on the mat in the kitchen, warming her hands near the stove as Uma aunty made her a cup of strong coffee with a little milk and two generous spoonfuls of sugar. Kaveri told Uma aunty how she had warmed up her coffee thrice that morning, eventually pouring it out onto the papaya tree after it had become undrinkable. When Uma aunty asked her why she had forgotten to drink the coffee – 'Anything on your mind, my dear?' – and placed a gentle, wrinkled hand on her knee, Kaveri's eyes unaccountably welled up with tears. She found herself with her head on Uma aunty's lap, sobbing, while the older lady stroked her hair gently – the coffee lying ignored by her side in its steel tumbler.

Later, as Uma aunty made fresh coffee for her (her banana tree having received this batch of coffee), Kaveri narrated the entire story to her: beginning with the murder of Ponnuswamy, and ending with how she'd felt when she'd seen Muniamma lying unconscious in the hospital.

'I'm so fond of Venu – he's such a sweet boy. His little frame is shrinking in on itself as he tries to shoulder the responsibilities of an adult while his brother is absconding, and his sister-in-law is in a coma,' she said.

Uma aunty nodded. 'I know the family well,' she said. 'Venu's grandmother, Hiramma, was my mother's servant when I was young. She used to oil my hair and comb it into two plaits every morning. She is a formidable person: takes life by the tail and shakes it. When Manju got a job in the hospital as an attendant, I remember how proud she was. If Muniamma dies, it will be a tragedy they won't recover from.'

Kaveri jumped up and said, 'Aunty! Let's go to the grandmother's house. Where does she stay? Maybe she'll give us some information that can help us solve the crime.'

Uma aunty turned and looked at her, surprised.

'Hiramma stays in the cowherd's colony in Halasur,

Kaveri. I have never gone there,' she began slowly, looking uncertain. 'My son is particular that we avoid the areas of the cantonment. We keep the barriers of caste strictly, as my husband did before my son's time.'

'Your son is not here,' pointed out Kaveri. 'How will he ever get to know?'

Uma aunty nodded slowly. 'You . . .' She hesitated again. 'You are a new bride. No, it is not right. What will Ramu say when he knows you have gone there?'

'He won't say anything,' insisted Kaveri. She remembered Ramu telling her that when he studied in the hostel, he used to visit the house of his close non-vegetarian friend Kala Gowda and had eaten many meals of mutton curry and rice there with relish. His parents had not minded, he had assured her, when she'd gasped. 'In fact I went with him before,' she told Uma aunty, 'and helped him take Muniamma to the hospital.'

'What will your mother-in-law say?'

'We won't tell her,' said Kaveri. 'Come on, aunty.'

With that, Kaveri practically dragged Uma aunty to the door, waiting with impatience until she had her chappals on her feet and closed the door. She had promised Ramu that she wouldn't venture out alone, but she hadn't said anything about going out accompanied by another person. Besides, she thought, it was not as though they were going to an unsafe area. Nowhere could be more crowded than the streets of Halasur.

The two women wrapped their saris around their heads to provide protection from the hot midday sun, and walked to the vegetable market at the corner of the road, where they hailed a cart. Climbing into the cart, they set off to the inner streets of the Halasur cowherds' colony: an area that traditional women like them would not dream of entering in normal circumstances.

The cart passed by Halasur Lake. With calm waters, cows grazing, and women washing clothes at the water's edge, it presented a beautiful panorama. Uma aunty pointed out the army barracks at the far end of the lake, next to which the landscaped Kensington Park gardens formed a scenic strip.

Kaveri stared at a woman standing in front of a large boulder, with two baskets heaped with cow dung at her side. She was shaping the fresh dung into small balls and throwing them with an expert flick of her wrist onto the boulder, where the dung flattened out into a chapatti-shaped patty, sticking to the rock with ease.

'She'll come back in the evening and remove these, once they are dried, and then take them for sale to the local market, to use as fuel,' Uma aunty explained as the horse plodded along the slippery mud lanes strewn with banana peels, discarded flowers and dung of various kinds – dog, human, donkey and pig. The horse's hooves clopped along a muddy *kutcha* road. Kaveri's sari received a splattering of mud as they moved over a puddle. The women held their saris higher around their calves, to keep the hems from getting dirty.

After paying the cart driver, they began to walk, deciding it would be easier that way to locate Venu and Manju's grandmother's home; there was barely any space for the cart to move along these narrow streets. Kaveri looked around in wonder. The entire atmosphere had changed. These streets were so unlike hers, which were silent, with the menfolk out at work and the women indoors, cooking and cleaning for their families. The streets of Halasur were filled with noisy chattering people, with bullock carts tied to the posts of houses, and bullocks eating hay tethered next to the carts. At the front of most of the houses was an empty cowshed, indicating that the cows had been taken out to graze.

People stopped everywhere to stare at the two ladies, young and old, Uma in a nine-yard sari tied in a distinctive style. The cowherds knew women like these well – indeed, they went daily to their homes to supply them with milk. They had never before seen them actually visit their part of the city. Their stares weren't threatening, though, but friendly and open with curiosity.

At each turn, the road grew narrower and more dusty, while the houses pressed close to the road. As they walked along, Uma aunty, nervous at first, slowly began to relax and absorb the spirit of the adventure. She pointed out the entrance to the famous Halasur Someshwara temple to Kaveri as they walked along, telling her that Kempegowda, the founder-king of Bangalore, was believed to have constructed and prayed at this temple. The women moved on past the market streets of Halasur, passing shops selling flowers, coconuts and betel leaves, steel vessels and clothes, gold and silver – constantly asking for Manjegowda's *ajji*'s house. Yes, that Manjegowda who worked in the hospital, the one whom the police were looking for. No, they were was not from the police and had not come to report the family, or get them taken away to the dreaded plague camps outside the city, they reassured several people on the way. They only wanted to visit and help the family, see how they were doing.

Asking directions, they were pulled further in to the deep bylanes of Halasur, reaching a small lane which ended at a tiny hut, built of limestone and mud brick, with a well repaired thatched roof. In comparison to the ramshackle lanes they had just left, this hut was spotlessly clean. The earth in front of it had been packed down until it was hard, and cleaned with water. Fresh *rangoli* had been placed there too. The cowshed was swept out and glistening with water, and a mound of grass had been placed in front of the cow, who was busy chewing. The strong, earthy smell of fresh cow dung mixed with hay filled the air.

Kaveri saw a small figure disappear around the side of the house. 'Venu!' she called loudly.

The figure started, then reversed course and came back. 'Kaveri *akka*?' called Venu, shading his eyes against the midday sun. Then, when he realised that it was indeed her, he yelled, '*Ajji*! Come, *ajji*, come quickly. Kaveri *akka* has come with Uma aunty.'

Venu's grandmother came out. She was a small figure, bent almost double. She walked over to them on spindly bow legs. Kaveri averted her eyes from her swollen varicose veins, looking like large distended blue and purple snakes writhing on the surface of her skin.

Inside the hut, the mud floor felt surprisingly cool on their bare feet after the heat of the blazing sun. Venu's grandmother's eyes filled with tears at the sight of Uma aunty, who was now sitting next to her, patting her calloused hands. Her high-pitched tremulous voice shook with age. 'Manju was my eldest grandson. Now he has disappeared, and no one knows where he is. And my granddaughter-in-law? What will I do if she dies? What harm did she ever do to anyone?'

At this, she broke down completely, sobbing as Venu stood by, helplessly looking on. Uma's eyes filled with tears as well, but she swallowed the lump in her throat, speaking more firmly than she'd perhaps intended. 'That's enough now, Hiramma,' she ordered. 'If you break down like this, you will fall sick. And then what will happen to your daughter and grandchildren, or your great-grandson, still a young baby? Pray for your granddaughter-in-law to recover. Then all will be well. Think of poor Venu here. He is just a boy, and shouldering the burdens of the house. Be brave, and don't make him take on more than he can handle.'

The sharpness in Uma's voice seemed to do Hiramma no harm. Indeed, she jerked and sat up straight, wiping her tears with her sari.

'We have come to see if we can help solve the crime,' Kaveri told Hiramma and Venu. 'To try and find out anything new. Tell us, did Manju's behaviour change recently?'

'That is what I keep racking my head about, but I cannot understand, Kaveri *akka*,' interjected Venu. Kaveri motioned for him to sit down next to her. 'Lately,' he continued, 'he'd stopped taking food from home. He started wearing perfume. He stopped giving us money, and would shout at me when I asked him for money to buy rice.'

'He even . . .' the grandmother said with a worried look, raising Venu's shirt.

Embarrassed at exposing his body in front of the two women, the boy flinched and moved away. 'Yes, Kaveri *akka*, he even started to hit me. My brother – never had he ever hit me before. But now, he even tried to hit *athige* once. I protected her. I told Manju *anna*, "How can you hit her? She has your baby in her stomach!" I stood in front of him and raised my hand to him. My mother came to drag me away, but I still stood there. Eventually, he went away.'

'Manju was so happy that day,' wailed his grandmother. 'I know the evil eye struck him, to compensate for his lucky streak.'

Kaveri looked up. 'What lucky streak?' she asked.

'Manju was very excited last week. He came to visit me after a long gap. It was the evening before he ran away.'

Kaveri nodded. The night before that eventful dinner.

'He said a mysterious well wisher had given him a gift of one hundred and twenty rupees. One hundred rupees paid off a debt he had, so he was left with twenty. He gave me five rupees before he left. That is what I have been using for the past few days to run the house.'

Kaveri was stunned. A hundred and twenty rupees was equivalent to a year's salary, a small fortune for someone like Manju. Who was the well wisher who would have paid Manju such a large sum of money?

17

A Secret Affair

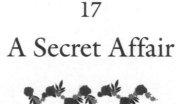

As the two women left Hiramma's cottage and stepped out into the narrow passage that led to the muddy lane outside, the afternoon sun pierced their eyes. The temperamental May sky, overcast and cloudy when they had entered the cottage, had gone through one of its quick mood changes, and the sun now blazed hot overhead. The lane, which had been a chaotic mass of puddles of mud a short while ago, had now dried, and flakes of mud peeled off the ground as they moved. Kaveri looked sadly at her sari border – the woven fringe of peacocks had become an unrecognisable grimy pattern, caked in mud.

As they made their way swiftly down the lane, a small figure darted around the gate of another home, and hissed at them. Surprised, they stopped. A woman wearing a grimy grey sari beckoned to them imperatively. Surprised, they looked at each other and paused. Should they enter? Uma aunty was uncertain. They did not know the woman, or the house. They looked left and right, but there was no one in sight. Then Kaveri impulsively took the decision to enter, moving forward.

'If we go back home, we will be no wiser than when we began, Aunty,' she whispered to Uma, not wanting the strange woman to hear her.

'Who is she?' Uma asked.

A voice rang out from inside the house. Uma had failed to keep her voice down.

'Who am I? Please come in, and you will find out.'

It was a surprisingly youthful voice; melodious, firm, yet confident.

They followed the voice in. And stopped, astonished.

The passageway was dank and narrow. Once they entered, they found themselves inside a surprisingly large and spacious courtyard. The house was surrounded by a garden, with a riot of flowers – purple, orange, scarlet, pink, yellow, white, blue – on all sides. Creepers hung down thick with flowers on a line of bowers, making a passageway fit for a newly wedded bride and groom to pass through. Kaveri and Uma had to press close to each other to make their way through to the entrance of the cottage. The scent of the flowers was overwhelming, imparting a soporific, languorous feeling to the air.

The woman waiting for them at the entrance took their breath away. She was clad decorously, in a thick cotton sari. Yet she stood next to a large, life-size portrait of herself, which provided a dramatic contrast.

Limpid kohl-lined eyes gazed at them from the painting, in a face surrounded by wild curls. Her lush lips were outlined in scarlet, and her eyes were framed by thick eyelashes. Kaveri's breath caught. The woman in the painting had left her hair loose to the waist – no decent woman would do such a thing. Her blouse was cut low in front, and her sari – of the thinnest chiffon – was draped across one shoulder, leaving her figure well exposed. Something about her figure and the way she had been portrayed in the painting caught

Kaveri's attention. *This* was the mysterious stranger who had been arguing with Manju that night at the Century Club. The woman Ponnuswamy had threatened.

Kaveri felt drab and dull in front of this gorgeous peacock of a woman.

'Well?' she asked, putting one hand on her hip and raising her chin. She was not going to stand here and feel insignificant in front of this stranger, no matter how beautiful she was.

From the corner of her eye, she noticed the woman who had beckoned them into the house standing in a corner behind one of the pillars. Hands folded, she was watching them carefully.

Uma aunty was quiet. She had clearly decided to follow Kaveri's lead.

'You wanted to speak to us?' Kaveri asked.

The woman held out a hand to Kaveri. A soft hand, well manicured, with scarlet nails. Kaveri took it, shocked by her own boldness. She remembered what Ismail had said that night at the Century Club. Ponnuswamy, the man who had been murdered, was a well known pimp, and Mala was one of his women. Panicking suddenly, she turned to clasp Uma by the other hand, gripping her tightly for security.

Hesitantly, they entered the building.

Belying its casual exterior, the house was luxuriously furnished. In every corner, there were precious objects – a marble box, exquisitely carved, studded with gemstones; a jade Buddha; a bronze Shiva dancing in a *tandava* pose; and – Kaveri lowered her eyes in confusion – statues of naked women, big breasted, flaunting their bodies.

The woman gestured to them to sit on the colourful mattresses that were spread on the floor with large pillows at the back.

'No,' Kaveri refused firmly. 'First, tell us why you called us here.'

'I would offer you water, but you would only refuse,' the woman said. 'Women like you will not drink water from the house of a woman like me.'

She said it matter of factly, and Uma aunty nodded, looking almost surprised that she would say something that was so obvious to them. Something inside Kaveri winced.

'I would love a glass of water,' she said. And felt rewarded when a look of surprise, then delight, spread over the mystery woman's face. She bounded up almost eagerly, and moved towards the mud pot placed on a stand, pouring water into an elaborately worked copper glass.

Ignoring Uma aunty's pointed glare, Kaveri drank the water. It was cool, just the thing she needed after walking in the heat of the sun.

'Do you want some, *Ammaavare*?' the woman asked Uma respectfully.

Her lips tightened, but she said, 'No, my dear,' civilly.

'Tell us why you called us in,' Kaveri said.

The woman nodded. 'Call me Mala,' she said. 'And this is Narsamma.' She nodded to the woman with the baskets, who had squatted down on her haunches in the far corner of the room.

'Narsamma told me you were visiting Manju's grand-mother. How . . . how is he?'

'Why do you care?' challenged Kaveri. 'What is he to you?'

A shadow crossed Mala's face.

'He was my lover. For two months.'

Kaveri and Uma aunty exchanged shocked glances. *During the time Manju's wife was pregnant.*

'It wasn't my idea,' Mala said after a pause. 'Ponnuswamy forced me to.'

'What was Ponnuswamy to you?' Kaveri asked her in a challenging tone.

'He was my brother's friend. My father died young, followed by my mother when I was only ten years old. My brother got into bad company, and started gambling. He joined a local gang. Everyone told him that a sister like me was an asset, one he should keep in tight control. He . . .' Her voice broke as she spoke. 'My brother sold me out to the highest bidder, when I was about twelve. He made me, a young girl used to playing with her friends, into a common prostitute.'

Kaveri winced. She had heard gossip when she was growing up about such cases. But to hear it from a woman's own lips? She turned her face away, sickened at the thought of Mala as a young girl, losing control over her own body.

'Over the years, with my earnings, we built this house. Then – suddenly, last year – my brother died. I thought I would be free, but Ponnuswamy took over from him and took ownership of my life.' Mala shuddered. 'It was bad enough having my brother in control of me. Ponnuswamy . . .' She closed her eyes. 'He sickened me. The first time he touched me, I threw up. I had to scrub myself clean, every inch of my body. He was much more violent than my brother. I was terrified of him.' She opened her eyes again, and said slowly, and with perfect sincerity, 'I have never been so glad in my life to hear of someone's death as I was the day they told me that he died.'

'Then why did you start an affair with Manju?'

Seeing the disapproval on Kaveri's face, Mala's eyes flashed.

'It wasn't my idea. Ponnuswamy forced me to entice Manju.'

'Why?' Kaveri asked again incredulously. 'He's a poor milkman. Not a wealthy businessman.'

'Ponnuswamy was after the bundles of cash stored in the hospital safe. The news was in the papers some weeks back, that the hospital had a large grant from the British government to buy new equipment. Ponnuswamy was obsessed with getting his hands on the money. He even created a file on all the staff who worked in the hospital, trying to see if he could get to the keys through any of them. Finally, he zeroed in on Manju. An attendant goes all over the hospital, in and out of each room, each day. A doctor normally sticks to his room, and the wards.'

Kaveri nodded slowly. It was beginning to make sense.

'Ponnuswamy wanted to get Manju into his hands, get him gambling, and encourage him to spend money on me. Once he had Manju in his control, through large gambling debts, he wanted to get hold of the keys to the safe, and make copies.'

Uma aunty looked horrified. 'Did he succeed?'

'No. Ponnuswamy had got Manju deep in debt, and started to turn the screws on him. Then Manju's grandmother Hiramma came to speak to me. Of all the people on this street, she was the only one who had ever shown any kindness to me. When I was a young child, she often sneaked parcels of *chitraanna* to me, calling to me and leaving them on the wall of my house before she quickly moved away. Her husband did not allow her to share food with others – they had little of their own, and many mouths to feed – but she saw how thin and starved I was. I remember how that rice tasted – like *amruta*. Food for the gods.

'So I have never forgotten Hiramma. Of course, after my brother sold me the first time, everyone on the street stopped speaking to us. They spat at us when we came near. The children threw dung balls and stones into our home. People jeered at me and hurled abuse when I came close. I soon stopped going anywhere down the lane.

'Hiramma never treated me badly. She never spat at me, as some of the other old ladies did. Only, she did not dare to give me food again. I did not need food by then. All I needed was a kind word from someone.' Mala sighed. And then looked, surprised, at Kaveri. Kaveri had reached out and clasped her hand tightly with her own.

'Hiramma fell at my feet. She begged me, through her tears, to let her grandson go. Told me that he had started to gamble all because of me – that he was now deep in debt, and had taken to drinking. He had begun to beat his wife and brother. And his wife – she was pregnant again . . .' Mala's voice trailed off. 'His grandmother was right. I was bad for him.' Her mouth turned up in a sour pucker.

'Manju was infatuated with me by then. He lavished money on me. Ponnuswamy got him to play cards, to gamble, to get money to buy me gifts. He got deeper and deeper into debt as Ponnuswamy watched, engineering the whole situation.'

She twisted her sari *pallu* into folds, pleating and unpleating them as she spoke.

'Manju was deep in the clutches of the moneylenders. He owed them a hundred rupees.'

Kaveri gasped. That was a large sum – more than a year's salary for an attendant like Manju.

'The moneylenders threatened to break Manju's arms and legs, to kidnap his grandmother, to beat up his pregnant wife. That's how they started to turn the screws on him. In a few days, they planned to beat him up badly, and then propose that he get hold of the keys to the safe and hand them over to Ponnuswamy to make a duplicate, in exchange for clearing his debt.'

Kaveri and Uma aunty exchanged a glance. It was all beginning to make sense now.

'Then Hiramma came to me, asking for my help.' Tears trickled down the side of her face.

'I was terribly afraid of Ponnuswamy. But I could not refuse Hiramma. She was right. My life was ruined anyway.

What right did I have to ruin theirs? But Manju refused to leave me alone. So I took to mocking him. I told him there was no way that a high class courtesan like me would ever make the mistake of falling in love with a common cowherd like him. I told him he reeked of cow dung. I had only taken him in because I thought he would be interesting, a change from the kind of men I usually slept with. He hit me, but I did not stop.'

Narsamma moved, then stilled again. Uma aunty wiped her eyes with her sari.

'I found all his weak points – his ego, his pride, his vanity – and shredded them to pieces. He lost all love for me, and was left only with hatred. Then he left.'

Kaveri looked at her, then said bluntly, 'Why are you telling us this?'

'I just . . . I wanted someone to know the truth. I did not want everyone to think badly of me. And I wanted to know about his wife. How is she? Even though it was not my wish, I have wronged her.'

Kaveri spoke up. 'Manju is missing. We don't know where he is. But Muniamma is still in a coma.'

Mala buried her head in her hands, sobbing quietly.

'I saw you that night, at the Century Club,' Kaveri said.

Mala raised her tear-streaked face. 'Did you? Where were you?'

'I was in the corridor that leads out from the ladies' room. Why did Ponnuswamy attack you afterwards?'

'Attack me?'

'Yes. He had his hand around your throat. And then I saw you later, running away.'

'I tried to keep it a secret from Ponnuswamy that I had rejected Manju and sent him away. But he suspected something was wrong, and followed me to the Club. He was furious when he heard me telling Manju to go away.' Mala held her throat reflexively. 'That's how he treated us – all the women he owned. To keep us in his control.'

Kaveri accepted a second glass of water. After a sidelong glance at her, Uma aunty accepted a glass of water as well. They sat a while longer with Mala.

Mala's story seemed genuine. But there was no denying that she would have wanted Ponnuswamy dead. Could it all be an elaborate set of lies? Kaveri could not help feeling bad for the woman, though. Her life had been shattered.

'Who is the secret well wisher who gave Manju one hundred and twenty rupees?' she asked. If Hiramma's account was true, this was an important question, a potential clue to solving the mystery and finding the attacker.

Mala looked at her, surprised. 'That was me! How did you know?'

'Manju told his grandmother. But you? How did you get the money? One hundred and twenty rupees is a large sum.'

'I sold my jewellery,' Mala said. 'One of my previous admirers had given me an expensive Burmese ruby necklace. I sold it and used most of the money to pay off Manju's debt. He refused to take it from me directly – it hurt his ego. That's why I pretended to be an anonymous well wisher. Even though his debt was only one hundred rupees, I left an additional twenty rupees so he could buy some things for the house. I knew he had stopped giving money to his house because of me. Hiramma will not take money from me directly, so I wanted to find another way to get some food to them.'

Kaveri sat quietly for a while, musing on this. What she had found today answered a number of questions. But it also brought them to a dead end.

She had a sudden thought. 'Who were the other women Ponnuswamy . . .' Her voice trailed off. She could not bring herself to use the word 'owned'. 'Ponnuswamy controlled?' she amended. 'Could they have killed him?'

Mala shook her head. 'I thought of that too. But the two other women – Gowramma and Yellamma – were out of town. There was a big meeting of industrialists, and Ponnuswamy had sent them to Mysore to accompany the men.'

Kaveri shuddered. Mala noticed, and gave her a weak smile.

'I am more fortunate than the other women. I have my house, and some money of my own.'

'Who hit Muniamma on the head then?' Uma aunty, who had been sitting quietly until then, spoke up. 'And why?'

'I don't know,' said Kaveri. 'We don't know who killed Ponnuswamy, and we don't know who hit Muniamma. Surely the two must be related.' She let out a frustrated sigh.

Kaveri had a sudden idea. 'What time was the attack on Muniamma?'

'Around five a.m.,' Mala said.

'This is a narrow street. Surely someone would have seen the attacker?'

'That early in the morning?' Mala looked doubtful. 'Everyone is up, but in their own homes, milking the cows before washing them and getting ready to take them out to graze. But I can ask around,' she offered. 'Some of my brother's friends may know.'

'See if you can find where Manju is hiding too,' Kaveri said. 'His grandmother is worried about him.'

Mala nodded. 'I will try and find out. Now you should go, otherwise people will talk. I will send a message through Narsamma if I hear anything.'

Narsamma got up and gestured to them. They followed her to the back of the house, past a dark corridor, and entered the back garden. Here, the layout was more prosaic than that of the front courtyard, more befitting a frugal housewife. Banana and papaya plants, weighed down with fruit, neatly lined the compound wall. In the corner, a drumstick tree stood tall, pods hanging from it. A vegetable patch was in a corner, next to a curry leaf tree.

Mala hailed them as they left. She passed over a bundle of drumstick pods, neatly tied with twine, to each woman.

'From my garden,' she said shyly. Then hesitated. 'Plants have no caste or community. I hope you can accept this.'

Uma aunty nodded and impulsively placed her hands gently on Mala's head – a blessing. Mala blinked. Then she reached down to touch Uma aunty's feet.

And with that, Narsamma took them to the corner, where they slipped out by an unobtrusive gate, finding themselves at the opening of a busy lane. No one noticed them. They made their way out to the Someshwara temple, and hailed a waiting cart to take them back home.

Uma aunty said a hurried bye to Kaveri, and slipped into her house. Her son would be home soon, and she had to start preparing the evening meal. Kaveri turned into her own home more slowly. Ramu would be back much later. She had the afternoon to herself.

Her thoughts in a whirl, she sat down with a paper and pencil and began to write down what they had learnt from Hiramma that day. She was looking forward to sharing it all with Ramu that night. Only, Uma aunty's words of caution rang in her mind: *Make sure your husband doesn't learn about our encounter with Mala. He won't like it. My son won't either.*

18

Complete Disclosure

Kaveri was resting her sore feet in a bucket of hot water when she heard the gate open. Ramu had come home early. She tried to jump out, but her sari got caught in the bucket. By the time she'd disentangled herself and stepped out, Ramu was in the compound, alighting from the car. He turned to her, impassive as ever, though she saw the sides of his mouth twitching. Kaveri murmured a hasty apology as she fled to the garden with the bucket in tow. Just as she reached the papaya plant, he called, 'Careful, Kaveri. Don't cook the papaya plant. The water must be hot.'

She could definitely see his face twitching now. She gave up, and began to laugh, wringing the moisture from the folds of her sari at her feet. Ramu smiled back.

'Did you sprain your leg?' he asked.

'It's a long story,' replied Kaveri. 'Let me get you your coffee and then I can tell you the details.'

Ramu sniffed as he entered the house. The drawing room was filled with the rich aroma of roasted curry leaves. 'Uma aunty told me how to make a different kind of rice *pudi*, with curry leaves,' Kaveri announced excitedly.

'Mmmm,' Ramu said, taking in a big breath. 'If it tastes half as good as it smells, I'll devour a full plate for dinner.'

Kaveri sat down with him on their front steps, placing two tumblers of hot, sweet coffee in front of them.

'I met Manju's grandmother today,' she said, so softly that Ramu had to bend to catch the words. He looked at Kaveri, puzzled, as she began to describe her visit to Uma aunty's house. As she spoke of taking a horse cart to Hiramma's house in Halasur, Ramu sat up, setting his coffee aside as he focused on her face.

'So we are back at square one,' he said, as she wound up her account.

Kaveri swung her legs restlessly. 'How is the attack on Muniamma related to Ponnuswamy's murder? It must be, otherwise it doesn't make sense.'

The sun dipped low on the horizon, and the silhouettes of the trees cast long shadows on the grass. As the wind blew, the trees swayed in time to the musical concerts of the bulbuls who flittered from branch to branch.

A black kite broke the spell of magic that the setting sun cast on them. It let out a keening cry of triumph as it swooped down from the topmost branch of the mango tree towards the grass, coming up triumphantly holding a frantically wriggling mouse in its hooked beak. Kaveri jumped in alarm as two crows came flying out of the jackfruit tree, shouting in their hoarse voices, and chased after the kite, pecking at its head to try and wrest the mouse from it.

'It's not the mouse who is the target, it's the kite!' Kaveri said suddenly, looking at the birds. Ramu turned to her in surprise. 'I mean, maybe Muniamma was not the target,' she said. 'Maybe the attacker intended to hit Manju, but attacked Muniamma by mistake.'

'Why?' Ramu objected.

'Perhaps Manju saw the murderer? Or the murderer thought he did.' Kaveri got up and paced around the garden restlessly. 'If only Manju had not run away. We could have asked him, instead of all this speculation.'

As they got up to go into the house, Kaveri turned towards Ramu with a challenging look.

'Are you angry with me?'

Ramu raised his eyebrows.

'For going into another community's house,' Kaveri clarified, 'and the house of a cow herder at that. My mother would be horrified if she knew that I'd disrupted the purity of our house.'

Ramu shook his head dismissively. 'Of course not, Kaveri. You know I don't believe in such outdated nonsense about purity and community. In fact, you helped resolve an important piece of the puzzle. I doubt Manju's family would have confirmed his story if I had brought them to the hospital and I or the other doctors had queried them.'

'Your mother would not have liked it,' said Kaveri slowly, her large eyes dark and uncharacteristically serious in the evening light.

'I am not my mother,' Ramu reminded her.

'What perplexes me is . . .' she began after a while.

'What?' Ramu asked.

'How did the attacker enter Muniamma's narrow lanes unchallenged? I hope Mala can tell us more.'

'Mala?' Ramu turned to her, surprised. 'Who is Mala?'

The words dropped like a stone into the suddenly charged atmosphere. She had forgotten Uma aunty's warning.

Ramu looked at Kaveri, sitting up straight, stiff with tension. He moved towards her, and gently set his hands on her shoulders.

'Come, sit with me. Tell me what it is you're hiding.'

'I need to heat up the milk,' Kaveri said.

'The milk will keep. Tell me.' His voice was implacable.

The story of Mala came out slowly, in fits and starts. Kaveri told him of their encounter with the mystery woman, describing how they'd met her and gone into her house. She cast sidelong glances at Ramu's face as she spoke, trying to get a sense of what he was thinking. The lamp cast long shadows on his face and body, and she could not read anything from his face.

All he said, at the end of her story, was, 'Never do this again, Kaveri. You must promise me never to meet this woman again.'

'She is a good woman.' Kaveri's eyes were angry, her voice fierce. Ramu shook his head.

'If you met her, you would understand. She is very nice.' Kaveri persisted.

'I don't want to hear any more.' There was a finality in his voice that warned Kaveri not to pursue the discussion any further. 'Come, Kaveri,' he said wearily. 'Switch off the lights, and let us go to bed. I'm completely exhausted.'

'I don't believe Mala is at fault.' Kaveri's face set in stubborn lines. 'No woman would want to be in her situation,' she argued fiercely. 'She could help us. I don't know why you're being so stubborn about this.'

'Kaveri . . .' Ramu gave up, as he saw his wife moving away from him towards the kitchen .

Kaveri and Ramu attempted no further conversation that night. Husband and wife went to sleep facing in opposite directions, their backs hunched away from each other.

In the morning, Ramu got up early, before the crack of dawn. He crept out silently without waking Kaveri.

When Kaveri woke up, her head muzzy with sleep, she was alone.

19

The Respectability of Good Women

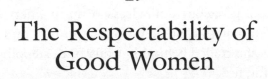

It had been a long time since Kaveri had thought of Ambujakshi. Yesterday, when Ramu had scolded her for meeting Mala, she remembered her old school friend with sadness.

Poor Ambujakshi, she never had a chance. Ambu had been the best student in their class of ten girls. She scored one hundred per cent in all of their tests, wrote in perfect copperplate handwriting, was an expert veena player, did excellent handwork and embroidery, and was the pet of all the teachers. Every parent held her up to their girls as an example of what they should aspire to be. If she were not so friendly and such fun to be with, they would have all hated her. As it was, they loved her – she was sunny, good natured and a joy to be with. Much of Kaveri's facility with maths and numbers was due to Ambu, who spent hours with her, teaching her patiently, and correcting her errors when the teacher had given up.

Ambu paid the ultimate price for her beauty, hard work and talent. Her fame spread far and wide, and she became a much sought after bride. Many prominent families approached her parents for an alliance, and she was eventually married to the eldest son from one of Mysore's wealthiest families when she was just fourteen. Kaveri remembered with a twinge how Ambu had looked the day she was married – like a gorgeous doll, dressed up in finery, her eyes large and stark with apprehension, her posture dull and submissive, as she trailed behind her husband, stepping around the wedding fire.

Two years later, she was back in her parents' home, thrown out by her in-laws because she had failed to give her husband children. Of course, no one pointed a finger at her husband – even though they all knew that he was too drunk to be capable of fathering children, and barely spent any time at home – he was too busy visiting the pleasure woman he kept in a separate home, thought Kaveri.

Assessing a woman's character seemed to be the favourite pastime of elders, both men and women. The burden of the respectability of the home was placed on one's womenfolk. Parents were constantly on guard when it came to their daughters, searching for and identifying 'loose' women – then warning away their children from any contact with them, to protect their reputations.

Ambu returned to school – but only for a day. The girls were thrilled to see her. So were her teachers, who had loved the child, and were devastated to see her married so early. But the parents . . . No, Kaveri corrected herself bitterly. The *fathers*. It was they who were, as always, the moral custodians of the honour of the family. The fathers got together and spoke to Ambu's father.

It was a pity, they said, that a girl who had brought the family such disgrace was permitted to come back to school.

It would bring shame on their own daughters to be associated with such company.

They were confident that Ambu's father would understand. It was all for the good, they assured him, as they drank his coffee, and left with fake smiles of good cheer and bonhomie.

Ambu never returned. In time, Kaveri heard that she had been packed off to their village, to live with their aunt, a child widow. Another woman discarded by society for failing to live up to its standards of 'good womanhood'.

Kaveri paced the room as she remembered the difficulty she'd had trying to trace Ambu's address. Her elder sister, married, had come home for a visit and Kaveri had managed to sneak over to her place when her parents were out, begging her for Ambu's address. Then she'd written a letter to Ambu. How to post it, though? She'd waited for days, hoping to find her father in a good mood. One day, when he was especially proud of her for a veena recital she'd given on Sankranthi, she handed over the letter to him, placing her hands around his neck and leaning her cheek against his, pleading with him to post it to Ambu. His face had darkened, and he'd pushed Kaveri away, crumpling the letter into a ball and throwing it into the waste basket as he left the room.

Kaveri wiped her eyes and squared her shoulders. She was no longer fourteen. And Ramu was not her father.

20

Tracking a Fugitive

Later that evening, as Kaveri walked towards the gate to close it, she saw a movement in the deep shadows. She stiffened.

'It's me.' Narsamma stepped out of the shadows. 'My mistress Mala sent me with a message.'

'What is it?'

'You asked her to find where Manju is hiding? She has found him. He is hiding out on the road to Closepet. Beyond the town, just after the road curves at the foot of the hill, there is an old disused temple on the side of the road. He is hiding there.'

'How did she find out?'

'She asked her brother's friends to help her. One of Manju's cousins, who is closest to him, lives in Channapatna. He is afraid to keep Manju in his house. The police have come there to search for him a couple of times. But he brings food and water when he can sneak out. Someone waited behind his home and followed him to the temple.'

Kaveri nodded, walking slowly back to the house. She

itched to hop into a cart and take it down to Closepet to confront Manju. But she knew what Ramu would say. And he would be right. This was a task for the police. She turned, hearing a sound from the gate. Aha! Ramu was just coming in. She hurried towards him, telling him what she'd learned.

'I'll go straight to the police station,' Ramu said, turning the car around.

Kaveri waited up for him, unable to sleep. He came in around midnight, his footsteps echoing in the silence. She sat up.

'Have you eaten? Shall I get you some food?'

Ramu shook his head. 'I had some bananas on the way back. I'm not hungry, Kaveri. I just want to get into bed.' He climbed in, holding her tight.

'What happened?' Kaveri asked.

Ramu stroked her hair as he spoke to her.

'We found him, hiding in the temple. We went ahead and parked at a distance, so that he would not be suspicious. Then we took off our shoes, and walked down the road in single file, silently. Two policemen went to the back of the temple, to secure the exit. Ismail and I went in towards the front entrance. Manju didn't even see us coming. He was fast asleep.

'Ismail stood aside in the shadows and signalled to me. We had decided how to approach it on the way in. I would speak to Manju first, and see how much I could get out of him. It seemed more likely that he would confide in me than in the police, whom he had no reason to trust.'

'Manju?' Ramu had shaken him awake.

'*Ayya?* Sir?' Manju was shocked awake. 'Is it you?'

'Yes, Manju, it is me.'

'How did you find me, sir?'

'Mala told me where you were.'

Manju sounded astonished. 'That bitch Mala!' Then hastily he added, 'I beg your pardon, sir. I . . . I just lost my temper, that's all. She led me on a fine dance. I planned to leave my wife and child, my old mother and young brother, for her. I was drunk on her love. I must have been mad. In the end, she was playing me for a fool all along. She was only having a fine time laughing at my expense.' Manju opened his fingers and curled them into fists. 'If I could have killed *her*, I would have. But never my wife.'

Ramu could hear the exhaustion in the man's voice. The tension of hiding out in the abandoned temple for several days, constantly on the alert for capture, must have driven him almost to the edge. He seemed close to fainting with exhaustion. The stench that he carried, after a few days in hiding, was indescribable. Ramu took out the bottle of water which he had carried with him, and placed it Manju's hands. The man drank greedily, as though he had not seen water or food in days.

Then all of a sudden, he placed his face in his hands and began to sob.

'My wife . . . how is my wife?' he pleaded.

'No different than before,' Ramu told him. 'She is still in a coma, but her condition has not worsened. And – it is almost a miracle – the heartbeat of the baby is still intact.'

Manju wiped the tears from his eyes. 'Sir. I beg of you. I don't care what happens to me. I just want my wife and child to survive.' He began to cry again.

'We have very little time, Manju,' Ramu said sternly. 'If you want me to help you, answer my questions truthfully. Otherwise, your wife and son will have to deal with the stigma of being the family of an accused murderer.'

Ramu's words finally got through to Manju. He stopped crying and wiped his eyes.

'Did you kill Ponnuswamy?'

Manju shook his head. 'No, sir. I ran away to Channapatna as soon as I saw Ponnuswamy's body. I knew the first person that the police would suspect would be me.'

'Why did you ask me for money last week?' Ramu asked next. He had heard Mala's version, from Kaveri, and told it to Ismail. But both he and Ismail were unsure if Mala was telling the truth, though Kaveri insisted that she was trustworthy.

'I . . .' Manju hesitated.

'I know you were gambling,' Ramu interrupted brusquely. 'How much did you lose?'

'A hundred rupees, sir.'

'To whom?'

'Ponnuswamy. He runs a gambling den at the end of the Chickpete main road, tucked away in a back alley. I wanted to buy Mala fancy clothes and jewellery. I started to gamble – he sucked me in. The first few times, he let me win. And then . . .'

Ismail, listening in a dark corner, nodded his head. He could fill in the gaps only too easily. It was a common trick used by many crooks. Bring in an innocent, ply him with drink, and hold out the promise of easy money and easy women. Let him win the first few times, and he was hooked. Then you could lure him in deeper and deeper.

'I'll ask you again, for the last time. Tell me truthfully. Did you kill Ponnuswamy?' Ramu pressed.

'I did not,' Manju protested vehemently. 'When I saw him, he was already dead. Ponnuswamy had threatened to send his henchmen to rough up my elderly mother if I did not pay off the debts. And then, like magic – when I went to the office that evening, just before the party in Cubbon Park, there was an envelope on my table. Inside was a bundle of notes. One hundred and twenty rupees. Enough to cancel my debts from Ponnuswamy, and leave a little money over for my family.'

Manju looked up at Ramu. 'I swear on my son's life, sir. I am telling you the truth.'

'Who paid off your debts?'

'I have no idea, sir. I think it must have been the devil in disguise who sent me the note – and I, like an idiot, thought it was a gift from God. I was so ecstatic. I went to the temple in Halasur, and from there, to my grandmother's house, to give her some money for food, and then made my way to the Club. I used the rest of the money to buy a sari for Mala. I sent her a note, asking her to come to the Club. But she . . .' His face darkened, and Ramu remembered Kaveri's description of the scene she saw that night. Manju pleading with Mala, and Mala moving back, gesturing 'no'.

Ramu stood up. 'The police are here.' Manju cringed against the wall. Ismail signalled to the other policemen, who handcuffed him and dragged him away to the car.

'Did you think Manju was telling the truth?' Kaveri asked Ramu once he'd finished narrating the events to her.

'I can't be sure, Kaveri. But he sounded sincere.'

'Did Mala kill Ponnuswamy then?' The room seemed to sway around Kaveri. She remembered the open, frank way in which Mala had spoken to her and Uma aunty, baring her vulnerability. It was not easy to be a woman in her situation. If she killed Ponnuswamy, it was with good reason. But that would not matter to the police, of course. She sent up a silent prayer, hoping Ismail would not turn his attention to Mala.

21
A Victim's Testimony

At the hospital the next day, Ramu walked restlessly up and down the room. He was unable to get the picture of Kaveri visiting a prostitute's home out of his mind. His wife was an innocent, kind hearted and forgiving, but still – what an idiotic thing to do. He hoped he had put all thoughts of meeting Mala again out of Kaveri's head. Still . . . He remembered uneasily that, although he had forbidden Kaveri to meet her again, she had not said anything in response.

Thimakka came into the room, duster in hand, and paused at seeing him striding furiously up and down the room. Ramu stopped, feeling faintly ridiculous.

'Any news from Muniamma, Thimakka?' he asked.

'I was sitting up with her last night. She moaned and opened her eyes once.'

'What?'

'Yes, sir.' Thimakka beamed at him. 'She seems like she may be regaining consciousness. Her mother will be so pleased,' she added.

Muniamma's mother had sat by her side since the day she'd rushed up from the village after hearing of her daughter's attack, leaving her only to eat and bathe. She even slept on the floor next to her daughter, on a thin straw mat, covered only with a cotton sheet – Ramu had told her many times that Muniamma was in a coma, and would not know if her mother was there or not, but she had refused to budge.

'I know you pack food for her, Thimakka.' Ramu opened his wallet, giving her some money.

'Oh no, sir, I couldn't take money for this. I bring her only simple fare, curd rice or lemon rice with a bit of lemon pickle on the side.'

'Yes, but it helps Muniamma's mother, who has little money, manage to pull through the days that she is here.' Ramu pushed the money into Thimakka's hands, feeling bad that he had not thought of it before. How little these people had, and yet how giving they were. He paused for a moment, suddenly feeling ashamed of himself for being so petty-minded about Mala. After all, she was also a woman in a difficult situation. But still – he could not like the idea of his wife spending time with a prostitute.

He ran downstairs to the ward where they were keeping Muniamma. Appia was there, changing her dressing.

'Muniamma's head injury is healing. Look.' He pointed to the wound. 'I took off the large bandage, and replaced it with a much smaller one.' Muniamma moaned as he carefully sponged her wounds with antiseptic, and shook her head, all the while with her eyes tightly closed.

Her mother stared at Appia with distressed eyes.

'Don't worry,' Appia reassured her. 'The fact that she is moving and making noises, however incoherent, is a good sign. She seems to be slowly coming out of her coma.'

Ramu was much relieved, as these were signs that Muniamma may be slowly regaining consciousness. He was also worried though – as the news that Muniamma may be recovering spread, as it surely would, what if the person who had attacked her tried to do away with her again?

When he went home that evening, Kaveri smiled at him tentatively. Ramu pulled her into a hug, whispering softly, into her hair, as he held her close, 'I'm sorry, Kaveri. I should not have shouted at you like that for going to Mala's home.'

Kaveri reached out and patted his cheek. 'It's all right.'

'She must be a good woman. But still, I don't feel comfortable about the idea of you spending time with her.'

Kaveri only nodded, and moved away to fetch him his coffee.

Later that night, when Kaveri asked him for his daily update on Muniamma's condition, he told her of Muniamma's mother's devoted vigil at her bedside.

'She sleeps there each night, next to her bed.'

'What about her food?'

'Thimakka brings it to her.'

'And clothes?'

Ramu raised his eyebrows.

'What about her clothes?'

'I mean, is she washing and wearing the same sari? Muniamma was struck down a week back. Her mother has been with her all that time, hasn't she?'

Focused on cleaning Muniamma's head wound and checking for the heartbeat of her unborn foetus – which thankfully still beat strong within her – Ramu had never thought of such prosaic details as what saris her mother was wearing. He took a thin cotton bundle containing two of Kaveri's old saris with him to pass on to her mother.

As he went in the next morning, it was still early, though the first rays of the sun had begun to filter through the cottonwool-like clouds that dotted the sky. The morning call to prayer came in strong and loud from the nearby mosque. As it wound down, the bells of the Hanuman temple began to ring loudly. It was Tuesday, Ramu realised – a special day for worshippers of Hanuman. The temple must be packed with a rush of devotees.

This early in the morning, the hospital was empty. Only Thimakka had come in, and was just beginning to sweep the floors. The rest of the hospital staff were probably still eating breakfast, or making their way to the hospital.

He opened the door of the patients' room. Muniamma's mother was sleeping on the floor. He moved carefully around her, placing the bundle of saris next to her, near her feet, so she would see it when she got up.

When he sat next to Muniamma, he blinked. Her eyes were wide open.

Ramu buried his head in his hands. Was he dreaming, he wondered? Only yesterday she had still been in a coma, moving restlessly and moaning, murmuring a stream of unintelligible words – mostly gibberish – but her eyes had been closed, and when he had taken a small hammer and tapped the pressure points on her knees and elbows, there had been no response. Yesterday, for all practical purposes, she had been dead to the world.

And today – she was looking at him.

He rubbed his eyes and sat up, placing a gentle hand on her wrist. Her pulse was faint, but steady.

'Ramu, sir?' she whispered.

'Muniamma.'

'What am I . . .' Her voice was raspy. She stopped and coughed.

'Water . . .'

Ramu hurried towards the mud pot that was kept in a corner of the room, filling a steel tumbler with the boiled and cooled water that was kept in the pot for patients and their families. He took the glass to her, and carefully levered her up to partially raise her head and shoulders, supporting her with his left arm as he dribbled a few drops of water into her mouth with his right hand. Her mother had done this several times a day, with a medicine dropper, feeding her milk and water, trying to keep her and her baby nourished.

Muniamma coughed, but managed to drink and keep down a few sips. She then nodded to Ramu, who levered her back onto the bed.

'What am I doing here? This is the hospital, isn't it?'

She gestured to her mother, lying at her feet on the side. And felt her bandage with her hands. Her voice was still rough, and she spoke with hesitation.

Ramu understood what she was trying to ask.

'You were found unconscious, near the entrance of the cattle shed. You had been hit on the head with a bamboo *lathi*.'

'How long have I been here?'

When Ramu replied 'a week', Muniamma gasped. Her hand flew to her rounded belly.

'The child is fine,' Ramu assured her. 'I can hear the heartbeat.'

When Muniamma still looked fearful, Ramu took out his stethoscope. Placing it to her belly, he positioned it so that he could hear the baby's heartbeat, steady and clear.

Placing one end of the stethoscope gently on her ear, he said, 'Can you hear your child?' He grinned at the happy smile that bloomed on her face.

Roberts and Appia were as pleased as Ramu to hear of Muniamma's recovery. Soon after Ramu had shown her the heartbeat of her child, she closed her eyes, and went back into a deep sleep – this time, a natural one.

Roberts had called the police room, and a policeman now sat, stolid and block-like in his uniform, at the end of Muniamma's bed. Muniamma's mother sat at the other end, near her daughter's head, frightened stiff of the police but trying not to show it. She had covered her face and entire body with her sari, and looked almost invisible, wrapped in folds of cloth. Only her hands peered out, tenderly smoothing the hair back from her daughter's forehead.

Muniamma stirred, and murmured something. Her mother stroked her hand reassuringly. Over the past week, Muniamma's petite body had lost a great deal of weight, the slim pickings of fat she had seeming almost to have melted from her bones. She looked like a snake who had swallowed a melon. It was a miracle that her baby had survived, Ramu thought with wonder.

Muniamma opened her eyes again, as suddenly as she had done in the morning. She reached out to her mother, clutching her hand. Then she searched the room again and again, looking for her husband. She flinched when she saw the policeman, and turned her head towards Ramu, looking for reassurance.

Ramu nodded at her. 'It's all right, Muniamma. The policeman wants to ask you some questions.'

Ten minutes later, Muniamma's voice had begun to falter and her eyelids to droop. Ramu gestured to the policeman, who closed his notebook. They tiptoed out of the room, leaving her in the care of her mother.

Muniamma's testimony was clear. Manju had not returned home since that night at the Century Club. She had waited for him all night, and then, as she had done the previous two days, she had gone out at dawn to clean the cowshed and give the cows fresh water and hay.

It had been dark still, the sun just beginning to rise. She'd heard a rustling sound near the entrance, and seen a dark shape in the shadows moving, out of the corner of her eye. Fearing it might be a leopard, she'd turned – then seen a large stick descending on her. She hadn't even had time to let out a cry. After that, she knew nothing. Only blackness.

'So, the intruder lay in wait for her at the cattle shed, a bamboo *lathi* in his hand,' Ismail said, as he sat with Ramu, handing him a copy of the police report.

'What should we do about Muniamma?'

'Can you keep her under observation a while longer?' Ismail asked. 'It's safer for her to be at the hospital. We don't know who her attacker is.'

'Are you planning to release Manju?' Ramu questioned.

'Not yet. We've taken his fingerprints, to see if they match those on the knife used to attack Ponnuswamy.'

Ramu leaned towards at Ismail. 'Even if you release him, can you make sure he doesn't go back and beat up Muniamma or Venu again?'

Ismail slapped his hand down on the wooden table. 'If the fingerprint report turns out negative, I'll put the fear of God into him before I release him. He'll not dare to even look at his wife or brother cross-eyed.' He nodded grimly.

22

A Not-So-Fallen Woman

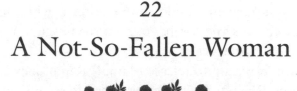

As Ismail and Ramu made their way to the hospital gate,
Ramu suddenly stopped dead in his tracks. Taking a
couple of steps ahead, Ismail noticed that Ramu was no
longer with him, and stopped too, looking over his shoulder
at the young man – who was staring with shock at the gate.
Ismail turned back to the gate to see Kaveri walking in, with
another, older woman.

Ismail watched Kaveri make her way towards them down
the road that led to the hospital, weaving her way through a
line of horses yoked to carts – and a pavement packed with
flower vendors, fruit sellers, and carts piled with fried snacks
and sweets for hungry hospital patients and their families.
She walked briskly, her eyes now focused on Ramu, who
continued to stand stock-still, the same stunned expression
on his face.

Kaveri held onto the arm of the older woman, and seemed
to be tugging her along in her eagerness to get to the hospital
and reach Ramu. Something about the way in which her
eyes sparkled as she neared Ramu made Ismail think with

nostalgia of his wife. He had been married for close to forty years, but he remembered clearly that his wife used to look at him like that when he reached home at the end of the day when they were newly wed.

The two women were now standing in front of them, staring at Ramu and Ismail expectantly.

'I . . . why . . . why are you here, Kaveri?'

Uma aunty shot him a pleading glance. 'I told her to wait for you until the evening. She did not listen.'

'And I told you he said he would be back late tonight,' Kaveri retorted. 'By which time it may be too late.'

'What may be too late?' Ismail stepped forward, his curiosity piqued.

Kaveri looked at Ramu and Ismail for a while without speaking. Finally, she sighed and moved back. 'It is not our story to tell. You need to hear it. Please.'

She gestured to one side, and Ismail suddenly realised there was a third woman in the team. An elderly woman in a crumpled sari, with *paan*-stained lips, she squatted in the shade made by the gatepost. Clearly an attendant of some kind. Ismail's attention was now firmly captured.

Fortunately, it was still early and most of the hospital staff and doctors were not yet in attendance. They needed to move soon, before they gathered an audience. Ismail nodded to Kaveri, gesturing for her to lead the way.

Ramu went ahead with Kaveri and Uma, and the attendant followed at a distance. Ismail gave them a few minutes, then walked on behind them. He noted with some amusement that Ramu and Uma seemed to be attempting to gently remonstrate with Kaveri, but without much noticeable effect.

They took a cart, which led them deep into the twisting and turning lanes of Halasur, the roads gradually becoming narrower, more muddy and potholed. The spectacular flowering trees that lined the British cantonment and areas around the hospital had given way to scraggly roadside castor plants and *ekke gida*, untidy scrubby plants and lanky coconut trees, laden with nuts and full of the screeching of monkeys and crows. Ismail had heard a British sergeant who had recently moved in to Bangalore dismiss the native areas of the city as a 'metropolis of monkeys'. The casual dismissal of the white colonists stung, but the menace of monkeys was real.

They alighted at the end of a small lane. The woman in the crumpled sari moved aside some fronds of vegetation hanging on a wall. And disappeared from sight.

A hidden door behind a green wall of vegetation. Very clever.

Ismail glanced around casually. Ramu, Uma aunty and Kaveri had also gone in, moving quickly so that they didn't attract too much attention. This time in the morning, few people were around. Most cowherds were out grazing their cows at Halasur Lake, and their women were at home, working – cleaning dishes, washing clothes, mopping the floor, and sweeping out the cowsheds with coconut brooms.

Ismail crossed the road and quickly slipped behind the hanging green fronds, finding himself in front of a small gate. Someone had left the gate open, and he was able to quickly get in.

He looked around. He was in the back garden of a house that appeared much fancier than the surrounding homes, which were little better than huts. This was a home arranged with some attention to aesthetics. And the beautiful creature that stepped out from the shade to greet him looked like she was born in this place – a *houri* of unsurpassable beauty, draped in a silk sari that clung to her lush body. Ismail turned his face away, embarrassed.

The woman in the crumpled sari hurried to her mistress's side – for her mistress it was, Ismail thought, studying the body language between the two. The beautiful woman turned to her and gestured. The attendant nodded, and brought her a thick shawl. She wrapped herself in the shawl, which covered her from head to foot. Ismail breathed a sigh of relief. Now he could look at her without torturing his mind with visions of impurity. He had met courtesans and prostitutes before – any man in his line of duty had to – but never one who seemed so pure and yet so attractive at the same time.

Kaveri stood supportively close to her, Ismail noted – and Uma stood protectively close to Kaveri. Ramu, who must be feeling as uncomfortable as Ismail was, stood away to one side.

'This is Mala,' announced Kaveri. 'She has something important to tell us. First . . .' She trailed off, placing her hand on Ramu's arm. Decent women could not tell a man, a perfect stranger too, what she needed to tell Ismail.

Ramu patted her hand. 'I have already told him everything that you told me when you met Mala last time.'

Ismail nodded. He had heard and seen similar stories before. A young woman growing up in a life of hardship with severe family responsibilities becoming trapped by an abuser, her body sold for hire. He looked at Mala directly for the first time. 'I have understood the background. Tell me the rest.'

Narsamma – for that was the woman attendant's name – brought chairs for Ismail and Ramu. The women settled down on straw mats, sitting cross-legged in the shade. Narsamma squatted down on her haunches in a corner, listening intently.

'When I heard from Narsamma that Muniamma was in the hospital, I was horrified.' Mala had an attractive speaking voice – low, melodious, without any of the coquetry Ismail had expected.

She continued, 'My brother brought me into this profession. He had a number of contacts with various people in gambling dens, thieves, pickpockets, murderers. When he was alive . . .'

'When did he die?' Ismail interrupted.

'Six months ago. It was sudden. He was drunk at night, and crossed the road without looking – a horse cart travelling at full speed hit him. The wheels ran over him. He died almost immediately.'

A snort came from Narsamma, sitting in the corner.

Mala's face hardened. 'I cannot lie and tell you that I was upset. He was not a nice man, even though he was my own brother, blood of my blood. My parents passed away when we were young – they were both single children without siblings, and my grandparents on both sides also passed away early. We had no one else. My brother mostly raised me. Almost as soon as I reached puberty, he sold me to a rich businessman for a month. I begged, screamed, pleaded. It made no difference.

'The one thing he soon realised was that he could make more money from me if he left me in control of my clients, rather than turning me out onto the streets. I soon met Narsamma – she was sleeping on the roads, having been discarded by her children because she was of no use to them – and I took her in. Until her, I had no one in the world – except my brother, who was more trouble than help. Now – we have each other.'

Narsamma's eyes misted with tears. She wiped at her face awkwardly with her sari.

'After my brother died, I was inconsolable. Not with grief,' Mala continued fiercely. 'With anger, sorrow, and so many mixed emotions. I knew that for the first time in my life, I was free. But then Ponnuswamy came and claimed ownership over me. He had some papers with him. He said my brother owed him some money – and he was going to use me to pay off his debts . . .' She glanced around defiantly.

Ramu shifted uncomfortably on his chair, but did not respond. They had all come to the house with their own deep-set biases – Kaveri, Uma, Ramu and Ismail. Yet this woman – this independent, beautiful, intelligent woman who had been, by her own account, subjected to horrific abuse and humiliation for most of her childhood and adult life – was a person of courage. She went on.

'Ponnuswamy wanted me to trap Manju in an affair so that he could get the hospital keys from him and gain access to the safe. Manju and I spent less than two months together, and in that time, Ponnuswamy managed to get him entangled in gambling debts. They threatened his family with harm unless he paid them back. Ponnuswamy was going to ask him for the keys to the safe, when Manju suddenly paid off his debts.

'You know how that happened,' she continued. 'After Hiramma came to me, I decided that I could not be a part of this any more. I needed to get Manju free, otherwise his family – including Hiramma – would be attacked by the moneylenders. I sold one of my necklaces, which an admirer had given me a couple of years ago – my brother did not know I had it; I had hidden it from him for a rainy day. It was a ruby necklace, and fetched quite a tidy sum. I used that to repay all of Manju's debts, and then got rid of him.'

She straightened the pleats on her sari with restless fingers, then continued. 'But Manju refused to stay away from me. He kept after me, coming to my home and shouting for me, banging on the door and creating a scene. I was beginning to get frightened of him. I came to the Century Club that night because Manju had sent me a note. He said that if he could only meet me once, he would not bother me again. But he lied. He only wanted to meet me to beg me for a second chance.

'I told him once again to stay away from me. I didn't realise that Ponnuswamy had followed me. He heard us speaking, and realised that I had broken with Manju. He shouted at me for going against his wishes and turning Manju away. He put his hands on my neck and choked me. I was frightened that he would kill me. I had never seen him so angry before.'

She rubbed her neck reflexively. Deep blue bruises still marked the sides of her throat.

'But I didn't call you for your sympathy.' She sat up straight, looking at Ismail fiercely. 'I wanted to give you a piece of information that may be useful. An old beggar sits on the corner of the road that leads to Manju's house. The morning that Muniamma was attacked, he said he saw a tall, thin man holding a heavy walking stick, walking down the road. As the man approached their gate, he hesitated, and looked to the right and left. The beggar was hidden behind a tree – he saw the man, but the man could not see him from that angle. Then the man entered Muniamma's home.'

'Did the beggar see the man's face?' Ismail pressed.

'No. He was wrapped in a large grey woollen shawl, covering his entire body, even his head.'

'How can I find the beggar?' Ismail opened his notebook and took down his name.

As they left, Ismail whispered in Ramu's ear, 'I'll get someone to bring in the beggar so we can question him in more detail. But do remember – and tell your wife – we must keep the fact that we have someone who may have seen the murderer secret. This man is dangerous, and has already attacked twice. He must not get even the slightest hint that we are on to him.'

23

Men Can Make Coffee

Kaveri overslept the next morning, after a night spent tossing and turning restlessly on her mattress, filled with questions. When she awoke, she was startled to find that the sun was already up, and light had filled the room – Ramu had gently placed a kerchief on her eyes to shade them from the sun.

Rajamma was on leave that day, to attend a relative's wedding, and Kaveri had planned to get up early to bring in the milk from Venu. She must have overslept, she realised, as she got up with a start. The sun shone through the wooden slats in their bedroom windows, forming a slanted pattern of banded strips of light across the bed. The aroma of fresh coffee filled the room. Surprised, she threw off her sheet and padded to the kitchen. Ramu was squatting in front of the stove, making coffee. He turned around.

'Morning coffee for you?'

Kaveri did not know what to say. Apart from her mother, no one had ever made coffee in the morning for her. She had never seen a man making coffee before. And for his wife – a thought of what her mother would say quickly flashed through her mind.

'Care to share the joke with me?' asked Ramu, as he gave her the sweeter tumbler of coffee, taking the one with less sugar for himself. She sent him a grateful glance, realising that he had noticed, and remembered, her love for extra sugar in her coffee.

She sat down next to him on the mat. For a couple of seconds, as they blew on the coffee to cool it, she thought about what to tell him. Finally, she admitted, 'I was thinking of what our mothers would say, if they saw you making coffee for me.'

Ramu laughed out loud. 'Horrors. It does not bear imagining. Let us agree not to tell them, then. Or they may decide to descend on us, to make sure we conduct our marriage according to their rules.'

They sipped their coffee companionably for a while. Kaveri drained the last sip in her glass with a sigh, putting it down and saying, 'This was so nice. My mother stopped making coffee for me when I was eight. My sister got the job of making coffee for all of us. She hated it. She wouldn't dare mess up the coffee she made for my parents and grand-parents, of course. For us, her younger siblings, she made terrible coffee, though. Poured the dregs of the decoction into the glass. I think it was her way of getting back at us for the fact that she was the oldest girl, and had to take the lion's share of the housework. That's when I developed a taste for extra sugar, I think. To disguise the bitterness of the dregs that she used for our coffee.'

Ramu nodded, following Kaveri as she took the glasses outside the kitchen to the washing area.

'Let us make a deal, Kaveri. During the week, you make the coffee. On Sundays, you sleep late, and I will wake you up with a cup of hot coffee. I can't equalise the situation for the week, since I have to leave earlier, before the milk arrives. But I can at least treat my wife to a good cup of coffee every Sunday. Over a few decades, I can slowly make up for all the bad cups of coffee you had growing up in your house.'

He spoke louder to carry across the sound of her washing. Kaveri giggled. 'Shh. Uma aunty will hear us, and then the news will be all across the neighbourhood. Rama Murthy's wife makes her husband give her coffee every day: the shameless woman.'

Ramu dropped a kiss on his wife's forehead, then took out a cloth and began to dry the glasses. 'I spoke to Ismail, by the way. Manju has been released – the fingerprint analysis came back negative.'

'What about Muniamma?' Kaveri looked worried. 'She's still recovering from the attack on her. If Manju returns home, she'll be in danger again.'

'Ismail told Manju that he'd put him behind bars for ten years if he dared to so much as look at his wife or brother cross-ways,' Ramu reassured her. 'He's asked a policeman to drop in every evening and check on them. And Roberts has also stepped in.' Ramu smiled as he told Kaveri of the dressing down that Manju had received from Roberts, who had been horrified when he'd seen Muniamma in the hospital and realised the extent of her bruises.

'Roberts wanted to sack Manju, but I restrained him. If Manju loses his job, then their entire family will starve. Muniamma is too weak to return to her job at Roberts' home for a while. But we've decided that we will not pay Manju directly. Instead, Thimakka will take his salary and hand it over to Muniamma. She's also promised to check in on Muniamma every day on her way home, to make sure she's all right.'

Kaveri smiled. The entire hospital had banded together to take care of Muniamma, it seemed.

'Yet the mystery of Ponnuswamy's murder – and of the attempt on Muniamma – has not been solved.' Kaveri sighed. 'I wonder if we will ever find out who did it.'

'Kaveri!' Ramu reached for her hand impulsively.

'What?'

'Never mind who attacked Ponnuswamy, or Muniamma. What does it matter to you or me? Muniamma is back home, and Venu is happy now that his brother is out of jail and won't be beating them any more. Let's forget about it all. I want to take you to see the zoo in Lal Bagh today. Let's pack a picnic lunch. I haven't taken you anywhere in Bangalore as yet, apart from the library.'

Kaveri nodded reluctantly. She didn't want to give up on the case. She didn't really care about Ponnuswamy, but she felt personally responsible for finding out who had attacked Muniamma. But Ramu was right. With the news that Manju's fingerprints did not match those on the knife, they had no further clues to investigate. And with the relief of hearing that Muniamma had recovered, and her child was well, she felt the need to celebrate. The tight knot of tension in her body was finally released.

A couple of hours later, they were in the car, rolling down the road. In the back they carried a picnic basket containing parcels of lemon rice neatly wrapped in banana leaves and tied with twine. The day was cool, one of those rare overcast days in mid May, and the sun – though high overhead – was not overwhelmingly strong.

Ramu looked so handsome in his grey coat, worn over a crisp white shirt and neatly pressed pair of grey trousers, a Mysore turban of white silk with gold embroidery on his head. Sitting next to him, Kaveri could not help stealing glances at him from the corner of her eye. She had dressed with care for the occasion. She wore one of the saris that her parents had given her for her wedding:

turmeric-coloured, with a border of bright pink, the colour of roses. She had run over to Uma aunty's house for a string of jasmine flowers, which aunty had ornately wrapped around her plait, all the while teasing her about her 'outing' with her husband. Kaveri felt ridiculously happy.

She smiled at Ramu, who said, 'What?'

'What?' echoed Kaveri, puzzled.

'This is the fiftieth time you are smiling at me. What are you smiling about?'

'Nothing,' she laughed. 'I'm just feeling so happy I could burst. Or float away, like a balloon.'

Ramu began patting his pockets, as Kaveri stared at him. 'Didn't bring a string with me,' he said with a straight face. 'Didn't know I needed one. Oh well. I shall just have to poke you with a stick if I need to let out some air.'

Kaveri thought back to the weeks just before she had moved to Bangalore, spent fretting about what kind of husband she had married, wondering if he would be kind and welcoming or stern and disapproving. Sitting next to Ramu now, she sent up a silent prayer of thanks to her patron saint, Sri Raghavendra Swamy, for giving her what surely must be the best husband in the world.

As they swung down the road, Ramu looked around for traffic. Seeing the wide road empty of people, vehicles and carts, he beckoned to Kaveri and drew her close, placing her hands on the steering wheel and holding it in place. Kaveri grinned with glee as she took her first impromptu driving lesson, learning how to swing the steering wheel as they approached a turn and picking up her sari to place her feet onto the accelerator and brake.

Her face lit with excitement, she turned to Ramu. 'Will you teach me how to drive properly?'

He wrapped her hand in his and pressed it warmly.

'I will.'

The gardens of Lal Bagh were lush and welcoming. Kaveri, chattering to Ramu about her school in Mysore, fell silent as they drove up to the park gate.

'What is that?' she whispered, as she stared at the massive black wrought-iron gates that flanked the entrance. The gates were spectacular, but intimidated her.

'The Cameron Gate: Mr John Cameron, the park super-intendent, commissioned them in 1891.' Ramu slowed down for a moment so that she could see the detailed metal work.

'I find them a bit overwhelming,' admitted Kaveri, as Ramu drove in.

'So many different kinds of plants?' she added, looking around at all the greenery.

'There are supposed to be three thousand, two hundred species here!' Ramu said, after they parked their car and walked over to a large banyan tree that provided a patch of shade. They sat down below the tree to eat their simple, satisfying picnic of lemon rice and curd rice, with mango pickle.

They strolled down to the zoo, laughing at the antics of the Madras langur, and staring in fascination at the Indian anteater, a strange animal with a bizarrely long snout. 'How can an animal grow so large, eating only ants?' Kaveri asked. 'He must eat a lot of them.'

She had spoken too loudly, and was shushed by a disapproving guard. Kaveri moved across to another enclosure, captivated at the sight of an Indian street dog nursing two small tiger cubs. Seeing her rapt gaze, the guard came over, explaining that their mother had refused to nurse them, but the village dog had adopted them without question.

Taciturn no longer, the guard went on to tell her all about his family, from his mother's digestion issues to the problems he was having with his truant son. Kaveri told him that Ramu worked at the Bowring Hospital.

'I know one of your doctors, Mr Bhagavantam Sastry,' the guard said. 'He visits Lal Bagh every Tuesday and Thursday with his young son. The orangutan from Sumatra is his son's favourite.'

'Son?' Kaveri turned to Ramu, startled. She remembered meeting Mr Sastry's wife, Indira, at the Century Club dinner. A slight, short woman, probably in her mid-thirties, she had been noticeably quiet when the other doctors' wives had spoken about their large broods of children. Mrs Reddy had looked at her sympathetically and whispered to Kaveri, 'Childless, poor woman. They've been married for fifteen years, but never been blessed with offspring.'

'Who is the boy that Mr Sastry comes to the park with?' Kaveri asked Ramu later.

'The guard must have been mistaken,' Ramu responded.

'I'm sure the guard knows him. I think it's very peculiar,' Kaveri insisted. 'Why would a man whom we know does not have children visit the park with a small boy?'

'Stop searching for mysteries everywhere, Kaveri. With Muniamma discharged, and Manju acquitted of Ponnuswamy's murder, I hope this will be the last of our problems. Whoever the culprit is, he seems to have long gone. I don't think we'll find him now.'

Kaveri refused to give up. 'That large policeman – Inspector Ismail – he won't forget, even if we do. He's looking for a suspect. What if he goes after Mala next?'

The temperature seemed to have dropped by several degrees.

24

A Second Arrest

The idyllic day in Lal Bagh was the last worry-free day they were to have for a while. The next morning, as Kaveri turned to go in to the house after seeing Ramu off at the gate, she was interrupted by a tear-choked voice calling, 'Kaveri *akka?*'

Kaveri turned to find Mala's maid, Narsamma, moving towards her. She looked unkempt and haggard – her sari was crumpled and dirty, her hair uncombed. Her eyes were wild with fear.

'Kaveri *akka*, my mistress needs help. Can you save her?' Narsamma choked out.

Kaveri froze. 'Mala? What happened to her?'

Narsamma pointed in the direction of the jail. 'The police came to our house in the morning and took her away. They say they found the bamboo *lathi* used to attack Muniamma in our garden. But I had never seen it before. It wasn't there even the previous evening. Someone must have kept it in the garden to frame my mistress. Can you help Mala? She'll die in prison. You know how they treat women prisoners. They won't let me in to see her even for a minute, or give her food.'

Kaveri's face was red with anger. 'I'll go straight to the police station.'

Ismail was speaking to a junior policeman when she burst in. He looked up in frowning annoyance as she asked, 'Why did you arrest Mala?'

Ismail gestured to the young policeman to leave, and pulled out a chair for Kaveri, sitting down on the other side of the large desk.

'We found the weapon used to hit Muniamma in her house.'

'That doesn't mean anything! It wasn't even there in her house the previous evening.'

'We received an anonymous note.' Ismail opened the drawer in his desk, and pulled out a pair of gloves. He put them on, and took out a long envelope from another drawer.

'I probably shouldn't be showing you this,' he said, as he took out a piece of paper, and turned it upside down so that Kaveri could read it. 'Don't touch it.'

The note was printed in block letters: WHY HAVEN'T YOU INVESTIGATED THE PROSTITUTE? LOOK IN HER GARDEN.

It was signed, 'A Well Wisher'.

She looked up at Ismail. 'Who wrote this?'

He shrugged. 'It was delivered to the police station early this morning, at six a.m.'

He pre-empted her next question. 'We didn't see who brought it. But a small boy, loitering on the street corner, said he saw a tall man, like a ghost wrapped in a long grey shawl, go past the police station.'

'Just like the beggar said.' Kaveri let her breath out. 'That must be the murderer. Don't you remember? Mala said there was an old beggar who sits at the corner of their lane, who saw a tall man wrapped in a grey shawl carrying a large bamboo walking stick, who went down the lane towards Muniamma's house just before she was attacked.'

'Yes, but until we find this mysterious man, what we have to go on is the evidence,' Ismail said. 'We found a large, heavy bamboo *lathi* in Mala's garden, propped against the wall, just inside the gate. It had traces of blood on it, and a few strands of black hair. It matches the wound on Muniamma's head.'

'Fingerprints?' Kaveri rubbed her hands hopefully. 'You used fingerprint evidence to clear Manju, Muniamma and Mala of Ponnuswamy's murder.'

Ismail shook his head. 'The *lathi* didn't have any fingerprints on it. The attacker, whoever it was, wore gloves.'

Kaveri couldn't believe it. 'Mala is too slim to wield a heavy bamboo *lathi* and hit someone on the head.'

'She could have hired someone, an outside killer perhaps, to kill Ponnuswamy, and to hit Muniamma – her rival for Manju's affections – on the head. She certainly had the motive for Ponnuswamy's attack at least. Ponnuswamy harassed her, and his death has made her free again.' Ismail folded up the letter, placing it back into the envelope.

Kaveri sat for a while, deep in thought.

'Can I see the fingerprint report that cleared Manju?' she asked eventually.

Ismail pulled out a file from his desk. 'I was waiting for you to ask, ever since your husband told me that you borrowed a book on fingerprinting from the library.'

'Aha!' She pulled out a piece of paper from the file, and brandished it at him triumphantly. 'Based on the Henry System of fingerprint classification, the fingerprints on the knife are different from Subject A (Manju Gowda) or Subject B's (Muniamma). Their thumbs have been worn smooth with manual labour, and lack a central whorl. In contrast, the partial thumbprint of the attacker, outlined on the knife, has a clear and prominent central whorl.'

'So?' Ismail shrugged his shoulders.

'Don't you see? Anyone whom Mala would have been likely to have hired would be a local man. The fingerprint book I read had a chapter on how difficult it is to get clear fingerprints from the labouring classes, whose finger ridges are covered by callouses, or rubbed smooth by years of physical effort. The attacker's thumbprint has prominent whorls. It seems likely to be someone educated, with money. Someone whose fingerprints are intact and clear.'

She continued, building her argument in full force, 'That anonymous note – it was written in English. It can't have been one of the men that Mala would have hired. They wouldn't know how to read and write in English. No, that note was written by an educated person. That person and the one with the unidentified fingerprints on the knife – they must be one and the same. That's the killer you should be looking for. Not Mala. Someone else framed her, by placing the *lathi* just inside the gate. You should be looking for the man in the grey shawl.'

Ismail sat back. 'You may well be right, Mrs Murthy. That's a very important point. But . . .'

Kaveri narrowed her eyes.

'The absence of evidence is not the same as the evidence of absence. I'm afraid your points, however compelling, will not convince a judge, or even a mere policeman–' he gave her a regretful glance '–to release Mala.'

'You have not spent time with Mala. I have,' she said, her dark eyes focused intently on Ismail. 'She is straightforward, without deceit. She had no reason to kill Muniamma. She was not in love with Manju. She had an affair with him only because Ponnuswamy forced her to.'

'A judge may not agree with you,' Ismail said. 'A good police lawyer will argue that Mala wanted to get rid of Muniamma because she was jealous of her, and wanted to clear the way for her continued affair with Manju.'

Kaveri kept her eyes on Ismail. 'You know how badly they treat women in jail. Last week, there was a story in the newspaper about the number of prisoners who died last year because the food was inadequate. How can you keep her in jail? Can't you release her? On a bond?'

'I wish I could. But I have orders from my superior officer. He wants the case solved quickly. Unsolved murders don't reflect well on us. There is already a journalist who has been poking around.' Ismail spoke to Kaveri quietly. 'I'm not convinced she did it either. But I have no choice. If you could find any evidence that proves her innocence . . .'

She nodded reluctantly. 'If I come to you with more concrete evidence, would you take it forward?'

'This is a woman's affair. Another woman may be able to find out more. But your husband may not like—'

This time it was Kaveri who interrupted. 'I'll take care of my husband.'

Ismail gave her an approving look. 'Then we have a deal. Let me know what you find out.'

Kaveri nodded. 'Can you give me a letter, addressed to the jail authorities, asking them to let me meet Mala?'

As Ismail handed her the letter, Kaveri pulled out her list of suspects, which she had brought along to show him.

'Very detailed,' commented Ismail.

'Did you check the steward, gardener, drivers and cleaners?' Kaveri asked hopefully.

Ismail nodded. 'All their alibis hold.' He gestured to the right hand column. 'I learnt a lot from my favourite novelist, Arthur Conan Doyle.'

'He's my favourite too.' Kaveri sat up, excited. 'I'm reading *The Sign of the Four* right now.'

Ismail smiled at her. 'Then you will recognise this famous line, by the incomparable Sherlock Holmes: *When you have eliminated the impossible, whatever remains, however improbable, must be the truth.* When the possible is excluded, look to the unlikely. And then the impossible.'

Kaveri stared at him. 'So, if we have eliminated all the staff – that leaves only the guests at dinner that night. That is, the doctors? But why would one of the doctors want to kill an outsider like Ponnuswamy?'

25

Chained and Fettered

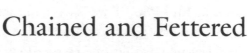

Kaveri could not find a horse carriage willing to take her to the jail. She cried continuously as she walked there. She had heard horror tales of how innocent people were tortured in jail, with women – especially beautiful women like Mala – at risk of molestation. Distorted images of swollen faces and bruised bodies floated before her eyes.

The heat of the morning had given way to a chilly breeze which set the coconut trees swaying. Thick dark clouds gathered overhead. It was noon on Friday – the call of the muezzin echoed from the ramparts of the mosque. Near the temple just ahead, Kaveri paused to give a few coins to the elderly women outside its walls. They were huddled around a small fire they'd lit with tiny pieces of wood, striving to keep warm.

In a short while, the walls of the jail loomed in front of her. Grim and forbidding, the blocks of stone seemed almost invincible, stacked one upon the other. The guard on duty managed to seem bored, suspicious and threatening all at the same time. He inspected the letter from Ismail with one grimy hand, keeping a firm grip on his bamboo *lathi* with the other. Then, with a curt, 'Wait here,' he disappeared into an inner room.

Kaveri looked around, spying a bulletin board on the tobacco-stained wall. There were over two hundred men confined within these walls, and thirty women kept in a separate section. They must be understaffed, she thought. The room seemed like it had not seen a broom or mop in months.

Then she heard a faint murmur of voices. The guard was back, holding a massive bunch of keys. She followed him down a long, dank corridor smelling of urine, faeces and human fear. Cells lined the corridor on both sides. Women cried out for help, holding and shaking the bars. Kaveri cringed and hurried behind the guard, not wanting to lose sight of him.

The guard stopped abruptly at a cell on the left side, near the end of the corridor. Kaveri almost careened into him, but managed to stop herself in time. Through the bars, in the gloom, she just managed to make out a glimpse of a couple of mats on the floor, and the people sleeping on them. The guard called out, 'Visitor!'

No response.

Kaveri stared at the people lying on the floor. At one end of the cell, near the wall, lay a thin figure with matted hair and bruises. Kaveri was reminded of Muniamma's fragile form, lying motionless on the floor.

The guard took a stick and poked it through the bars, prodding the figure near the wall. Kaveri let out a small cry, only then realising that the figure on the ground was Mala. She couldn't recognise the beautiful, confident woman she had met twice, in this abused form.

The guard poked Mala with the stick again and barked, 'Are you deaf? I said, you have a visitor.'

'Don't hit her,' Kaveri said fiercely. 'I just want to speak to her.'

The guard held his stare for a minute, then lowered his eyes.

'Yes, madam,' he muttered.

The guard opened the door and moved aside. He gestured with the stick, forcing Mala out. She shuffled out like an old woman, gazing blankly at Kaveri. Kaveri flinched when she saw Mala's feet, chained with fetters. She tried not to retch at the stench.

'I need to speak to her privately. Downstairs.' Kaveri stared down her nose at the guard.

The guard began to laugh derisively. Kaveri stopped him.

'Inspector Ismail's orders. Mala is a prisoner who needs to be handled with care. The Inspector will have a word with your Deputy Superintendent to demand an explanation for this conduct if it gets to his ears.'

She had no idea if this was true, but it seemed to work. The guard blanched and stepped back.

From her initial discomfort at being trapped inside this dungeon-like establishment, to disgust, Kaveri's emotions had now transformed into fierce anger. The inhumanity of keeping prisoners wrapped in chains, and confined in narrow places that reeked of human excrement and misery! Worse than cattle and animals, she thought. These people were confined like slaves.

The guard opened a door to a smaller room without windows. Kaveri entered, and sat down on the single chair behind the desk in the corner. Mala came in slowly. She looked gaunt, with hollows below her eyes. Kaveri itched to order the guard to remove her fetters, but she knew there was no point. The man would only refuse, and her authority would be reduced. Instead, she ordered the man to bring in a glass of water, then leave her alone with the prisoner.

Once the guard had gone, closing the door behind him, Kaveri turned to Mala. She could see that she was almost falling down with exhaustion, and took the chair over to her. She wished she had thought to bring some food for her. She took a glass of water and placed it in her hands, refusing to let herself flinch from the nauseating stench that emanated from her. The woman drank greedily, as Kaveri thought, *They probably don't even give them water.*

Then all of a sudden, Mala placed her face in her hands and began to sob.

Kaveri glanced at the clock on the wall. Five minutes already. The guard had permitted them fifteen in total.

'We have very little time, Mala,' she said. 'If you want me to help you, answer my questions.'

Kaveri's words finally got through. Mala stopped crying and wiped her eyes. Kaveri opened the door and called for another glass of water, carefully blocking the guard from seeing into the room and noticing that the prisoner was seated in a chair. Mala sipped the second glass of water more slowly.

'Did you kill Ponnuswamy?' Kaveri asked her.

'I swear on my life, I did not,' Mala said passionately. 'But why would anyone believe me?' She let out a defeated sigh. 'No one will believe the word of a common woman such as I.'

'I believe you.' Kaveri held Mala's gaze with her own. 'We must find out who did it. Do you have any information that can help us?'

'No.' Mala's shoulders drooped.

The guard's heavy footsteps approached. He opened the door.

'Don't worry,' Kaveri said. 'I will speak to Inspector Ismail. We will get you out of jail. Don't lose faith in us.'

As Kaveri left the building, she couldn't shake the memory of Mala's eyes. Hopeless, defeated. She stumbled out into the sunshine, her own eyes filled with tears.

She returned home in a foul mood. 'We need to do more investigating,' she said, brandishing her list of suspects at Ramu, now creased after having been folded and refolded many times. 'Can't you find out a way for us to spend more time with the doctors? And the Roberts too – they may have heard something about the other doctors.'

26

An Invitation to Lunch

Ramu was in the hospital, assembled with the other doctors for their monthly meeting, when Dr Roberts arrived. Sipping steel glasses of hot tea, and eating fried *pakoras*, the other doctors greeted him, and he moved into the centre of the room and regarded them over the tips of his steepled fingers. Otherwise genial and friendly, when it came to work, Roberts was an exacting administrator, with small forbearance for failure and mistakes. He could excite fear as well as an attitude almost amounting to worship from his subordinates. Appia came under the latter category. Painstakingly detailed himself, he appreciated Roberts' maniacal zeal for sanitation and hygiene, and considered the results that they had achieved over the past two years since Roberts had taken over as the head of the Bowring and Lady Curzon Hospitals nothing short of miraculous.

'We have purchased eight Mayer's Hand Pumps, placing them in dense native habitations like Halasur, Blackpalli and Chickpete, and in native temples, churches and mosques, to provide safe drinking water. Four iron tubs have been purchased for a hundred and twelve rupees for the Epidemic Diseases Hospital.'

Roberts' voice droned on, describing the items they had purchased in their refurbishment of the hospital facilities. Ramu tuned him out. Roberts could go on for a long time when he was on a roll.

When Roberts finally wound down, Ramu threaded his way across to the table to get a fresh cup of tea. He bumped into Dr Iyengar, who greeted him warmly. 'Rama Murthy. Just the man I wanted to meet. How is Mrs Murthy? No after-effects from that disturbing event at the Club the other night?'

This was the opening Ramu had been waiting for. 'We need to meet the doctors informally,' Kaveri had insisted over breakfast that morning. Freeing Mala was all she could think of now. 'The fingerprint evidence suggests that the murderer is an educated person – someone not from the labouring class. It could be one of the doctors. We have to get to know them better.' Her dark eyes had been insistent.

'My wife is well, thank you,' Ramu told Dr Iyengar. 'In fact, she's a bit lonely, as she doesn't know many people in the city as yet, and my mother is away for a month to help her sister out. Would you care to come for lunch next Sunday?'

As easily as that, the plan was made: Ramu invited the other Indian doctors in the room home for lunch the next Sunday, with their wives. They accepted with some surprise – all except for Appia, who said he was heading out to Coorg that weekend. Ramu did not demur. In any case, Appia and his wife had not made an appearance at the Club on the night of the murder, and were not on Kaveri's list of suspects.

That evening, Ismail called on Ramu at the hospital. He closed the heavy wooden door to Ramu's room, making sure that no one else could listen in. Ramu feared that Ismail would be annoyed that he had brought his wife into his plans. On the contrary, Ismail sounded very pleased.

'Your wife has quite the mind for detection,' Ismail chuckled, rubbing his hands together briskly. 'What does she plan next?'

'Actually, Inspector, we plan to host the doctors for a meal at our home on Sunday,' Ramu said. 'That way, both Kaveri and I can get to speak to them in an informal setting, and see if we can get any clues to any unusual behaviour.' He told Ismail about their visit to Lal Bagh, and the unexpected news of Mr Sastry who had visited there with a son whom no one else was aware of.

'Excellent, Dr Rama Murthy, most excellent.' Ismail patted Ramu on the shoulder with delight. 'Remember – you must stir the pot. Stir the pot, and see what emerges.'

That evening, Ramu and Kaveri strolled down the road to the nearby Basavanagudi Dodda Basavanna Temple, with its massive Nandi bull statue. Ramu's pants seemed uncomfortably tight around the waistband. He made a mental note to himself that he needed to watch his appetite, now that Kaveri seemed bent on experimenting on him with new and tasty dishes.

The *pujari* at the Shiva temple at the base of the Bull temple welcomed them as they arrived in time for the evening *puja*. They climbed the roughly hewn steps to the top of the large granite hillock on which the temple was located. The steps were slippery and covered with green lichens after the recent rains, and Ramu placed a steadying hand on Kaveri's arm as they navigated the steep climb. From the top, the view of the city was breathtaking, with the scarlet May flowers from the Gulmohar tree in full bloom.

Ramu pointed out the niches carved into nearby Bugle Rock to Kaveri as they went by. 'These were carved during a previous ruler's time to guide sentries to the lookout tower on top of the rock.'

The niches glowed in the dark, filled with oil and lit with cotton wicks by local women in worship. An elderly lady passed them, her stick clattering on the stone steps.

They placed their slippers underneath the massive banyan tree outside the temple, and entered, walking clockwise around the temple three times before they stopped in front of the large Nandi idol. Kaveri knew the story of the large bull that had ravaged the nearby groundnut fields at night. The temple had been built to appease him. The idol, originally small in size, had grown each year, local residents claimed, to reach its current impressive size.

A young couple accosted them, stuffing a couple of bills into their hands before moving swiftly away. Kaveri scanned the sheets of paper. A call for subscription to the nationalist Indian National Congress. She held them out to Ramu.

'As a doctor working for the British government, I won't be permitted to join.'

'But I can, can't I?'

'Yes, of course. I wish I could join openly, but I have my duty as a doctor to fulfil. Thank goodness you are not bound by the rules of my employment. We must each do our bit, small as it may be.' Ramu spoke with some sadness.

Darkness had fallen as they made their way back home. In the distance, the howling of street dogs filled the air. Kaveri looked around nervously, and pulled her shawl tighter around her.

'Feeling scared?' asked Ramu. 'Why? There is no need. This is a safe neighbourhood. And I am with you.'

'Perhaps I am just not used to going out of the house so late,' Kaveri murmured. 'My mother never allowed me and my sisters out of the house after dusk, though my brothers would come back late. The night seems scary, somehow.' As Ramu opened his mouth to protest, she added, 'It was in the dark that Muniamma was hit on the head, wasn't it?'

27

A New Phase of Investigation Begins

There were still a few days to go until the lunch on Sunday. Kaveri, fretting about Mala, was too worked up to sit still at home. Seeing Uma aunty's head over the compound wall, after a quick glance left and right to confirm that no one was watching, she jumped across. In the past few days, she had really become quite an expert at this, she thought, as she bent down to brush the mud off her feet.

Uma aunty looked sombre as soon as Kaveri mentioned Mala. 'What can we do, Kaveri?'

'There is one thing. I don't know if it's relevant to the murder or not, but it's certainly odd. We met a guard at the zoo who said that Mr Bhagavantam Sastry from the hospital visited often with his young son.'

'No, my dear. I know his wife Indira. They are a childless couple. It is her one deep sadness, that she could not have children.' Uma aunty scanned Kaveri's belly for telltale signs of new life.

Kaveri blushed, but stayed on track. 'No, aunty,' she insisted. 'I'm sure the guard said he came on Saturdays to the zoo with his family.'

'A mystery,' mused Uma aunty.

'Yes, aunty, and with Mala in jail, we need to do some further investigating.'

'Really? Let's find out then,' said Uma aunty. 'I know Sastry's house. It's only ten minutes away: they also live in Chamarajapete, around the corner. Indira will be happy to see us.'

Before Kaveri could say anything, Uma aunty had hustled her out of the house, and into a rackety horse cart. As the cart jolted along the roads to Mr Sastry's house, Kaveri missed their comfortable car. Ramu had offered to take her driving a couple of days back, but she had refused, saying she needed to work on her list of suspects. She would ask Ramu for a driving lesson as soon as she could, maybe even today, she decided, settling back against the uncomfortable, poky cane frame of the cart.

The Sastry home was a pretty, whitewashed little bungalow on 4th Cross Road, just off the Albert Victor Main Road in Chamarajapete, with a monkeytop gabled roof. The cottage was set back in a charming little garden, with a gate bordered by a wrought iron arch. A flowering Rangoon creeper entwined the arch, and pink flowers burst out of the creeper in all directions, filling the road with their fragrance as the two women reached the gate.

Indira, wearing a vibrant sari of grassy green, was sitting in the portico, a heap of flowers piled in front of her on a thin white towel. She was deftly weaving a garland, placing the stalk of one flower into the other to create a chain.

'Uma aunty. How nice to see you.' Indira opened the gate and touched Uma's feet, greeting her respectfully. 'Please come in. I had just finished all my morning work, and was just thinking how nice it would be to have visitors. You know, in Tumkur where I grew up and lived before my marriage, we would never have had to spend a moment alone. In this large anonymous city, Bangalore, no one comes to our home at all.' She turned to Kaveri. 'And who is this pretty young girl? One of your nieces? Or a daughter-in-law?'

'Don't you remember her? This is Kaveri, my neighbour. Kaveri's husband, Dr Murthy, also works at the Bowring Hospital. I think you met at dinner, at the Century Club.'

'Of course! Do forgive me for not recognising you. I think we met only briefly that night,' Indira said, ushering them in.

A few minutes later, the obligatory exchange of greetings over, the women were sitting in the living room, sipping cups of coffee. Indira brought in a plate of steaming fried *ambades*, which Uma aunty seized upon with delight. '*Ambades*, Indira? I was just thinking of making these, as I had a craving for them.'

'I saved you the hard work, then, aunty. I made much more than we can eat. Just the two of us, and my husband is rarely home for lunch – like yours, I think,' she said, turning to Kaveri.

Was this loneliness what all childless women felt? Kaveri wondered. Ramu left her at home for most of the day, but she was usually happy to be alone for some time, to work on her maths, read the news, and catch up with her music. Indira seemed to have no life of her own.

But now she had stayed silent for too long, and Indira was staring at her, puzzled. Kaveri forced a smile and said sweetly, 'These are delicious. I was just thinking that my husband, too, would love these. Are they very difficult to make?'

Uma aunty turned to Indira and explained, 'Poor girl, she does not know much about cooking. Newly married, you know. And her time at home was spent studying: a mania for books, this girl has. You will not believe how much time she spends reading her textbooks. Now she has discovered that her husband likes good food, so she is eager to learn new recipes to cook for him.' She dug Kaveri in the side with her elbow and went off into peals of laughter.

Kaveri's cheeks burned, but Indira turned to her reassuringly. 'Not at all, my dear, they are very easy to make. I'll write it down for you.'

Uma aunty continued to engage Indira in casual conversation, asking her if she had ever been to Lal Bagh. She shook her head vigorously. 'Never. My husband would not hear of it. He has often told me that the public areas in Bangalore are hotbeds of indecency, where the British troops move around. He says no respectable Indian woman would find it fit to venture there.'

'But Lal Bagh is quite nice, especially on weekends,' ventured Kaveri. 'I have heard they have a star attraction. An orangutan with a best friend – a small doll, which it pushes around in a perambulator.'

Indira shook her head. 'My husband does not approve of my going out alone. And he is too busy to accompany me.' She spoke with resigned finality, and a deep undercurrent of sadness.

Over coffee later that day, Ramu heard of their visit to Indira's home. He also tasted the fruits of the visit, in the form of *ambade*: crisp fried ovals of dough, made of *kadalabele* with curry leaves and green chillies. Indira's recipe, written down and explained to Kaveri, was a success.

'I have more inside. I'll bring them for you.' Kaveri jumped up and ran into the kitchen. Ramu's stomach protested, but he quelled its rumbling, thinking to himself, 'I'll go for a long walk later tonight to digest the food.'

He coaxed Kaveri to eat much of the second plate, though, resorting to feeding her the last two morsels, watching his wife's face with pleasure as she ate. She was beautiful, this young wife of his, whom he had met and married almost by accident. Ramu thanked his stars, and chanted a silent prayer to his patron saint Raghavendra Swamy, thanking him for giving him the wisdom to hold his tongue when his mother had insisted upon the marriage.

As had become their daily habit now, he moved into the kitchen, chopping vegetables while Kaveri prepared dinner. As she cooked, Kaveri raised a question to Ramu. Why did Mr Sastry go to Lal Bagh so regularly, and why was his wife unaware of it? They argued the matter back and forth, unable to reach a resolution. There could be a quite innocent reason for the visits, argued Ramu. Perhaps Mr Sastry liked to go and look at the orangutan, and his wife did not. If so, Kaveri responded, why was Indira *akka* unaware of it all? And why did she specifically mention that her husband had told her that he never visited the cantonment area, and warn her not to go, unless he was doing something he didn't want her to know about? Ramu had no answer.

After dinner, when they came out into the garden, they could just see a dark shape squatting in a corner near the door. Kaveri let out a small scream and moved close to Ramu.

A hoarse voice came from the figure. 'It's me. Narsamma.'

'Have you been able to send food to Mala?' Kaveri asked her. Furious at the way Mala was being treated, she had stormed back in to Ismail's office after visiting her in jail to demand that Narsamma be allowed to send food and fresh water to her mistress.

Narsamma nodded. 'Thank you for speaking to the police. I take a parcel of food to the jail twice a day, along with water. Without that . . .' Her voice trembled. She looked up in surprise as Kaveri moved forward to hug her impulsively. Behind her, Ramu shifted uncomfortably, then made an excuse and moved into the house.

'Don't worry, Narsamma. We'll find a way to free Mala soon,' Kaveri promised, forcing herself to sound more confident than she felt.

'I hope you do, *akka*.' Narsamma's voice was thick with unshed tears. 'Otherwise, my poor lady's beauty will waste away in that place of horrors.'

28

Stirring the Pot

The day of the doctors' visit arrived too soon for Kaveri, who was fretting about how she would manage to cook lunch for so many.

'I can help you,' Ramu offered. Kaveri arched her eyebrows at him and then laughed. 'I was planning to ask Uma aunty to help. I don't think she would know what to do with you if you were in the kitchen.'

The vegetable vendor brought a selection of fresh vegetables, heaped high on a wooden cart, to their front gate, just as Uma aunty arrived. Kaveri was surprised to see her so early.

'I told my son to take the child to his sister-in-law's house for today so that I could be free,' she told Kaveri airily. Then she stared at Ramu, who had just sat down to help his wife chop vegetables. 'Do you plan to be here?' she asked him, with an edge in her voice. Ramu took the hint and excused himself, promising to bring the visitors for lunch at noon.

As the guests began to arrive, Kaveri went to meet them with some curiosity. She greeted the Reddys with pleasure, feeling like Mrs Reddy and she were old friends by now. Mr Sastry looked like a quiet man: short, with a youngish face, but with lines of worry deeply etched in it. He seemed to have prematurely greyed. Next to him Indira seemed young and extremely pretty, wearing a leaf green and scarlet silk sari with a border of mangoes, embroidered in gold and dark green. Kaveri was introduced to Indira, and smiled politely and greeted her. Ramu, who was of course in on the secret, kept his face blank, but studied her closely, curious to see this woman whom his wife had spoke about with such keen interest.

The men sat outside on the stone benches next to the large pillars that supported the semi-circular verandah that ran around the front of the house. The women were ushered inside by Kaveri, to sit on straw mats – *chaapes* – that she had placed on the cool red-oxide floor.

As always, the men ate first. The food was served with elaborate care, like a festival meal. Indira helped Kaveri to serve, unobtrusively guiding her on the correct order and placement of the various items. First the salt, on the leftmost corner of the leaf, followed by sweet *payasa* on the bottom right. The salt was then followed by *kosambari* to its right, then the vegetable, *sondige*, and *ambade* – and a teaspoon of mango pickle at the top right corner of the leaf. Then rice was served – in heaping mounds at the centre of the plate – with heaped teaspoons of heated ghee, naturally. The men ate appreciatively.

Once the men had completed their meals, Ramu took them out into the courtyard, where they had set out chairs under the shade of the mango tree.

'That was an excellent meal, Rama Murthy. Please give our compliments to your wife,' said Mr Reddy, looking like a very well fed and satisfied cat, as he leaned back ponderously in his creaking chair.

'Do you always eat like this?' asked Iyengar. 'How do you keep your slim figure, man?' He patted his protruding stomach. 'I used to be slim too, you know, when I got married. After fifteen years of marriage – Mrs Iyengar cooks very well, you know – well, my stomach now seems to have a life of its own.'

Silence reigned for some time. In the cool shade of the tree, after that massive meal, the men seemed relaxed, content to lean back in their chairs and look at the sky, while their stomachs began the hard work of digesting mammoth quantities of food.

Meanwhile, Kaveri had cleaned the floor and laid out fresh banana leaves for the women in the kitchen. Away from the men, the women relaxed and began to talk of children, cooking, mothers-in-law, and other domestic matters, slowly getting to know each other.

Mrs Reddy, resplendent in an ornate burnt ochre silk, ate everything with delight, asking for second helpings. The other women also asked for an extra helping of this or that, eating with enjoyment.

Mrs Iyengar spoke at length of her daughter's wedding, which appeared to have been an expensive affair, involving a lot of gold.

'We invited five thousand guests from both sides of the family – hers and his. Iyengar families, you know . . . all large.'

She was decked out in jewellery, wearing six gold bangles on each wrist, and a thick *kaasina sara* – a chain of gold coins strung together – around her slender neck.

Through it all, Indira sat quietly, taking in all the conversation, but not saying much. As Kaveri moved across the room, making sure that everyone had a glass of water and anything else they needed, she caught snatches of conversation.

'Oh, my husband came into an inheritance about eighteen months ago. Since then, we have become quite comfortable. One of his aunts, a most distant connection. Under her will, he gets money in instalments, every few months.' That was Mrs Iyengar. She moved her hair behind her ears, so they could admire her new earrings. 'My husband bought them for me last month, for our wedding anniversary. A new design – Burmese ruby in the centre, surrounded by six diamonds, and then again by twelve diamonds.' The earrings looked gorgeous, thought Kaveri, but must be incredibly heavy. Probably pure torture to wear. She remembered that Lalita Iyengar had also been heavily decked out in gold, wearing a thick chain, and multiple large bangles jangling on each hand as she swam. It seemed an uncomfortable price to pay for the pleasure of flaunting your wealth.

Mrs Reddy was now chatting to Indira. 'My mother-in-law simply cannot keep her mouth closed. *Vata-vata-vata*, she goes on talking. Such a loose tongue. Anything you tell her, she tells it to the entire neighbourhood.'

Indira, after much urging by Mrs Reddy to visit their home, looked rather distressed and said faintly, 'I must check with my husband. He doesn't like me to go out without informing him.'

As Kaveri put coffee onto the stove, Ramu poked his head in. 'Do you need any help?'

'Not with the coffee, but could you get me a fresh cleaning cloth from the study?'

Ramu went into the study. He was surprised to see the door closed. He was sure he had kept it open. He turned the handle, then stopped short. Dr Iyengar was in the room, with his hand on Ramu's desk.

Iyengar jumped and turned around. Ramu looked at him in shock.

'I was looking for a piece of paper.' Iyengar sounded embarrassed. 'I wanted to write down the address of my plumber for Reddy. I looked for you, but you seemed busy in the kitchen, so I thought I would look for a piece of paper and pen myself.'

Ramu nodded, though it made no sense to him. Why had Iyengar not just waited to ask him for a piece of paper? And why would he have closed the door?

After coffee, Kaveri and Ramu stood at the gate, seeing off their guests. Then they went in, and Ramu sat down with a sigh.

'I need to take a nap,' he said.

'No!' Kaveri exclaimed. 'Before we forget, we need to go over the list. Now where did I leave it?'

She frowned at Ramu. Ramu frowned back at her. 'I'm afraid you left it on my desk. In my study.'

'Why afraid?'

'Because Iyengar was in there.'

'What?' Kaveri sat up bolt straight.

'Yes, it was very strange. He said he was looking for a piece of paper and a pen, to write down an address for Reddy. But why did he close the door?'

'Do you think he saw my list?'

'He may have,' Ramu admitted.

'Well, anyway. I'm going to write down a fresh list.' Kaveri went into the studio and returned with another piece of paper.

She ran her eyes down the earlier list. 'We need to change the names of the primary and secondary suspects.'

'Who was on your primary list again?' Ramu peered at the list, frowning in concentration. 'I can't remember. I've only seen it – let me think – yes, about a hundred times. Nowhere near enough to remember by heart.'

Kaveri swatted at him. 'You need to take this more seriously,' she scolded. 'We have to get Mala out of jail.'

Ramu sobered immediately. 'How is she?'

'Narsamma came to see me again yesterday. After I spoke to Ismail, they moved Mala to solitary confinement. It's meant for notorious criminals, but it has the advantage that she's safer alone, where others can't harass her. And Narsamma is able to get food to her regularly. But she's losing weight, fretting away.'

Ramu nodded. Ismail had warned him that the case might come to court in the next couple of weeks. 'We need to do something soon. If we don't find the murderer – all the circumstantial evidence points to Mala. They'll lock her up in jail and throw away the keys.'

'Or even . . .' Kaveri paled, unable to complete her sentence. They both knew that the chances of Mala getting the death penalty were high. It would be so easy, to convict the prostitute for the murder of the pimp, and the attack on her lover's wife. Who would take the trouble to listen to her side of the story? Not everyone was like Ismail, who was a rare kind of policeman.

They looked at the list.

'We can cross Manju and Muniamma off the primary list. On the evidence of the fingerprints.' Kaveri struck them off the old list. 'And Mala as well. For the same reason.'

She turned to the list of doctors she had put in the second column, reserved for the less likely suspects. 'Whom should we move to the primary column?'

They crossed out Appia and his wife, who had not been to the Century Club for dinner that night. They'd had to go to a niece's wedding.

'We should also remove the Urs family. They left early, remember? Even before the dessert course. Their son had exams and they wanted to get home early.'

That left the Iyengars, the Reddys and the Sastrys. Kaveri noted them down in the first column.

They stared at the names for a while.

'I think we're going about this all wrong, Kaveri. We need to look at what seems suspicious to us.'

Kaveri nodded. 'I'll start on another sheet of paper.'

She counted out suspects on her fingers.

'One. Sastry. What is he doing in Lal Bagh? Who is the small child with him?' She wrote Sastry's name on a new list, titling it 'Really Suspicious Characters'.

'Two. Iyengar. What was he doing in your room? That's really suspicious too, if you ask me.' Iyengar's name went on the new list.

'Is that it?' Ramu asked. 'Don't you want to add the unknown Mr X? The man with khaki pants and a walking stick?'

'That's right!' Kaveri added a third name to the list. 'The Mysterious Mr X.'

'Can we learn anything from the anonymous letter Mr X wrote to the police?' Ramu wrinkled his nose. 'I did a course on handwriting analysis once. A trained analyst can tell you so much about the person, just from a sample of their handwriting. Whether man or woman, old or young, rich or poor.'

Kaveri shook her head. 'The anonymous note the police station received was written in an educated hand, though disguised. It was carefully printed in capitals. That shows us the letter writer is someone educated, who knew that they needed to disguise their handwriting.'

They sat back and looked at the list.

'This looks really thin,' Kaveri said doubtfully.

'Yes, I feel like we're grasping at straws,' Ramu said. 'Have we missed anything important? What about the people at our table?'

Kaveri threw her hands in the air. 'Surely you don't want me to add the two of us as suspects? Well, I'll put down Dr and Mrs Roberts as suspects.' She added them in the second column, and looked at the names for a moment. 'We need to find out if the Roberts know anything that may be useful. Perhaps Daphne saw something that evening when she went to the washroom to clean her dress. How do we arrange to meet her? I can't gatecrash her house again without warning. She looked at me most peculiarly when she found me outside her gate with Muniamma.'

'I can't invite them here.' Ramu glanced around.

'Why not?' Kaveri asked, a bit annoyed. 'What's wrong with our home?'

Ramu looked flustered. 'Nothing's wrong with it. It's just that many British officers and doctors don't want to visit Indian homes. My father tried inviting them home a couple of times. It was very embarrassing. I'd rather not.'

'Well, then. Can you get us an invitation to tea at their residence?'

'I can't see how I could do that. Just go up to Roberts and ask him for an invitation?' Ramu grimaced.

'No . . .' Kaveri leaned forward, tapping her knee with a pencil. 'I've got it. Yes, this might work. When we met for dinner, Daphne said that Dr Roberts was getting a violin shipped to her from England. It should be here now. I mentioned that I'd like to hear her play, as I learnt the violin for a couple of years too, but in a very different style. Why don't you ask him if the violin has arrived? I'm sure he'll invite us over to see it then.'

'And meanwhile, we'll figure out how to clear up the mystery of Sastry's zoo visits.'

29

Driving Towards a Solution

Ramu returned home early with an invitation from the Roberts to tea. Kaveri's plan had worked.

Kaveri winced.

'I thought you asked me to do this,' protested Ramu, looking upset.

'I did. I do, I mean. But she's such an odd woman. Do you remember I told you the way she spoke to me – *and* looked at me – when she found me unexpectedly on her doorstep that day? She did everything but tell me directly to leave when she was done pumping me for information.'

Kaveri dressed carefully in her most elegant sari, of palest blue, embellished with a border design of parrots in purple, green and gold. She looked at herself in the mirror, adding a delicate necklace of seed pearls, needing the reassurance that she was looking her best. Inspired by Mrs Roberts' striking sleeveless gown, she had asked her tailor to create a sleeveless blouse for her.

She came out of the room, nervous about Ramu. Would he object to her bare arms? But Ramu's eyes rested approvingly on her. 'How beautiful you look. Is that a new blouse?'

Kaveri beamed, humming under her breath. Ramu held out his arm for her, as he led his wife out to the car, which he had polished and waxed to perfection that morning.

He guided Kaveri to the driver's seat, as her mouth fell open. By now she had taken several driving lessons with Ramu in Lal Bagh and Cubbon Park, and was now fairly confident about her driving abilities there, where few people were around. But to drive on the streets?

'Why not?' Ramu urged her on. He watched with pride as his wife drove, steering the car with panache towards the Roberts' home on Residency Road. She turned deftly into the gate held open by the startled security guard. Daphne and her husband stood at the door to welcome them. Daphne clapped her hands.

'Oh, well done, my dear, absolutely spiffing in fact. You've absolutely inspired me,' she declared, nudging her husband with her elbow. 'I'm going to have to learn to drive too.'

Daphne seemed in a better mood today, thought Kaveri thankfully. Or perhaps she behaved herself when her husband was around. A while later, after Daphne had played the violin for Kaveri, they were comfortably ensconced in the Roberts' living room, replete with tea and cake. Kaveri and Daphne were sitting side by side engrossed in the latest copies of the *Weldon's Ladies' Journal*, flipping through dress designs. Daphne was enchanted by Kaveri's sari, and wanted to know where she could get a similar length of silk to fashion into a dress. Kaveri was fascinated by the varieties of neck and arm designs that the magazines displayed, sketching out ideas for new sari blouses in her mind.

'Thank goodness the news of the murder is fading from her mind.' Roberts leaned over and spoke to Ramu in a low voice. 'My wife was prostrate for days. We will all be happy to return to our quiet, normal lives, with the men engaged in work, and the ladies in fripperies and beautiful things – as indeed they should.' He nodded at the two women, a full head of shining jet-black hair next to a golden bun.

Ramu nodded noncommittally. He was glad that Kaveri hadn't heard Roberts. She would have had an earful to say, Ramu was sure.

'I have heard that Green's store supplies yards of Burmese and China silk,' Kaveri was saying to Daphne just then. 'Mr Reddy told me, when we went swimming.'

'Oh, do you swim then? We have a lovely swimming pool at the back of our house.' Daphne waved her arm excitedly, almost knocking over the attractive tiered cake stand in front of them. 'You should come over and swim with me. How about—' Daphne picked up her calendar, naming a date a couple of days away.

Kaveri nodded. She had wanted to speak to Daphne about the murders – but it seemed odd to do so when they were having tea, with the Roberts' young girls coming in and out of the room with their governess. She didn't really feel like she wanted to spend more time with this woman. But perhaps she could pick up some clues from a conversation with her as they swam.

The slight delay would also give her time to pick up a new swimming costume from Greens.

'Mrs Reddy said one could wait there, while it was stitched,' Kaveri told Ramu, as they left.

'We can go there today. And we can get ice cream while we wait,' he said, seeing the happy grin on her face.

They drove down Krishnarajendra Road, lined by towering banyan trees on either side, and made their way towards Greens. A cramped little store on Parade Street, it was piled high with silks, velvet, chiffon and other fabrics, imported from China, Burma and other parts of the world. The proprietor, a bluff, hearty middle-aged Anglo-Indian man, nodded when Kaveri hesitantly mentioned swimsuits. He opened a tiny door inset into the rear of the store, and called out. His wife emerged, holding a tape measure, and beckoned to Kaveri, taking her inside to the measuring room, where she took her measurements.

Kaveri flinched, unused to having a stranger's hand rest so intimately on her body. Mrs Green seemed to understand how she felt, engaging her in a constant stream of meaningless conversation that kept her distracted from the unfamiliar sensation of being touched by a stranger, as she made detailed notes in a thick notebook.

When they came out, they found Ramu in conversation with Mr Green, browsing through bolts of silk. He had kept some aside for Kaveri to inspect.

He pointed to a blue and green combination.

'This will suit you beautifully.'

While Mrs Green got busy sewing, they drove down to Blighty's and ordered two bowls of ice cream. Ramu looked on appreciatively as Kaveri dug into it with her spoon. She squealed a little as the ice cream melted on her tongue. 'I have always wanted to eat ice cream.' She let out a happy sigh. 'Now my day is complete.'

Her excitement didn't last long. The road outside Greens was busy, and they had parked the car at a distance. They walked down the busy South Parade street, towards the car. Kaveri saw a small boy waving a cheap printed Kannada newspaper: a sensational tabloid, quickly printed and sold for a few *annas* to make a quick profit when there was an event that attracted attention – a local murder, theft, or fight was prime grist for the mill.

'Prostitute Murders Pimp', the rag screamed in large print on the front page. The paper contained a gossipy exaggerated mix of fact and fiction, claiming that Mala was an accomplished prostitute and a dangerous wicked woman responsible for a number of other murders and thefts, as well as the break-up of families across Bangalore. The trial had been allotted a date. *Just two weeks away!*

Kaveri tore the bundle of papers out of the hands of the astonished urchin, and ripped them to pieces, stalking away angrily. Ramu reached into his wallet and thrust a handful of money into the boy's hands, apologising to him as he ran after his wife.

'He's only doing his job, Kaveri. You can't blame him for that. He has a living to make, too.'

'I know.' Kaveri raised a tear-streaked face to Ramu. 'But I couldn't bear it any more. No one is going to believe in Mala's innocence. And the trial is in two weeks. We're running out of time.'

Ramu held his wife as she sobbed against him.

30

Shadowing a Suspect

'Let's go back to the first item on our list of unknowns. Why does Mr Sastry go to Lal Bagh so often? And who is the small boy with him?' Kaveri was bursting with the need to do something.

'The guard said he goes to the zoo on Tuesdays and Thursdays,' said Ramu. 'I'll take some time off on some pretext, and go to Lal Bagh an hour before it's his time off. Let me find a quiet place to sit and watch him.'

Kaveri jumped, nearly spilling the ladle of hot *saaru* that she was pouring over a heap of rice on her plate. 'That's a brilliant idea,' she exclaimed. 'Only do be careful.'

'I'll be careful. I'll sit at a place where nobody else can see me,' promised Ramu.

The next day, Ramu set out to Lal Bagh early during his lunch break. He looked around for the chatty security guard, and was relieved to find him absent. It was probably the staff lunch break, for no one was around – except for the animals, of course. Ramu searched around for somewhere to hide. He climbed onto the grilles of an empty cage. From there, he swung himself up onto the solid branch of a nearby mango tree, where he was screened by the branches and leaves, and could get a good view of the animal cages.

After a while, lulled by the afternoon sun, he fell into a fitful sleep. He woke up to a harsh screech made by a parakeet sitting somewhere above him, bumping his head on the branch. A woman was aggressively sweeping leaves with a coconut broom. A donkey cart laden with water drums made its way slowly up the steep road, accompanied by a man leading the reins and occasionally shouting encouragement at the beast.

Ramu spotted Sastry, sitting with his back to him, at a distance. Next to him was a small boy. The man had an arm around the boy's shoulders, and was rubbing his hair affectionately. Sitting under a tree, they were watching the famous orangutan. The boy was still, and looking at the animal in rapt fascination. After a while, the boy started to jump around, imitating the orangutan. Ramu saw his face. The resemblance was unmistakeable. He looked exactly like Sastry, alike enough to be his son.

Ramu's back was stiff, he had a headache from the sun, his pants were stained with mud, and he had torn his shirt while climbing down from the tree.

Kaveri took one look at him and said, 'You're tired – you had a long day. I'll bring the food.'

Ramu muttered, 'It's all right, I'm not hungry. You eat.' He lay down on a mat, and placed a wet handkerchief on his forehead, almost moaning in relief as the cool cloth started to take some of the heat off his throbbing head.

'Is the boy who comes with him related to him? A nephew perhaps? But that doesn't seem to be anything to hide.'

'I am as confused as you, Kaveri,' Ramu admitted. 'The only thing I can think of is… maybe… Sastry is having an affair. And this is his illegitimate son.'

Kaveri let out a squeal of anger. 'That charlatan! Lying cheat.' She exploded as she walked up and down.

'Kaveri, calm down' Ramu said, catching her hand as she stormed up and down. 'We don't know if he is having an affair. We can't accuse him without any proof.'

'Well, we can make sure Indira catches him in action, and then gets an explanation from him' Kaveri said grimly.

At noon the following day, as had become their habit now that lunchtime was drawing close, Kaveri and Uma aunty quickly completed their morning's activities and walked to Indira's house.

Kaveri and Uma had seen a visible change in Indira since they had become friends. Indira, initially lonely and melancholy, had become very different: open, laughing, even teasing them back. Kaveri, who had missed her own home sorely after she had married, felt for the first time that she was happy, with a larger circle of friends around her, and a husband with whom she was steadily, and deeply, falling in love. She wished so much that Indira could find some peace and happiness in her marriage too. Were they doing wrong by Indira by taking her to Lal Bagh under false pretences? But no, if she was indeed being cheated, she had a right to know. And then to take whatever decisions she wanted to.

'My grandson is so naughty,' remarked Uma fondly, cutting a piece of ridge gourd into neat, small slices. 'Before he comes home from school every day, I need to make sure that all the sharp implements are placed on the topmost shelf of the kitchen, pushed back out of his reach. Otherwise, who knows what he will take it into his mind to cut: his toes, or fingers, perhaps.' As the women laughed, she turned to

Indira and asked, 'What about you? I know it has been many years since you have been married – perhaps I should not pry . . .'

Indira gave her a wry smile. 'It's all right. Back home, people had no trouble asking me that question – my mother-in-law, sisters-in-law, practically the entire village. Indeed, I sometimes find it strange that in Bangalore, it's not the first thing that people mention after meeting me.'

Kaveri impulsively reached out and hugged Indira. The older woman looked startled: Kaveri realised that she was unused to gestures of affection, and her heart ached for her.

'It must be very hard for you,' Uma aunty added gently

Indira looked at her with dry, hard eyes and said, 'I have not stopped asking the Gods for years now, why they did this to me. Did I not serve them enough? Did I not take good care of my in-laws? Have I not been a respectful and dutiful wife to my husband?'

Her eyes brimming with hot tears, Kaveri tried to focus on Indira's hands restlessly twisting and unwinding her sari *pallu*, as Uma told her gently, 'You can adopt a child . . . some relative's youngest son, perhaps, someone from a large family who is willing to give their child away to a family who can provide well for him. That is the way these things are done. Why do you not do this?'

'My husband is against it,' replied Indira. 'I have asked, so many times. Begged, pleaded, wept. He shakes his head, and leaves the house if I get too persistent. I have given up, Uma aunty. It is my fate, to be cursed like this. The worst part is that my mother-in-law blames me, deeply and openly, for this. A few years after we were married, my husband's younger brother also died, just when they were looking for a bride for him. My mother-in-law not only blamed me for bringing ill luck on the family, but also – now she has only one son left – blames me for being the reason for the end of the family line. I am terrified each time we have to go home for a family visit. My husband does not like it much either, I think. He defends me to his mother, and that makes her angrier. These days we go rarely – perhaps once a year at the most.'

Indira's face was set in careworn lines, and she suddenly seemed older and weary, very different from the pleasant, cheerful woman who had greeted them in the morning.

Uma aunty leaned across and patted Indira's hand. 'Sharing makes the heart lighter, child. I think you have been lonely for a long time, but you are lonely no longer. We are friends, and can share troubles, not just joys.'

Indira said nothing, but a tear rolled down her cheek.

'You need to get out of the house,' Uma said, firmly. 'Kaveri and I will take you out to the Venkateswara temple in the Fort. Once you see a little of the city, get some air, breathe and look around, life will seem very different. More interesting, and well worth living.'

Indira nodded, but looked troubled. 'What would my husband say . . .?' she began.

Uma broke in. 'I was married for fifty years before my husband passed away. Men are important, but not as much as they think they are. If you think he will disapprove – well, do not tell him, then.'

'If he finds out . . .' said Indira, shaking her head.

'Well, he will find out if people tell him. And they will tell him that you were with me. I knew both your mother and your mother-in-law when they were little children, and nobody who knows would dare to call me less than respectable company. Tell him that I have been doing a special *pooja* for you to have a child, and I need to take you out to the temple. Even his mother will not object. We will not lie. I'll begin the *pooja* tomorrow. And we will visit the temple. We'll just visit other places as well.' The wrinkles on her face congealed into grim lines. She looked every inch a respectable elderly lady, pillar of the community, as she firmly advised another respectable woman that she must lie to her husband.

Kaveri rocked back and forth. She couldn't wait for the encounter in Lal Bagh.

31

Spying on Husbands

Kaveri and Uma aunty reached Indira's home at midday on Thursday. Uma aunty took them to the Venkateswara temple at the Fort, asking them to tie a red thread dipped in turmeric around the peepal tree outside. A symbol of fertility, the tree was ringed by hundreds of red threads tied by married childless women. Indira was quiet, only her eyes revealing how fervently she hoped that the temple visit could help her achieve what she wanted the most from life – a child to love, and hold close to her lonely heart.

The three women sat in the shade of the temple. Uma turned to Indira.

'Let us go and see Lal Bagh. It is close by, and very nice. My husband took me there some years ago,' she added wistfully.

'Yes, Indira *akka*,' Kaveri joined in, seeing Indira hesitate. 'My husband and I went there last week. It is a very respectable place. Indian women like us, from good families, go there in large numbers.'

Indira shook her head again. 'My husband—' she began.

'– will not know unless we tell him,' Uma aunty finished Indira's sentence for her.

Ramu had spoken to the guard at the zoo, and described the pattern of Mr Sastry's visit to Kaveri in detail. To catch up with him, they only needed to ensure that they were near the back entrance of the zoo at around 2.30 in the afternoon. The women walked slowly, moving towards the zoo. Docile as ever, Indira deferred to Uma aunty and came along, though she kept reminding them that she needed to be home well in advance of her husband's return. Uma aunty dismissed her objections.

'Your husband only comes home at dusk, right? We will be back well before that,' she said, pulling Indira along.

They found a shady spot below a comfortable tree and settled down behind it, Uma claiming that she needed to rest her feet. Indira was looking more and more uncomfortable by the minute, clearly worried that her husband may arrive home early. Kaveri began to worry that she may bolt for home. Where was this man?

Just when Kaveri was beginning to get restless herself, they saw Sastry come in, leading a small boy by the hand. Indira jerked upright, confusion clear on her countenance. As Sastry sat down with the boy on his lap, obviously comfortable with him, smoothing his hair back and showing him the orangutan, the three women watched him with unblinking stares. Soon, he felt the weight of their stares, and slowly turned.

His face became ashen as he saw his wife.

'Indira,' he mouthed, but no sound came out. The boy squirmed off his lap, and raised his hands, demanding to be picked up. The resemblance between them was unmistakeable. Indira looked at the boy's face, then back at her husband's face. Then fainted dead away, in Kaveri's arms.

* * *

That night, when Ramu finally returned, Kaveri had much to tell him. She recounted the entire story, then said with a triumphant flourish of her hands, 'The boy is his nephew. Not his son.'

'He has only one sibling – a brother who is dead,' objected Ramu, who knew something of Sastry's family from the conversations over lunch at their home.

'Yes, this is the problem. His older brother had formed a relationship with a woman from another community, a Christian woman. Afraid to tell his family, he kept the relationship a secret, only telling his brother that they had married each other in a quiet church ceremony, with only her mother in attendance. He died three years ago, unexpectedly, when his wife was pregnant. Unfortunately, she passed away too, eighteen months ago. Ever since, the boy has been with his grandmother in a house in Halasur. But Sastry visits him several times a week, and takes the child outside, including a regular trip to the zoo.'

'Why didn't he tell Indira?'

'He was afraid she would either leave him, or force him to leave the boy. He seemed to be a nicer man than we gave him credit for. The reason he forced Indira to stay inside the house is because he was worried that if she went out, she might somehow get to know. Quite a few people have now seen him, and begun to talk. It's been worrying him a lot, which is why he's become so silent and withdrawn.'

'What did Indira say?' queried Ramu.

'She was at first very shocked – then very relieved. When she saw him, she said her first thought was that her husband was having an affair, and that this was his child. I think she'll try to convince him to let them adopt the child. She has longed for a son of her own for so long. I'm sure they can come up with some story that will satisfy his mother – they can say that a distant relative of Sastry's died, and left behind a child which they have adopted. They need not reveal the fact that the mother was of a different community.'

'So, this is Sastry's guilty secret,' concluded Ramu. 'Well, I must say I am happy for your friend Indira that it turned out to be something as innocent as an orphaned child. It brings us back to square one though, when it comes to looking for the attacker and thief. And Mala's trial is getting closer by the day.'

Kaveri nodded excitedly. 'Yes, but there's more. Indira told us something else. Something very important to the case.'

'Yes?' Ramu looked expectantly at her.

'Sastry was being blackmailed. By Iyengar!'

'What?'

'Yes!' Kaveri banged the table in triumph. 'He had come to Sastry's home one day, for a meal, and snooped around in his desk. Sastry said he found a photograph he had had taken of himself with the boy, who looks just like him. Ever since that day, Iyengar has been blackmailing Sastry. And it's not small sums of money he's taken from him. He takes half of Sastry's salary. That's another reason he's been so careful, keeping Indira largely at home, not allowing her to go anywhere she could meet new people without him accompanying her. He's been petrified that Iyengar will tell her the truth, or that someone else who's seen him with the child in public places will let the secret out.'

'I wouldn't have believed it of Iyengar if I hadn't seen him do something similar in our house when he came for lunch,' Ramu said. 'He seemed like such a nice man, so jovial and helpful. But Sastry's story is so similar to ours. The day I found him snooping around in our house, in my desk. He closed the door, so that he couldn't be seen, and told me some cock and bull story about looking for a piece of paper to write down an address.' Ramu paced up and down the room. 'He must be a serial blackmailer.'

The rays of the setting sun threw long shadows into the darkening room. The couple turned to each other.

'That makes sense,' Kaveri said, with growing excitement. 'Mrs Iyengar always goes about laden with jewellery. So does her daughter Lalita. She told me that her husband came into a great deal of money about eighteen months ago. That must be around the time he started to blackmail Sastry.'

Kaveri took out her list. Ramu watched as she crossed out Sastry's name and highlighted Iyengar's name with a red pencil.

'I'll take this to Ismail as soon as the police station opens tomorrow,' promised Ramu.

Kaveri settled back happily in her chair. 'Soon, Mala will be released.' She hummed under her breath.

'Not so fast, Kaveri,' Ramu cautioned. 'Iyengar may be a blackmailer. That doesn't make him a murderer too. We can't be sure he was the one who killed Ponnuswamy and hit Muniamma on the head yet.'

32

An Unexpected Attack

The next morning, Ramu and Ismail went around the hospital in search of Dr Iyengar. Ismail had sent a police-man to Sastry's house to take down his statement, as evidence of blackmail. He had also recorded a statement from Ramu, about how he'd found Iyengar rummaging in his desk that day, with the door closed. With both statements in hand, they had decided to confront Iyengar, hoping to take him to the station and surprise him into a confession.

But they could not find Iyengar anywhere.

As he stood near the entrance of the laboratory, Ramu heard a muffled groan. It was a dull sound, almost obscured by the calls of children playing with a ball on the open grounds nearby. It seemed to come from the clump of trees nearby. Between the stems of a large intertwined banyan and peepal tree, he could just make out a piece of crumpled white cloth.

That evening, Ramu narrated the story to Kaveri as they sat down for dinner.

'I moved closer, and saw Dr Iyengar, lying motionless in a pool of blood behind the tree. A large wound on his temple was still bleeding, and the soil behind him was saturated with blood. His face was pallid – he had lost a lot of blood.'

Kaveri gasped. 'Was he hit on the head too?'

Ramu nodded. 'Just like Muniamma. But this time, the attacker left the weapon nearby. A long bamboo *lathi*, covered with blood. And no, there were no fingerprints on the *lathi*,' he pre-empted Kaveri's next question.

'Where did you find him exactly?'

'At the back of the tamarind grove, behind the *ashwath katte* with the banyan tree. It was a perfect place to hide a body. It was only because I heard a groan that I looked in that direction. Even the flash of white cloth that I caught sight of was quite by accident. Iyengar's *lungi* was carefully wrapped around his legs, with the extra loose cloth pushed below a trailing root, secured with a large stone. The wind must have blown hard and one edge of the cloth had become unwound and fluttered in the breeze. That was what caught my eye – that unexpected flutter of movement.

'We were lucky to have found Iyengar in time, Kaveri. He had been hit on the head very hard, and was concussed and in a coma. He hasn't recovered consciousness, and the wound on his head is deep – as I said, he lost a lot of blood. If he'd lain undiscovered in the back of the grove for a few hours more, he may have died.'

'Could it be a robber?' Kaveri asked.

Ramu shook his head definitively. 'Why would a robber hit him on his head, then leave his wallet and jewellery?'

'It must be related to the other murder then.'

'It has to be.' Ramu got up, folding his banana leaf in two. 'But now we are stuck again. We thought Iyengar could be the key to solving the mystery.' He looked at the printed calendar hanging on the wall next to the door. Neither Kaveri nor he spoke of what was uppermost in their minds. Mala's trial was just a couple of weeks away. With Sastry's innocent secret revealed, and the news that Iyengar was a blackmailer, they thought they had made progress. But who had attacked Iyengar, and why?

Their investigation had reached a dead end. Only a miracle could help them find the murderer and save Mala from jail. Or even worse, the gallows.

As Ramu drove in to work the next morning, he saw a cart drive up to the hospital entrance and stop. A young man of about twenty helped a lady – Mrs Iyengar – out of the cart. The young man held his mother's hand as she climbed up the steps stiffly.

Ramu took them into the room where Iyengar lay breathing heavily.

Mrs Iyengar's face crumpled as she saw her husband lying motionless on the bed. She hid her face in the folds of her sari, surreptitiously wiping her tears.

Dr Appia came in just as Ramu was answering the family's questions. He checked the unconscious patient's pulse and blood pressure, telling Ramu, 'Still strong.' He turned to Iyengar's wife. 'God willing, he will pull through this.'

'When?' she sobbed.

'It has been less than a day,' said Ramu. 'Some people come out of a coma in two days. Others can linger for weeks.' He did not add, as he would have if speaking to another doctor, that some patients also died without ever returning to consciousness.

Leaving the family in the room, Ramu went out with Appia. The older doctor looked gravely at Ramu. 'He is unlikely to recover. His superficial head injuries are light, but I fear something has broken within his head. I had a patient two years ago, in Madras. A Sub Inspector of Police, he was set upon by a gang of thugs one night, lying in wait for him near his house. He lapsed into a coma, lingered for about a week, and then one night – he just died. Peacefully, in his sleep.'

'That may be the best we can hope for,' admitted Ramu. 'If he wakes up, with a severe head injury—' He did not continue, for Appia knew well what he was going to say. A patient with a severe head injury who survived without his mental capacities intact . . . Taking care of such a patient could be devastating for the family.

'It is in God's hands now. We can only watch, and pray,' said Appia, clapping a hand on Ramu's shoulder and turning towards the wards, where the mass of daily patients waited.

Ismail had sent a note across to Ramu the previous evening, asking about Iyengar's condition, so Ramu sent a message across with Thimakka to let him know that there was no change A few hours later, there was a knock on his door, and Ismail looked in.

'Can I see him?'

'Of course.' Together, they walked to Iyengar's room.

'I think we need to find a safer place for him than this,' Ismail said, gesturing at the hospital room where Iyengar lay, with patients, attendants and doctors moving in and out. 'The person who attacked him may want to try again. If he wakes, even for a minute, we must ask that his wife send for one of us immediately. I'm sure he holds the clue to the attacks.'

Deep lines of worry were etched into Ismail's face. Narsamma had come into the police station the previous evening to plead with him to release Mala. Time was scarce now.

Ramu had a quick conversation with Appia and Roberts, who agreed with Ismail that Iyengar needed to be kept safe.

Ismail had cautioned Ramu and Sastry not to tell anyone about Iyengar being a blackmailer. 'The fewer people who know about it, the better our chance of catching the murderer unawares,' he had said. All Appia and Roberts knew was that there was a dangerous killer on the loose, one who seemed as proficient with a knife as he was with a bamboo stick.

Appia went to Dr Iyengar's family and told them that he thought it was unsafe to keep him in the hospital any longer. Trembling, his wife instantly agreed to move her husband to their home.

'Keep him secluded,' Appia warned. 'Away from visitors.'

A bullock cart was summoned by Thimakka from the cart stand opposite the hospital. Dr Iyengar was moved gently onto the cart by four attendants. His son sat up with him, holding him in place, while his wife went ahead with Appia.

Ramu's head swirled as he left the hospital that evening. Ismail's warning echoed in his memory: 'Remember, the person who committed the attack thinks that he has escaped notice. The fewer people who know about the details of the attack, the better the chance we have of discovering the truth. Act normal with your fellow colleagues, but keep the investigation going. We simply cannot afford the chance of having to deal with another murder attempt, after the three we have already faced.'

Ismail's face had set in grave lines as he'd looked at Ramu. 'Murder becomes easy, after a while. Whoever has done this is now becoming desperate. And he's likely to strike again, unless we do something fast.'

33

Visiting the Patient

W hen Uma aunty called to her across the compound
wall a few days later, Kaveri was very excited to hear
that Indira was back in town. The two women immediately
decided they would go to visit Indira. Kaveri hurried across
to Uma's house, carrying a large umbrella to shield the two
women from the summer sun.

When they reached the Sastry home, the women paused.
They heard unfamiliar noises coming from the house, which
used to be so quiet. Squeals of excitement sounded from
inside, as a child raced around the verandah holding a toy
windmill in his hand. The door was open, and Indira sat
cross-legged in a corner of the verandah. She was peeling a
large mound of peas, while the child – a small boy of about
three – kept running to the bowl and flinging handfuls of
shining green peas into his mouth, squealing mischievously
as she tried to grab him.

Indira looked up in surprise as she heard the gate open.
The child stopped his circuits and ran to her, hiding behind
her back. Only his head was visible, his eyes peeking out at

the new visitors with avid curiosity. Indira got up and hurried towards them.

'Come in, come in. We just came back from town two days ago . . . I wanted to send word to you to come visit us, but I have been so busy with this naughty boy.'

She reached behind herself with one hand and gently drew the boy forward, clasping his slight figure to her body possessively.

'This is Krishna. My son.'

The women smiled at each other in mutual delight.

An hour later, the boy had finally tired of playing, and was lying fast asleep in a corner, curled up like a puppy on a straw mat. As the boy lay sleeping peacefully, his stomach rising and falling with each breath, Indira smoothed his hair back from his forehead, and placed a hand on his arm, patting him gently. From a shy, nervous woman, she had blossomed into a happy, confident parent. The pinched, drawn and anxious look had gone from her eyes. And the child had clearly bonded well with her.

At least one good thing has come out of this entire mess, Kaveri thought.

Ramu arrived home early that day, and went out for a short stroll to stretch his legs. His neighbour, the lawyer Subramaniam Swamy – a nosy, obnoxious 'British toady' as Kaveri referred to him – called out to him, leaning against his gate. Ramu smiled politely, inwardly cursing his luck. He despised the man, and had no desire to engage in desultory neighbourly conversation with him. Swamy's eyes were bright with ill-disguised curiosity.

'No car today?'

'No,' Ramu responded curtly. 'I wanted to stretch my legs, so I came out for a walk.'

'Ah.' Swamy rubbed his hands unctuously against his brown waistcoat. 'I thought perhaps –' he gave Ramu a knowing look '– perhaps your wife has taken the car out, and left you to walk.' He laughed uproariously at his own joke. 'You should take my advice, young man. You need to make sure your wife stays at home, and keep a tight leash on her. You should start as you mean to go on. Otherwise you'll end up a henpecked husband. Whatever will your wife want to do next? Get a job? You better watch out, or she'll be wearing the pants in the house, and you'll be the one making coffee and serving her next.' He laughed again, the sound grating on Ramu's ears.

Ramu clenched his fists, itching to plant the obnoxious man a good facer. Then he thought of a better idea. He smiled, and put his hands into his pockets, whistling cheerfully. 'That sounds like a good idea.'

'What?' Swamy looked genuinely confounded.

'I have started as I mean to go on, and she may want to get a job. In fact, I'm heading back home right now – to take your advice and make my wife a nice hot cup of coffee.'

Ramu turned back home. After a few steps, he stopped and looked over his shoulder. The older man had come out of the gate and was standing on the road, staring at him. His mouth hung open foolishly.

Ramu laughed, his irritation suddenly evaporating in the wind. How petty this blowhard was. 'You should try it sometime,' he called over his shoulder.

'Try what?'

'Try being nice to your wife for a change. See what a difference it makes to your life.'

He put his hands in his pockets and whistled to himself as he strolled back, eager to see Kaveri's face flushed with pleasure as he handed her a cup of freshly made, aromatic coffee.

* * *

Later that evening, Ramu and Kaveri went out for an evening stroll, in the direction of the Basavanagudi Public Square. It was another cloudy evening, and the temperamental monsoon winds had gathered in the sky. The air was filled with smoke from the wood fires that the security guards had lit on the sides of the road. Ramu took her elbow gently, and nudged her along. He wished he had thought of bringing a shawl to keep her warm. Kaveri urged him on. Her happiness at seeing Indira and her son had evaporated from her mind, and her stomach now churned with fear about Mala, whose trial was now just a week away. She wanted – no, *needed* – the walk, to help her focuses.

'Isn't it fairly difficult to hit someone on the head with a *lathi*?' she asked.

'Yes. The man, whoever he is, must be quite strong. And tall. Both Iyengar and Muniamma were hit on the top of the head. That means the assailant was taller than Iyengar, who must be about five and a half feet,' Ramu replied.

'Why would anyone want to attack Dr Iyengar? He was second on our list of suspects, after Manju,' mourned Kaveri. 'Now what are we to do? We still don't know why he was rummaging in your desk. You didn't have anything in there, did you?'

They sat down on a stone bench. At this hour, there were few people around. The park was brightly lit by electric lights, newly mounted on wrought-iron columns. A beggar woman squatted in a corner, in a pool of shadow. Only her hands were visible, thrust into the circle of light, raised piteously out for offerings. Ramu dropped a few coins into her palm. She moved into the light and smiled, exposing rotten teeth in a wrinkled face, calling benedictions to Kaveri as they passed. 'May you die a *sumangali* – a married woman. May you be blessed with a thousand sons.'

On the opposite side, a man stood with a cart, selling boiled peanuts mixed with chilli powder and salt in twists of paper to hungry and cold passersby, going or coming from shifts of work. Puffs of steam rose from the large aluminium vessel, placed on an untidy mound of sticks, on which the peanuts were kept simmering in water. Ramu squinted. Just behind him he saw a mound of people – the peanut vendor's family, he assumed, sleeping on the pavement. He shivered and pulled Kaveri closer to him, suddenly thankful that he had a nice warm house to take his wife back to after their walk. The children of the peanut vendor were fated to live their entire lives on the street, whether in the bitter cold of the winter or the harsh heat of the summer. They would be put to work early. No childhood full of games for them.

Ramu suddenly thought of the children they would have – he and Kaveri – deeply thankful that they would not grow up in poverty. Marriage had changed him. No – Kaveri's move to Bangalore had changed him, made the marriage finally become real in his mind. He felt very protective of his wife and their future children. He moved even closer to Kaveri, taking her elbow protectively in his hand.

Kaveri shot him a startled glance. Her mind was not on the beggar woman or the peanut seller. Focused like a mongoose intent on attack, she was still mulling over the reasons why someone would have wanted to attack a respectable doctor like Iyengar.

'We need to get to know Dr Iyengar better,' she said, absentmindedly tugging her hand from Ramu's and moving further away from their house. Ramu stopped and pulled her back. Beyond this junction, the road lay dark.

In the distance, he could hear the sound of a heavy *lathi* being tapped against the cobblestones. 'Thap! Thap! Thap!' A constable patrolled the roads in the darkness. Still, it was not a safe place to take Kaveri. Anything could lie there . . . snakes, rats —even human beings, more dangerous than snakes and rats.

'Kaveri,' he said patiently. 'Iyengar is in a coma. How can he tell us anything?'

'Let us go to his house tomorrow,' Kaveri suddenly decided. 'I'll sit with his wife and see what information I can get from her. You go sit with Iyengar. Maybe there will be something there that provides us with a clue.'

Ramu did not think much of the possibility. But they needed to scout out every chance, however slim. He turned back, agreeing that they would head to Dr Iyengar's house the next day.

The next morning, at 10 a.m., three people made their way to Dr Iyengar's home; Uma had joined them. Her son had taken Ravi to visit an aunt, but Uma had declined to go along with them. She had now well and truly caught the sleuthing bug, and did not want to miss anything.

Uma kept up a continuous stream of conversation with Ramu the entire way, as they drove down to Dr Iyengar's home. Kaveri was engrossed in sombre thoughts about Mala, only half-listening. When they reached Malleswaram, she perked up. She had never been to this part of Bangalore before.

As Uma chattered, Ramu drove on, thinking of how they could get more information from Dr Iyengar. In the light of the morning, his earlier doubts about the suitability of their visit had dropped away from his mind. He agreed with Kaveri. They needed to find out more about Iyengar. What had he been doing in Ramu's study, and why had he had such a note hidden in his desk?

It was a long shot. With Iyengar in a coma, and his wife possibly prostrate with grief, they might well return home no wiser than they were before.

It was a risk they had to take.

The wide roads began to give way to narrow, congested lanes. Ramu parked the car under the shade of a magnolia tree. Kaveri breathed in the fragrance of the white blossoms appreciatively, as Ramu began to ask around for directions. Dr Iyengar's home was not easy to find. This was Malleswaram, after all, an area full of Iyengars.

They asked a woman selling heaps of marigold, neatly coiled into mounds. Woven into garlands for the God, they were sold near the temple next to piles of coconuts, incense sticks and other offerings that devotees could purchase to take into the temple. The woman shook her head – she did not know. They asked a cobbler repairing slippers on the side of the road, who waved them on. An elderly man, arms folded across the gate, a small girl on his hip, hailed them with some curiosity. Ramu patted the chubby cheeks of the gap toothed girl – who continued to suck contentedly on a sticky lump of jaggery which she kept clutched fast in a small, grimy, chubby fist – and asked the man for Dr Iyengar's house. But he wasn't able to help them. They even asked a beggar, but to no avail.

'He told me he lived in Malleswaram,' muttered Ramu in frustration. 'Close to the Kadu Malleswara temple.'

Suddenly, they saw the uniformed figure of a postman, dressed in khaki, carrying an unmistakeable satchel of parcels and letters, cycling past. Ramu stopped him. The postman dismounted.

'We're looking for Dr Iyengar's house,' Ramu explained.

'The doctor who works in the Bowring hospital?'

34

Scouting for Suspects

From there, it was easy. Ramu walked ahead, scouting for directions. The women walked slightly behind, covering their heads with their *pallus* – they were in a more congested place now, and there were too many curious gazes on them. The Iyengar house was massive, with four magnificent wooden pillars supporting a verandah with a tiled gable roof. No one seemed to be around outside. They opened the large, creaking iron gates – clearly they had not been oiled in a while – and entered the large, well kept garden. They climbed up the steps to the verandah. A large, wooden door, ornately carved with a picture of Rama and Lakshmana, each holding bows, and Sita standing demurely between them, was surrounded by a frieze of red and green wooden parrots, carved into the door frame. The knocker was heavy. Ramu picked it up and knocked on the door twice.

After a long silence, punctured by the calling of a rooster in the distance, footsteps sounded within. There was a snick, as the shutter to the spyhole embedded in the door moved on the other side. A disembodied eye gazed out at them.

Then, having recognised who they were, there was a clatter and a clang as a heavy bolt was removed from within. Clearly, Dr Iyengar's son had taken the possibility of a renewed attack on his father seriously, and following Dr Appia's warning, had kept the house well secured.

The young man opened the door. 'Come in, come in. I'm sorry for the delay in opening the door,' he murmured. Ramu hastened to assure him that it was nothing. He ushered them into a dark living room, and pulled aside heavy curtains to reveal the light. The room was lined with lush Persian carpets.

Dr Iyengar's son muttered something about bringing his mother, then disappeared. Ramu, Kaveri and Uma aunty waited for some time. Then he came in again, and invited Ramu to come to the bedroom, where his father lay, still in a coma.

'We cannot leave him alone,' he explained apologetically. 'If we sit there, you can also check on him. Dr Appia comes twice a day to check on him and change his dressing. This is the weekend though, and he has gone to Coorg. No one will come for two days. We are alone. And my mother . . . she gets anxious. If you could see him . . .' His voice trailed away.

Ramu felt ashamed. He had spared little thought for Iyengar's family. Frankly, after hearing that the man was a blackmailer, he had lost all regard for him. But it was not fair to his family.

'Didn't anyone else come to visit him?'

'A couple of doctors from the hospital did visit. Mr Reddy and Mr Sastry. But the Inspector had told me not to let anyone in, except Dr Appia and you. They were not happy about it, I'm afraid.'

Ramu nodded. Mentally, he agreed with Inspector Ismail – there was no such thing as being too careful in this case. He went in to Iyengar's bedroom with his son.

Dr Iyengar's wife was sitting in the living room, an emaciated, hollow cheeked figure hunched into the sofa. The woman who had chatted with them in Kaveri's house seemed reduced to a shadow of her former self. Kaveri and Uma came over to sit with her.

Tears rolled down Mrs Iyengar's cheeks, and she wiped at them ineffectively with the back of her hand. Kaveri, moved to tears herself, squeezed her hand. They sat together silently for a while, until a woman wearing a grey cotton sari entered – their maid, guessed Kaveri.

'Where is Lalita?' she asked Mrs Iyengar.

'My son sent her to my sister's home. She was distraught looking at her father. He felt she needed a change.'

The maid brought in tea on a tray. Mrs Iyengar closed her eyes and took a long slurp. She sat up straighter, visibly struggling to regain control of herself.

Uma aunty patted her hand. 'Don't you have any relatives to help you? You should not be alone at a time like this. You need another woman for company. Should I stay with you?'

'My married daughter is coming today. She lives close by, in Kolar. She will stay for a few weeks and help me out.'

'In Kolar?' exclaimed Uma. That was her home town.

'Yes. She got married a year ago. She married so well – into a grand family, very well known.' Mrs Iyengar mentioned the name of her daughter's family. Uma aunty nodded – she had heard of the girl's father-in-law, a well known industrialist and philanthropist.

'We conducted such a grand wedding,' Mrs Iyengar continued. She did not realise that she was repeating what she had said to Kaveri at lunch in their home. 'We seated the bridegroom on an elephant, and had a uniformed band with twenty people playing music as the wedding procession walked down the street.

'Some years ago, my husband came into a lot of money from an old great-aunt. We have been fortunate. My husband

228

has a lot of elderly relatives who left him money over the years. We had never met her, but she died and left him a lot of money. After that, we bought this house and moved in.'

The conversation trailed off. Her head drooped to one side and her eyes began to close with fatigue. She leaned against the wall and gentle snores emanated from her open mouth.

The two women gently tiptoed out of the living room and went to the bedroom. Ramu was sitting with Dr Iyengar's son. Dr Iyengar was still in a coma, with breathing that sounded alarming even to Kaveri.

'Let's go?' Kaveri mouthed. Ramu nodded.

He got up, patting the younger man on his shoulder. 'We will pray for him.'

Dr Iyengar's son turned and faced Ramu. Young as he was, he appeared mature beyond his years. And determined to see his mother out of this.

'Tell me, Doctor. The truth. What are his chances?' He looked Ramu squarely in the eyes.

'We cannot tell for sure.' Ramu looked back at him frankly. 'However, if I were you . . . I would prepare your mother for the worst.'

The younger man's face crumpled. He dabbed at his eyes with a kerchief.

'Thank you, Doctor. I appreciate the honesty. I need to tell my mother. I need to . . . I was studying, to be an engineer. I think I need to return home now, permanently, and take up a job. This house—' He looked around. 'I don't know what our father has done with all the money he inherited over the years. I think he spent it all, on the house, my sister's wedding, my mother's jewellery. I can't find any money in his bank account.' He squared his shoulders. 'I think the house is too large for us. We'll sell it – I'll convince my mother somehow – and move to Kolar. My sister's family can help me get a job. And I think my mother needs a change.'

He turned to Ramu again.

'How much time does he have left?'

Ramu looked grave.

'His breath is shallow. He is struggling. I don't think you have very much longer. Maybe a day or two. The end of the week, at the most.'

'Thank you, doctor.' The young man looked down at his hands. 'My sister is coming today. That will be a source of strength for us.'

He escorted them out of the house. They waved goodbye to him as he stood at the verandah and watched them leave, a lonely figure carrying a burden beyond his age.

35

Evidence of Blackmail

Ramu went straight to the police station the next morning, and was rewarded by the sight of Ismail wearing a crumpled but still spotlessly white *kurta*, sporting grey stubble on his chin, and a tired look in his eyes. He was sitting at his desk, leafing through a pile of papers. When he saw Ramu, his eyes sparkled. A boy was just coming through the door, swinging a steaming hot copper kettle of tea in one hand. In the other hand he held a stack of tumblers, neatly stacked one inside the other.

The two men sat looking out of the window at the trees outside, sipping tea flavoured with ginger and cardamom. Ramu read the headlines on the *Daily Post* on Ismail's desk. Mohandas Gandhi was visiting Bangalore in August.

Ismail saw him looking at the newspaper, and handed it over to him. 'Gandhiji is going to speak at the Eidgah Khuddus Saheb mosque on Millers Road. We have been drafted into duty that day to take care of him,' he added with obvious pride.

Ramu nodded. After they had been given the flyers, Kaveri had sent off for a subscription to the Indian National

Congress by mail. Ramu wondered if Ismail was a member. It was a sensitive question, and he hesitated to ask him. After all, Ismail worked for the British government too. *How many of us work for one government, while holding loyalty in our hearts to another*, he thought. He only wished he could see a transition in his lifetime.

Once they had finished their tea, Ismail gestured to the boy – who, Ramu noticed, had left his heavy burden on one of the wooden tables in the room, and was squatting on his heels in a corner. In an instant, the boy sprung up and took both their cups with him. Then, taking a few coins from Ismail, he picked up the kettle and his pile of glasses, and sped off.

'A good boy,' Ismail said, watching him as he sped off through the streets on a dilapidated cycle, calling 'Chai . . . chai . . .'

'I picked him up from the streets last year – his older brother was drunk and had kicked him out of the house a few days before I saw him. He was filthy with grime and covered with bruises. A few days more and he would have been picked up by one of the gangs roaming the streets at night.' Ismail wiped a weary hand over his eyes.

'I . . . ahem . . . convinced his brother to let him back home. I send a constable around every week, so his brother knows we keep an eye on the house, and is scared to do too much to him. He refuses to give him and his mother any money, though. So we took up a collection in the station and bought him a second-hand cycle. His mother makes tea in the morning and evening, and he does a few odd jobs during the day. He earns enough to support them, and is even able to save a bit on the side now. Soon he will be able to move out and have a small shop of his own, where he can sell sundry items.'

What a good man Ismail was, Ramu thought, marvelling not for the first time at his own misconception. Previously he had believed all policemen to be corrupt and incompetent. This policeman – he inspired confidence.

The office was empty. As Ismail sat benignly watching the street, Ramu told him of the events that had transpired on Saturday. When Ramu began by saying that it had been his wife's idea to go to their house, Ismail chortled.

'Your little lady is a treasure beyond reckoning. I hope she retains her spirit.'

Ramu looked at him, surprised.

'She reminds me of my eldest daughter,' Ismail said. 'Many may tell you that she is too intelligent or assertive for a woman. They say the same to my son-in-law about my daughter. I tell you – any man would be lucky to have a woman such as her in his life.'

Ramu nodded. It was true – many men would have been shocked at the idea of a woman being educated, let alone discussing business affairs and even a crime with her husband. And making friends with a fallen woman. Speaking to a policeman. It would be grounds for divorce in many families. Ismail was right, though. His wife was a treasure beyond any man's measure.

Ramu continued with the narration. He had something to tell Ismail – something that Kaveri knew, but Uma did not.

'When I was with Dr Iyengar, his son excused himself briefly to go to the bathroom. When he left, Dr Iyengar moaned and shifted, trying to get into a comfortable position on the bed. I supported his upper body, lifting it off the mattress, and smoothed the sheet, which had bunched up into folds and could have caused bedsores. While doing so, a corner of the sheet came out, and I picked up the mattress to fold the sheet back. I saw a small piece of paper sticking out of the wooden slats in the bed below – it had been carefully folded into a small square and pushed into a narrow crack in the side of the bed. I pulled it out and put into my pocket, and hurriedly put the sheets back into place just in time, as I heard the young man's footsteps in the passage outside.'

Ramu handed over the paper to Ismail. It was a sheet of blotting paper, which held the impressions of a letter. There were only a couple of sentences, scrawled in a firm but untidy hand:

'I saw you that night, with the knife in your hands. You have the blood of a man on your hands. Unless you want the entire world to know about what you did: keep five hundred rupees in a plain brown envelope, and place it in the hollow of the banyan tree at the back of the hospital by Friday night.'

The letter was unsigned.

'More blackmail,' Ismail said, his bushy eyebrows rising almost to his hairline.

'Yes,' Ramu said, nodding. 'I recognised Iyengar's handwriting at once. I suspect Iyengar was quite the blackmailer. His wife said he came into a large inheritance from a distant relative, whom she has never met – and he gets this inheritance every few months. His son says he can't find any trace of the money in the bank. I think he must have been blackmailing any number of people, for several years, keeping it hidden from his family.'

'So, now we have the missing link.' Ismail picked up the sheet of paper again. 'That night at the Century Club, there was an eyewitness to the murder. Iyengar. He must have come across the murderer in the act of striking Ponnuswamy that night. Instead of informing us, he chose to try and use the occasion to his advantage.'

234

'Stupid man,' Ramu muttered. 'Didn't he realise the risk he was taking? The murderer has attacked twice already. He would not scruple to attack a third time.'

Ismail raised an eyebrow. 'Some men are just greedy.'

'Will you discharge Mala?' Ramu asked him.

Ismail pursed his lips gravely. 'You are an intelligent young man.' His deep voice rumbled through the room. 'You and I both know that someone has tried to frame Mala.'

Ramu nodded. 'But we need to catch this killer. He is a man without a conscience. If we do not catch him this time, he is likely to repeat his crimes again, now that he has caught the taste of blood.'

'I cannot release Mala,' Ismail said. 'I have no evidence of whom Iyengar was blackmailing in the letter. A clever lawyer could argue that Mala killed Ponnuswamy, and the finger-print evidence is unreliable. He could say that Iyengar was blackmailing Mala – and that, from jail, she hired someone to attack him. It is possible – even plausible – for someone who only sees Mala as a prostitute, involved with a gang of crimi-nals, and not a woman with character and integrity.'

Ismail saw Ramu's face fall. He knew Ramu was thinking of what Kaveri would say at the thought of Mala being forced to spend more time in jail. He put up a large hand. Ramu fell silent.

'I'll see to it that Mala is not treated too badly. I'll even try to see if we can postpone the date of her trial. But my hands are tied.'

Ramu nodded reluctantly.

'I am becoming increasingly sure that our unknown killer has some medical knowledge,' Ismail continued. 'The intensity of the attack and the severity of the head wounds on Muniamma and Dr Iyengar tell us that it was done swiftly, with one expert blow. Ponnuswamy was also killed with just one thrust of the knife. The killer must have had a good knowledge of where to hit to create maximum damage, with minimum blood.'

Ramu sorted out his thoughts. 'Why did the killer leave the *lathi* propped against Mala's gate? It's almost too obvious. Manju would have to be a complete idiot to hit Muniamma on the head with a *lathi*, then leave the *lathi* in the most obvious place anyone would think of searching – in her house, propped against the gate.'

Ismail nodded. 'But even this kind of a common trick could have been effective. Unfortunately, our criminal justice system does not always look beyond the obvious. How many will have been willing to convict Mala and hang her on the basis of such evidence?'

'That's what my wife said,' Ramu muttered.

'Oh?'

'Yes. She plans to go sleuthing in Mrs Roberts' home tomorrow. She invited Kaveri for a swim in their pool a few days ago, and she wants to use this as an excuse to get her into conversation.'

Ismail looked startled. 'Why the Roberts' home, of all places?'

'That's what I said too. Surely Mrs Roberts can't have anything to do with Ponnuswamy's death, or the attack on Muniamma. She moves in very different circles. But Kaveri thinks perhaps she heard something that night at the Century Club. Do you remember, we told you that she left the table briefly, to clean up her dress? There's a small chance she saw something, or heard something in conversation that might be useful to us.'

Ramu shrugged his shoulders. 'I still think it's futile. She would have told us if she had seen anything. Roberts knows how critical this case is. Still, I guess there's no harm in it?'

He glanced at Ismail.

36

Conversations Around the Pool

'This house was built for the former Surgeon-General of Bangalore,' Daphne said as she welcomed Kaveri the next morning, noticing her visible surprise at the size of the grounds behind the house. They passed a man in khaki uniform, hacking away at a large bamboo in a clump, swearing a little as he nicked himself. Next to him, a line of bamboo sticks were piled up in the grass. Kaveri narrowed her eyes at him. Bamboos were grown in gardens. Could the man who was seen outside Muniamma's house have been a gardener? Not this fellow, though. He was small and tubby. The beggar had clearly said he'd seen a tall thin man.

The pool was tucked away at the back. They passed a little shack, where another gardener was busily engaged in washing his cowdung-stained khaki pants – Kaveri wrinkled her nose at the unmistakable smell – on a stone. He was puffing on a hand-rolled cigarette, a *bidi*. He was bent over almost double, and she couldn't make out how tall he was. Hearing the women coming, he hastily stubbed out the *bidi* and made as if to rise. Daphne waved a careless hand at him.

'Really, these Indian servants,' she exclaimed. 'Always lounging around. And when they hear one of us coming, they pretend to be busy. We can't hire just one, you know. They come in droves.'

Kaveri smiled politely. Inwardly, she was fuming. Daphne had told her that she was the daughter of a policeman, and had grown up in a modest home. Roberts came from a wealthy family. She was sure Daphne wasn't used to a large house with many servants when she grew up. But many British wives liked to lord it over the 'native' servants when they came to India. They didn't care how much work it took to turn hot, tropical India into a miniature version of the English countryside to satisfy their whims.

The pool was surrounded by a tall hedge, discreetly screening them from view of the main house, or the staff. Daphne rapped out a command to one of the maids, who scurried into the house to fetch a tall pile of towels, which she placed neatly on a chair next to the pool. She then moved away to stand at the entrance to the pool, her back to them.

Kaveri raised her eyebrows at Daphne.

'I can't stand having people coming to stare at us,' she said tersely. 'These garden fellows. Drooling when they catch a glimpse of white skin.'

Kaveri looked away, shocked, as Daphne strode into the changing room – another shack, this one neatly painted. Such a stark contrast to the gardener's dilapidated room, with its peeling paint and mouldy patches on the walls, she thought.

Daphne was a mercurial person. Kaveri seemed to encounter different versions of her each time, from the aggressive woman full of questions whom she had had dinner with at the Century Club, the hostile, suspicious woman who had invited her in when she found Kaveri unexpectedly at her doorstep, and the warm hospitable woman she had met over tea just recently. She seemed like another person again today. Moody, irritable. And bigoted. Definitely bigoted.

Daphne came out wearing a gorgeous swimming costume. Cut daringly low, it was sleeveless, and stopped at mid-thigh. Kaveri willed herself not to stare at her. What an athletic woman Daphne must have been in her heyday. Even now, though she must be at least forty, her arms and legs were fit and muscular. A regular swimmer, Kaveri supposed.

'Oh yes, I absolutely love swimming,' Daphne said when Kaveri joined her in the pool. Kaveri admired the speed at which she wove in and out of the water. 'My father used to say I was like a fish.'

'Do you swim often?' Kaveri asked curiously.

'I swim at least thrice a week. And I play tennis at the Club–' referring to the British-only BUS Club '–on weekends. I would go mad here if it weren't for the exercise.' She suddenly realised that she was speaking to an Indian, and gave Kaveri a half-apologetic smile. 'I mean, it's different for you. You were born here. I miss my home. There's very little to do here. The servants do it all. My daughters have an excellent governess who takes care of all their needs. My husband is busy in the hospital from morning to late evening. What am I expected to do? I was a VAD, a voluntary nurse, for a few years just after I got married, you know. I worked on ill soldiers in the war. I've patched up bleeding men, even helped with amputations. I'm not good at spending my time on make-up and fripperies – or drinks and party gossip.'

Kaveri nodded. She knew that the British held weekly parties at each others' homes. She had even heard whispers of some of the wild things that some of them got up to. Wife swapping, drunken orgies, even drugs. But despite her love for flamboyant flapper dresses, Daphne seemed too healthy, with her obsession for exercise, to have indulged in drink or drugs.

As the women got out and towelled themselves dry, Daphne barked an order at the maid, who trotted back into the house and brought out two robes in gorgeous light purple silk. They settled into two chairs in the shade.

'Now what will you have to drink?' Daphne turned to her. 'Lime juice? Buttermilk? Or would you prefer tea?'

'A cool glass of lime juice would be lovely after the exercise, thank you.' Kaveri looked up at the sky. The sun was out, and the air was warm. A black kite soared high in the air, emitting a faint 'kee-yooo' keening sound. In the distance, she could faintly hear Roberts shouting at some unfortunate servant that his boots were muddy.

'What on earth have you been doing with my shoes? Damn your impudence. I know I didn't go anywhere muddy. Have you been using them to roam around at night? You bloody rascal.'

Picking up a tall glass of juice, Kaveri tried to ignore him. Ramu said he was a kind boss at the hospital, but he seemed to have quite a temper at home. Gosh, she would hate to be a servant in *this* house.

Daphne seemed unperturbed. Clearly, raising voices at the help was just another part of daily life here.

Kaveri thought of a way to bring the topic around to the murder in the Club. 'I hope you've recovered completely now,' she ventured.

Daphne flashed her a look of surprise. 'Recovered? From what?'

'From that dreadful murder. I was so shocked myself. It took me days to recover my appetite.'

Daphne nodded. Her mood seemed to have gone through another mercurial change. After the exercise, she was in noticeably better spirits.

'Yes, I was down for a bit. It was such a shock. But then I recovered. Anyway, that dead man, and men of his ilk, are the dregs of the earth. Scum. Better off dead. My husband told me he was a well known local ruffian.' She tossed down her glass, and poured herself another juice from the jug.

'Did you see anything when you went to clean your dress?'

Daphne shot her a quick glance. 'Like what?'

'I don't know – just anything out of the ordinary.' Kaveri cast around for a plausible reason for her question. Daphne was staring at her oddly. 'Mala – one of Ponnuswamy's women – has been arrested for the murder. That's what my husband said last night. I was only thinking, how difficult that must be. To be forced into prostitution, and then arrested for murder.'

'Forced?' Daphne banged her glass on the table so hard, Kaveri thought it might break. 'That woman was a harlot. She deserved everything she got. Luring good men from respectable families into sin. I know women like that. They deserve to be punished. Besides, I'm sure that's not the only murder she's committed. I heard that the milkman's wife was also hit on the head. But why are you asking all these questions?' Daphne narrowed her eyes at Kaveri. 'You seem awfully interested in the murder suddenly. You're the one who found the knife, aren't you?'

'I was just thinking,' Kaveri said slowly. 'You and I were in the corridor leading to the women's room just before dinner. What if the murder had taken place then? We could have been witnesses. And then we could have been next in line.' She pretended to shiver.

Daphne reached across and patted her. 'Never you worry, my dear. We move in very different circles from this riff-raff. And now that the woman has been caught and is behind bars, we'll be safe.'

Kaveri decided not to say anything further.

Daphne jumped up suddenly, and looked at her wrist. 'Heavens, is that the time already? I almost forgot.' She turned to Kaveri. 'I'm so sorry, my dear. I have an appointment with my hair stylist at ten. I must run, or I'll be late.'

'I'll make my own way back,' Kaveri reassured her. 'Do you mind if I stop on the way and ask your gardener for a cutting? I saw some lovely poinsettia plants, in deep scarlet. I'd love to have them in my garden.' *And I can speak to the gardener then*, she thought to herself.

Daphne beamed at her. 'Of course. Speak to the gardener. Take whatever plants you want.'

37

Disappearing *Lathis*

Later that evening, Kaveri waited impatiently for Ramu to return home. She was bursting with news to tell him, but paused, looking at his face with concern. 'What happened? Why do you look so exhausted?'

'A boiler burst at a local factory. There were so many injured men.' Ramu closed his eyes, reliving the memory of that long day. 'Thankfully, they all made it. But we need to keep them in hospital for the next few days, and watch them carefully.'

He sat down, exhausted, and gratefully gulped down the piping hot glass of coffee that Kaveri brought him, leaning his head back against the wall as Kaveri watched him with some concern. After a while, he sighed and opened his eyes.

'Did you have a good time with Daphne?' he asked.

'Are you sure you want to talk about this?' Kaveri asked doubtfully. 'Maybe you should lie down and rest for a while.'

'I'm fine. I need to talk about something else, to take my mind off today.'

Kaveri snuggled next to him, wrapping her arm in his.

'I had a very strange time with Daphne. She seemed like such a different person.'

'Really? In what way?'

'She's been so nice to us, but I saw a very different side to her today. She said such nasty things about her "native" servants. I don't think I want to visit her house again.'

'That bad? Roberts isn't like that at all.' Here Kaveri repressed the urge to roll her eyes, remembering this same Mr Roberts cruelly shouting at a servant. 'He's very genial, even friendly, with all the attendants in the hospital. Knows about their families, buys them packets of sweets for their children for Christmas.'

'Well, Daphne is nasty.' Kaveri shuddered. 'I wouldn't want to be a servant in her house. Do you know, the gardener was washing his pants – they had cow-dung stains on them – and she rebuked him for that. She said the gardeners were always looking for some excuse to shirk their work.'

'Cow-dung stains?' Ramu was curious. 'They live in such a posh part of the city, in the cantonment. You don't find cows roaming the streets there, like they do here.'

'Yes, that's what I wanted to tell you about.' Kaveri got up and paced up and down. 'The gardener's shack had a large grey shawl hanging on a hook. And two lengths of bamboo have gone missing from their garden. Do you think one of the gardeners may have been the person who attacked Muniamma and Dr Iyengar?'

'Slow down, Kaveri. I can't make sense of anything you're saying.'

Kaveri sat down next to Ramu. 'I saw one of the gardeners cutting a length of bamboo from their garden into long sections. Just the size of walking sticks. Or *lathis*.'

Ramu stared at her.

She continued. 'He's a short man, too short to have been the man the beggar saw near Muniamma's home the morning

244

she was attacked. But Daphne had left, so I stopped and chatted to him. I asked him what he wanted with so many sticks. He sounded irritated. He said –' she touched Ramu's arm '– that since *lathis* kept disappearing from the garden, he might as well cut several new ones.'

'Disappearing?' Ramu sat up.

'Yes, disappearing.' Kaveri leaned forward, poking Ramu's arm for emphasis. 'They keep a *lathi* in the gardener's shack, to kill snakes with. There are a number of cobras and kraits in the garden, and Daphne is terrified that they may bite the children. One *lathi* disappeared last week. Just around the time that Muniamma was attacked. A second went missing more recently. This one, around the time that Dr Iyengar was attacked.'

'Do you think one of the gardeners was having an affair with Mala? Or was an associate of Ponnuswamy?'

The couple gazed at each other.

'Mala would know,' Kaveri said. 'I need to speak to her again.'

'Well, I'm not having you go to the jail again,' Ramu said firmly. 'You know how worried I was last time.'

Kaveri shot him an angry glare.

'Kaveri. It's not safe,' he said patiently.

'She won't speak openly to you. Or to Ismail. I have to speak to her.'

Groaning, Ramu conceded. 'At least let me ask Ismail to bring her down to the police station. We can meet there tomorrow morning.'

38

What the Doctor Ordered

Ismail looked pleased to see Ramu the next morning. He handed Ramu a dry fruit *laddu* from the seemingly inexhaustible supply he carried around in the tiny steel *dabba* in his pocket. Today he was in *mufti* – plainclothes – wearing a turmeric yellow *kurta* over crisp white, voluminous *salwar* pants.

'The disappearing bamboo *lathis* must be related to the case somehow,' Ramu told him.

'Hmm hmm,' Ismail said noncommittally.

Ramu continued, undeterred. 'And somehow, the gardeners in Dr Roberts' house seem to be connected with this mess. The khaki uniform seems to tie into it. The question is, why would a gardener want to hit Dr Iyengar on the head?'

'Who is to say why a man is hit on the head with a bamboo *lathi*? The reasons can be many. As many as there are bamboo *lathis* in Bangalore.' Ismail's voice rumbled, echoing through the empty building. Most of the policemen had gone home after a long night's work, and the morning shift was out on their daily beat on the streets.

'Dr Iyengar was a blackmailer. But surely he wouldn't want to blackmail a gardener.' Ramu tapped his fingers on the wooden desk. 'This case is getting more and more confusing by the day.'

'Who does your wife think is the killer?' Ismail leaned back in his chair, his fingers steepled over his ample paunch.

'If we consider it is one of the doctors . . .' Ramu began. 'Well then. It has to be someone who had a grudge against Ponnuswamy. And against Muniamma.'

'Of course.' Ismail nodded. 'And someone with a guilty secret. Whom Dr Iyengar was blackmailing.'

'Iyengar was a serial blackmailer. He had blackmailed Sastry for several months. From the copy of the blackmail note I found, it seems likely that Dr Iyengar saw something related to Ponnuswamy's murder. Perhaps he saw the murderer himself.' Ramu sat forward, drumming restlessly with his fingers on the table.

'A slim man, with a long grey shawl, carrying a long *lathi*, wearing hobnailed boots, using safety pins. Perhaps an old soldier? A powerful man, to be able to fell people with one blow of the *lathi*. And tall, if one considers that he hit Dr Iyengar on the top of his head.' Ismail continued to summarise, ticking off points on his fingers as he spoke. 'Doesn't fit the description of any of the doctors. Sastry is too short, Reddy is too fat. It can't be Iyengar. And Appia was not at the dinner. And so we are at a dead end again. We know this much, but are no nearer to finding the man's identity.'

'Except for this new clue,' Ramu interjected, 'of the missing bamboo *lathis*. Surely it is no coincidence that two *lathis* went missing from the Roberts' garden at the same time that two *lathis* were used to attack Muniamma and Iyengar.'

Ismail nodded slowly.

'My wife wants to speak to Mala. She feels that there is more to this than we know. Perhaps Mala knows something that will help us solve the case.'

'And you do not want her to go to the jail,' Ismail guessed, looking shrewdly at Ramu.

'What time did you ask your good wife to come here? I assume you want me to fetch Mala to the police station, so she can speak to her?'

A couple of hours later, Mala stood before Kaveri in the police station. She looked thin and fragile, but not as bad as she had done when Kaveri had seen her, the first day they'd put her in jail.

'Sit down.' Kaveri moved her to one of the chairs.

Mala began to sob. Kaveri let her cry for some time, moving her chair close and patting Mala softly on the shoulder. She gave Mala a handkerchief to wipe her tear-streaked face. 'We need to find a way to get you out of jail before your case comes up for trial.'

'I'll never leave the jail,' Mala laughed bitterly.

'We have found some new evidence that may help.' Kaveri put an insistent hand on her knee. 'But you have to help us make sense of it.' She began speaking quickly, telling Mala all that she had seen and learnt in Daphne's home.

'Gardener?' Mala looked confused. 'Ponnuswamy did not hire any gardeners. I know all his men. And I did not know anyone from there either.'

Kaveri felt defeated. 'Can I call in my husband?' she asked Mala. 'And the Inspector? Maybe they'll think of something else.'

But Ramu and Ismail were stumped too.

'Let's look at the list again,' Kaveri suggested. 'The key lies with Mala, I'm sure of it. Can you think of any way in which you are connected to the Roberts' house?'

'The house?' Mala sat up. 'Well, I have been to their

house. But only to the back entrance. Near the bamboo clump.'

'What? Why would you go to the Roberts' house?'

Mala trembled visibly. 'I'd rather not say.'

Ramu and Kaveri exchanged glances. Ramu took Ismail by the arm, and the two men left the room.

'Now you can tell me.'

Mala turned away from her.

'Mala!' Kaveri lost patience with her. She moved to stand in front of her. 'Do you understand what the outcome of your silence might be? If you don't speak openly to us, the judge will condemn you to death when your case comes up for hearing. They'll hang you.' She felt dreadful at having to say it so bluntly, but she could not bear the thought of Mala's pretty, vivacious face disfigured by a hangman's noose.

She paused, then tried another approach. 'What will become of Narsamma if you die? Who will look after her then? She'll be reduced to begging on the streets.'

At last Mala looked up. 'I went to visit the English doctor. Ponnuswamy took me. They say he is expert at treating men and women with my condition.'

'Your condition?' Kaveri didn't understand.

'I picked it up from one of the men I was with.' Mala pointed to her groin. 'I had boils. Severe pus and itching. The whole area was so painful. Ponnuswamy said that there were good English medicines which could cure me. He took me to visit the English doctor.'

'When was this?'

'A few days ago. Just before the full moon night.'

The night before the dinner at the Century Club!

'And then? Did Roberts make a pass at you?' Kaveri was horrified.

'Not at all,' Mala assured her. 'The English doctor was

very discreet. He could not treat me without looking at me first. I felt very scared. I have never had a white man look at me before – and a doctor at that! But he was so kind. He took Ponnuswamy and myself into a small room next to the pool – where they change into their clothes after swimming. He asked Ponnuswamy to turn his back while he examined me, and then gave me an ointment from his medical case. He said that I would be fine within a couple of weeks. And I was.'

Mala reluctantly agreed to give her statement to Ismail, and so Kaveri explained the gist of their conversation to the two men.

'So Mala had a venereal disease. And Roberts came to treat her,' Ramu said. 'I don't understand it at all. Is it Roberts then?'

'Impossible,' Kaveri suddenly said loudly.

The two men turned to face her.

'Don't you remember?' She turned to Ramu. 'We were at the same dinner table. When Daphne and I went in from the ladies' room to dinner, Ponnuswamy was alive. I had just seen him. And Roberts was with us the whole time from then to the time they found Ponnuswamy's body.'

Mala flinched under their combined gaze, and looked away nervously.

'Mala, you have to be sure to tell us everything.' Kaveri gripped Mala's hands in hers. 'Are you sure you've not kept anything back?'

'Nothing,' said Mala. But she would not meet Kaveri's gaze.

'There *is* something you're not telling us,' Kaveri insisted. 'Mala, if you don't tell us, soon the trial will be here. The judge will convict you. Think of Narsamma.'

After a long pause, Mala spoke quietly.

'The English lady saw me go in with the doctor into the room. She waited till he left, and then barged into the room.

She screeched at me, and tried to scratch me. She called me all kinds of names, loud English names that I could not understand.'

'Why?' Kaveri was puzzled.

'I don't know. I think she thought that I . . .' Mala stuttered to a halt. 'That Ponnuswamy had brought me there as a woman. For the doctor.'

Ramu and Ismail were nodding well before Kaveri understood. Daphne thought that Ponnuswamy had brought Mala to service Roberts. How could she think that of her own husband? Did she not know the man?

'I have never been so frightened as I was that day. Ponnuswamy managed to fend her off and helped me put my clothes back on. We fled from the small gate at the back of the lawn. I was wrapping my sari around me as I ran. She was shouting after me.'

Kaveri said, slowly, looking at Ismail, 'Do you remember what you told me, when we discussed Sherlock Holmes in your office? *When you have eliminated the impossible, whatever remains, however improbable, must be the truth.*'

'Roberts did not get up from the dinner table. But Daphne got up for a while. To clean her dress,' Kaveri said, her voice dropping so low that Ismail and Ramu strained to hear her.

'Do you mean that Daphne is the murderer?' Ramu asked bluntly.

'We thought the blows were struck by a man,' Ismail said. 'Because of the height from which they were struck, and because of the force and strength that must have accompanied the blows. We arrested Mala, but we were doubtful about her ability to commit the attacks.' He pulled over a chair and sat down heavily.

'Daphne is tall, and strong. She swims and plays tennis regularly,' Kaveri said. 'I saw her in a swimming costume. She's quite well built.' Even though Kaveri had come up with the idea, it still seemed farfetched to her. 'How could she have stabbed Ponnuswamy?' A thought suddenly occurred to her. 'Surely there would have been bloodstains on her dress?'

Ismail looked at her with some respect. 'The stab wound was deep and forceful. It was in a place where it could cause maximum damage, straight into Ponnuswamy's lungs, between his ribs. It seems likely that it was inflicted by someone with medical knowledge. That is why we thought it may have been one of the doctors.'

'Daphne told me that she was a volunteer nurse, a VAD, in the war,' Kaveri said. 'Before she and Roberts had children. So she definitely has the medical knowledge this would require.'

'Why would she have wanted to attack Ponnuswamy though?' asked Ramu.

'I don't know.'

'Could she have seen Mala visiting her husband, and become suspicious? Been angry with Ponnuswamy? And then decided to frame Mala for his murder?'

'It is plausible. But is it possible?' Ramu asked. Ismail shrugged.

'What can we do now?' Kaveri asked, facing Ismail.

'The problem is the lack of evidence,' said Ismail.

'We may have some evidence. The fingerprints on the knife. Could they be Daphne's?' Kaveri interrupted.

'There's absolutely no evidence to suggest it may be so.' Ismail sat back, shaking his head heavily. 'Her husband is a senior British doctor. I can't walk into her house and ask for her fingerprints on the strength of such a flimsy sounding narrative. I'd lose my job.'

'I have an idea,' Kaveri announced, rocking on her toes.

'What do you suggest?' Ismail held up a large hand as Ramu began to expostulate, waving him to silence.

The two men leaned forward as Kaveri began to sketch out a plan, her small hands moving in the air.

39

A Denouement

Kaveri stood at Daphne's doorstep. She was sweating with nervousness. She wiped her damp hands on her sari, and pulled the folds of cloth around her arms to disguise the sweat patches on her underarms.

Ramu was pacing outside the house. At first he had forbidden her from going to see Daphne. But Ismail had intervened.

'We have no other way of getting Mrs Roberts' fingerprints,' he said. 'Can you imagine my going to my superiors with a cock and bull story like this, and getting permission for a warrant to take the fingerprints of a British doctor's wife? I'll be tossed out without a hearing.' He smiled wryly at Ramu. 'I would be lucky if they don't strip me of my post and uniform.'

'And Mala would rot away in jail. Or die at the end of a hangman's noose,' interrupted Kaveri, laying a hand softly on Ramu's arm. 'Please. You have to let me do this.'

Ismail nodded.

Ramu crumpled a piece of paper and threw it across the room.

'I'll be waiting for you outside. If you feel in danger, call out. The moment I hear a noise, I'll come in.'

But it was not possible for him to stand outside the gate. The guard had looked at him expectantly, asking if he should open the gate. Ramu murmured something about coming back later, turned on his heels and left. Ismail was waiting for him at the corner of the road, standing with a couple of constables under the shade of a tree.

'What do we do now?' Ramu asked. He cast a worried glance towards the house. 'We need to be in earshot. In case she calls out for help.'

'Let's go to the lane behind the house,' suggested Ismail. 'That's a conservancy lane. There won't be anyone around at this time.'

They went down a side lane, and took another turn, standing in the narrow path that led to the back of the Roberts' house. The tall hedge shielded them from view.

'Kaveri described this part of the house,' said Ramu, striding forward purposefully. 'This is the area just behind the swimming pool. She said there was a dense clump of bamboo to one side, and tall trees with a bougainvillea creeper on the other side. Look.'

He pointed to the trees. A riot of blood red bougainvillea flowers cascaded from the branches.

'Between the trees and the bamboo clump, there should be a small wicker gate, hidden behind creepers. There.'

They moved down towards the clump, and stopped, belatedly realising that they might be in full sight of anyone on the road. Thankfully, there was nothing on the road except a family of monkeys capering on the branches above.

Ismail placed a finger on his lips, motioning them to silence. He felt under the creepers. There was an iron gate with a large lock.

How would they get it open if they needed?

Meanwhile, Kaveri was in the drawing room, having been ushered in by the maid. She perched herself at the edge of the sofa, waiting for Daphne to come in.

After a short while, Daphne came in.

'Mrs Murthy? How delightful to see you. So unexpected, though.'

Kaveri tried to look embarrassed. 'I'm sorry, this is an imposition,' she began. 'I should have sent a note ahead to enquire if you were free.'

'Well, it's not like I have anything important to do anyway,' said Daphne, a slight edge to her voice. 'Only playing at being the lady of the house.'

'But tell me –' she stared keenly at Kaveri '– what brings you here?'

'Oh, I was just at home, looking at my music book,' Kaveri said, with what she hoped was a casual laugh. 'I remembered our conversation about the violin. You told me you had also learnt to play the flute in the Western classical tradition. I found my flute. I had packed it away in a box of books when I moved to Bangalore. You told me your flute looked different from the ones you had seen being sold in Indian shops, so I thought you might like to see mine, up close.'

She took out her flute from her purse, holding it carefully at the edge. It was a shiny piece of wood, polished to perfection. Ideal to take fingerprint impressions on. She had polished it with a piece of soft cloth, taking care to remove all fingerprints before she'd wrapped it in a piece of cloth and placed it in her purse.

She almost thrust the flute into Daphne's hands. Daphne picked it up, looking at it closely.

'It's beautiful. This is very different from the flute I saw in an Indian store. That was long, and much wider than this.'

'That must have been a *bansuri*, a North Indian flute,' said Kaveri, trying to prattle on in normal conversation. She could feel her heart beating, and worried that Daphne may hear it, it sounded so loud to her ears.

'Our flute is different. Do you want to try playing it?'

Daphne made as if to put it to her lips, then stopped. 'No, maybe some other time,' she said softly. 'I'm afraid I have a bit of a headache today.'

She gave the flute back to Kaveri, turning back to fiddle with the framed family photographs of her husband and children displayed on the ornate rosewood dresser against the wall.

'I'm so sorry,' Kaveri apologised to Daphne's back. She watched Daphne carefully, then quickly opened her purse, arranging the flute within the folds of the cloth. 'So stupid of me, to bother you when you're unwell. I'll go now, and return another time, when you're feeling better.'

'Not at all.' Daphne turned around again. She seemed to have undergone one of her mercurial mood swings again, flashing her a brilliant smile. 'It gets so lonely here without another adult to talk to. My husband is gone all day, and I welcome the chance to have some conversation, woman to woman.' She patted Kaveri on the shoulder. 'Do sit. Let me get you a glass of lemonade. It's too hot for tea.' She picked up a magazine from the table in front of them, fanning her face with it, then placed it down and went into the kitchen.

Kaveri's feet itched. She wanted to run out of the door and take the flute straight to Ismail for fingerprinting. But that would have been too obvious. So she sat down, flipping through the pages of the magazine.

She heard murmured voices from the kitchen, as Daphne spoke to her maid. She strained her ears, but could not hear what was said. The kitchen door closed, as the maid went out. Kaveri stiffened. Why had the maid left through the side door?

Daphne came in, carrying a tray with two glasses of yellow liquid. She handed one to Kaveri. 'Drink up!' she urged her. An odd smile lurked at the corner of her lips.

Kaveri took a cautious sip. The juice tasted odd. Almost bitter.

'What's in it?'

'Drink!' Daphne urged her, her voice rising higher. 'It's a herbal remedy, distilled from leaves in my garden. It's good for the heat. Very cooling. My maid makes it for me. You'll get used to it once you take a couple of sips.'

Kaveri hesitated. The room seemed too large suddenly, and Daphne's voice rather loud.

'DRINK.' Daphne's voice boomed in her ear. Suddenly, she was right next to Kaveri. Holding her hands firmly, she brought the glass close to Kaveri's lips, forcing them open.

Seeing Kaveri gasp, Daphne hissed in satisfaction. 'Didn't think you'd be found out, did you? Well, you're not so clever as you think you are. I saw your reflection in the glass.' She gestured to the wall above the dresser, on which hung a polished glass painting.

Too late, Kaveri realised. 'You saw me put the flute in the cloth.'

'Fingerprints, is it?' Daphne laughed. A wild, almost maniacal sound. 'Clever little missy. But not as clever as me. Drink up now, there's a good girl.'

Kaveri's head was whirling. If she drank the rest of the glass, that would be the end of her.

She made one massive effort to concentrate. 'What's in the glass?' But it came out feebly, distorted, like she was half asleep.

'Morphine. Did you know that half a grain is enough to kill a man? I put eight grains in your cup. Now drink up.' Daphne moved closer to her.

But I only took a small sip! Kaveri thought furiously. *What can I do now?*

Instead of moving away from Daphne, she swayed, leaning closer to her. Slowly, and with great deliberation, she picked up her left foot, thankful that she had selected a pair of shoes with hard wooden heels. She brought her foot down force-fully on Daphne's toes.

'Ow!' Daphne let go of Kaveri, reflexively moving her hand to her injured toes. Kaveri threw the glass onto the table. It smashed into several pieces, splattering yellow liquid all over them.

'Now look what you've done.' Daphne's eyes glittered with rage.

40

Back to the Pool

Kaveri sprang up from the couch and ran towards the door. Daphne grabbed her from behind, and put her arm around Kaveri's throat. Kaveri stilled, as she felt the cold hard blade of a knife touch her neck.

'You're hurting me,' she cried out.

Daphne pressed the knife deeper into Kaveri's throat. She stifled a cry. She could feel the knife pierce her skin. A trickle of blood flowed down her throat.

'You're not going anywhere unless I tell you to.'

Daphne grabbed Kaveri by the wrist and pushed her back down onto the couch. She stood over Kaveri, eyes hard.

Kaveri felt nauseous. Bursts of light came and went in front of her eyes. The poisoned juice that Daphne had given her – for poisoned it must have been – was making her feel dizzy. 'Let me go,' she said, trying to get the words out clearly.

'After all this?' Daphne demanded, gesturing to the mess that lay around them. 'No.'

Kaveri turned frantic eyes towards the door. Where were Ramu and Ismail? Surely they would realise that it had been a long time since she had disappeared into the house, and come in to find out what was happening?

Daphne followed her eyes. 'Searching for someone to rescue you? There's no one here except for you and I. The girls are with their governess and won't be home for a couple of hours. My husband will come back late this evening. I sent the maid out, telling her to take the gardeners and go to the Lal Bagh nursery to collect some seedlings for the garden. You and I, my dear, are going to take a little trip to the swimming pool. Where you are going to have a most tragic accident. An unfortunate drowning incident. I will, of course, be inconsolable when I come back from the kitchen with two glasses of lemonade, and find your body in the pool.'

Kaveri could feel her pulse race. She made an effort to control her breathing, focusing on the *pranayama* breathing technique her yoga teacher had taught her in school. Two counts in, four counts out. She looked around the room. Ramu was bound to come. She needed to keep Daphne talking, to buy time.

Daphne grabbed Kaveri by the wrist and pulled her up roughly, keeping the knife at her neck. 'Come on! We don't have that much time. I need to get you into the pool, then come back and clean up this mess.' She pointed to the shards of glass scattered over the table, and gave Kaveri a little nudge in the small of her back. Pushing and tugging at her, she got Kaveri out of the door and walking towards the pool.

'There's no need to pretend with me any more,' Daphne said, snarling at her, teeth bared. 'You play acted the role of ingénue so well. I almost fell for it.' She linked her arm in Kaveri's, dragging her across the stone pathway, keeping the knife at her throat. Her tone was almost conversational. 'When did you realise it was me?'

Kaveri was silent.

Daphne pressed the knife deeper into her throat.

'When I saw the gardener cutting the sticks of bamboo,' Kaveri cried out.

'I thought so.'

They'd reached the swimming pool. Daphne pushed her down onto one of the chairs, and sat down on the other, opposite her, breathing heavily.

'I looked out of my bedroom window as I was leaving that day, and saw you speaking to the gardener. You pointed at the bamboo sticks, and both of you turned to look at the grove. Did you really think I was so stupid?' Daphne's face contorted. 'I went straight to the gardener after you left and asked him what you were both talking about. Since then, I've been waiting for you to come back. I knew you were going to snoop around again.'

Daphne gestured to the pool. 'Well, we're here now. Do you want to ask me anything before you die? To satisfy your curiosity? Or do you know it all by now?'

Ramu and Ismail looked at each other in horror. The sound of the conversation carried out into the lane where they stood behind the hedge of trees.

Ramu tried to open the gate, but it was locked. He turned to Ismail. 'We have to go back through the front gate.'

The two men set off at a run, followed by the two constables.

'Why did you kill Ponnuswamy?' Kaveri asked weakly. She looked at the ring on her finger and prayed to her patron saint. *Please God, let Ramu come quickly!*

'Do you think I was going to let my husband consort with a whore?' Daphne spat out the words. 'I saw them at the changing room in the pool. I went after her – I wanted to kill her that day. And her pimp. How dare he bring a woman like that into a respectable house like mine? But when I went after her in my house, that large man – her pimp – he pushed me aside and dragged me away.

'That night, when I saw you in the corridor – both of them were in the garden. I knew they must be waiting to speak to my husband again. So I looked for them again when I went to clean my dress, to warn them to keep away. The whore was missing, but I saw the man. He was standing near the kitchen. I went after him to warn him away from my husband. But he made a fatal mistake. He laughed at me. I came after him to slap him, but he pushed me. I fell onto the grass. We were right behind the kitchen, near the washing area. I looked up at the washing stone. A large meat knife had fallen onto the grass. It was lying on top of a pile of cleaned vessels – I must have touched it when he pushed me and I fell onto the grass. I picked up the knife, and lunged at him, pushing it deep into his body. He fell instantly.' She giggled. 'He made one small squeak of a sound. Like an astonished pig being killed. And then he was quiet.'

She was breathing heavily.

'No one laughs at me and gets away with it. No one.'

'And Muniamma?' Kaveri prodded.

Daphne's eyes dilated as she stared at Kaveri. 'Curious little thing, aren't you? So many questions you have. Well, you're not going to live too long, so I suppose I can tell you. I didn't want to kill her. I was looking for her husband. The milk chap. I thought I saw him looking at me. I saw a large dark shape peering at me from the other side of the kitchen. So I went to his home, to get rid of him. But luck was really not on my side. I ended up hitting his wretched wife on the head.'

She giggled again, making another high pitched hysterical noise.

'But I was clever enough to figure out how to turn things to my advantage. I borrowed my gardener's clothes again, and left the bamboo stick in the whore's house, with an anonymous note at the police station.' Daphne bared her teeth. 'Finally, it was all right. The whore was in jail, and the pimp was dead. My husband was back in my control. And then – my ill luck – the man who spied on me in the Club turned out to be that wretched doctor. Iyengar. He had the effrontery to send me a blackmail note. Can you imagine that? Blackmail *me*?'

She looked genuinely astonished. 'I pretended to agree, and sent him a note asking him to meet me in the hospital in the early hours of the morning, behind the grove of trees. He thought a woman would be no danger to him. Foolish man.'

Kaveri nodded her head vigorously. Her head felt as if it was stuffed with cottonwool. Her thoughts moved slowly. *Keep her talking!* she thought, wondering if Ramu and Ismail would be able to get to her in time.

'How clever you are,' she murmured. 'How did you get to Muniamma's hut unobserved?'

Daphne's lips pressed together in a parody of a grin, as she bared her teeth. 'You didn't guess that, did you, little missy detective? I borrowed my husband's boots, and took a shawl from the gardener's shack. I wrapped it tightly around myself, so no one could see my hair clearly.'

'You used a safety pin,' Kaveri said.

'How did you know that?' Daphne's attention wavered for a moment, and Kaveri wondered if she could wrest the knife away from her. But it was only momentary.

'Did I drop the safety pin somewhere where you found it?' Daphne hissed, cutting a gash in Kaveri's neck. Kaveri squeezed her eyes closed as she felt the blood trickle down her neck.

If this is the end, please God, let it be quick.

Ismail and Ramu had reached the gate. They asked the startled security guard to open it, leaving one of the constables with the guard to make sure he didn't call out. Then they took off their shoes and socks and crept down the garden towards the back of the house, tiptoeing on the grass to avoid making any noise. Ismail motioned to Ramu to follow in his footsteps, avoiding the dry sticks that might snap under their feet.

Sitting in chairs at the edge of the water, the two women could make a pretty picture, thought Ismail. Both dressed so elegantly, sitting on chairs dappled in shade. Only if you looked closely would you see that both women were stiff with tension. And the taller golden haired woman in a purple and green summer frock was holding a wicked switchblade to the neck of the shorter, black haired Indian woman in a chocolate brown sari.

Daphne turned away from Kaveri, towards the pool. Then she faced Kaveri again.

'No need to play detective any more. This is the end now. Go lie down on the floor, stomach on the floor, and close your eyes. I'll make it easy for you. You won't feel a thing. Except when I hit you.' She bared her teeth at Kaveri again. 'I'll say you fell and hit your head against the side of the pool, then fell in and drowned. No one will be more upset than I.'

Kaveri swallowed hard. She looked at Daphne, measuring the distance between them. There was no hope of Ramu reaching them in time now.

'Lie down,' Daphne commanded.

Kaveri went and lay down obediently on the ground next to the pool. Her thoughts raced as she tried to figure out how to escape from this insanely capable woman.

Daphne kept her knife pointed at Kaveri, backing away slowly as she moved towards the wall. She picked up a tall bamboo stick with her left hand, plucking it out from behind the hedge.

Kaveri held her breath as Daphne came closer. Ramu strained to go towards Kaveri, but Ismail held him back with a reassuring hand on his shoulder.

As Daphne came closer, Kaveri held her breath, waiting for the right time. As Daphne stood right next to her, Kaveri started a silent count. *One, two, three* . . . Daphne began to raise her hand, holding the stick above her head. On the count of five, Kaveri grabbed Daphne's ankles and pulled hard.

Daphne fell on the ground with an audible thud. She began to curse, foul words dropping from her mouth in an unending stream.

Ramu ran towards Kaveri, and hugged her hard, feeling tremors shake down his body and hers. Ismail kicked the bamboo *lathi* and knife away from Daphne, then picked her up from the ground where she had fallen, holding her arms as she cursed and tried to kick and scratch him.

The constable moved towards her, a pair of manacles in his hands. He turned his face away as she spat at him.

'What took you so long?' Kaveri asked, burying her face in Ramu's coat in relief.

41

A Most Dreadful
Scandal

A week had passed. Kaveri and Uma aunty sat on the steps of their home, chatting to Mala, who sat on the floor at a distance from them. She had refused to come in when they invited her, saying firmly, 'It would not be appropriate.' Narsamma, ever-present like a faithful shadow, sat next to her mistress.

'You have lost a lot of weight, Mala,' commented Uma aunty, leaning forward. Kaveri looked at her. You would never have realised that Uma aunty had at first taken a dislike to Mala, she thought, watching as the old lady smiled fondly and urged a plate of *laddus* on her. 'Eat up. I made these with homemade ghee, and lots of dry fruit. They'll help you pick up your health in no time.'

Mala laughed, poking Narsamma with a stick. Her face, still gaunt, had lost its haunted look. Narsamma had told Kaveri earlier that she had been haunted by nightmares, but was slowly beginning to sleep more peacefully at night. 'I have no space left in my stomach! This woman here would feed me all day, yes, and all night too, if she had her way. I'll become like a round football in a month.'

Narsamma held out a large cloth-wrapped parcel to them.

'Here are Ponnuswamy's notes. He'd left them with one of his henchmen for safe keeping.'

'How did you get them?' Kaveri demanded.

Narsamma smiled, exposing crooked teeth with a black gap in between.

'Ponnuswamy's men are running around like headless chickens, now that he is dead.' She cackled, and turned aside, expertly spitting a stream of saliva, coloured red from the beetle nuts she chewed, into the garden.

'They don't know what to do next. I told them that Mala will take care of them. But first, we need these papers to help Mala take over his enterprises. As easy as that – they gave me the papers as soon as I asked.'

Uma aunty's jaw dropped open. Mala and Narsamma, leaders of the underworld?

'The first thing we did was to set the other women free,' Mala said soberly. 'Ponnuswamy owned shares of property in multiple places. I'll put it together, and use it to run a better business. A fair one, where people can earn a decent living. I have offered the other women jobs, if they want them.'

Kaveri beamed. It sounded like a good plan to her. Women would run a good underworld business, a clean and fair one.

A small boy came running in with a note for Kaveri. She read it as the women around her looked on with curiosity. It was from Ramu.

Be ready in half an hour, he had written, in his untidy yet confident doctor's scrawl. *I'll come home and pick you up. Roberts has invited us to his house.*

Kaveri shuddered as she remembered how stricken Roberts had looked when they had summoned him from the hospital.

He had come home to find his wife raving like a madwoman, her pretty golden hair in disarray, her hands curled like claws as she attempted to gouge the face of anyone who came too close.

Kaveri and Ramu had been hurried out by Ismail. 'Go home. Rest. I'll take care of this,' he had insisted.

After a week's leave, today was the first day that both Ramu and Roberts had returned to the hospital. Kaveri knew that Ramu had dreaded facing his boss again. Though he knew that they were not to blame, he was worried that Roberts may be angry, nursing a grudge against Ramu, and even derailing his career. As Rajamma helped her dress, Kaveri thought about a very similar evening just a few weeks previously, when she had been getting ready for dinner at the Century Club.

Was that really only a few weeks ago? she wondered, as Rajamma shook the folds out of her sari again. This time she had selected a heavy silk in a sombre grey colour, as far from festive bright shades as was available in her wardrobe.

The couple were silent as Ramu steered the car towards Roberts' house. Roberts stood at the doorstep, waiting for them. A forlorn figure in a grey suit, he seemed to have shrunk into himself.

Kaveri did not know what to do when she reached him. How could she express what she was feeling? She reached out impulsively, and hugged him. He looked exactly like her favourite uncle had, when his wife of forty years had passed away after an unexpected heart attack. As though the very light had gone out of his life.

Roberts looked startled. Then he hugged her back tightly. Ramu looked on in astonishment. He had never seen his boss look so vulnerable before.

Roberts took them indoors, where the same maid came in with glasses of lemon juice. Kaveri shuddered, remembering the poison-filled glass that Daphne had tried to force on her. 'Only water, please,' she said politely.

Roberts looked at her with haunted eyes, noticing the plasters on her neck. Kaveri put her hand to her neck reflexively. Daphne's knife had left deep cuts on her neck that were still healing.

'I'm so sorry,' Roberts said quietly. 'I don't know what to say.'

Kaveri reached out and gripped his hand tightly.

'Where are the children?' she asked after a moment.

'I sent them with their governess to our friend's home. In Closepet, nearby. He and I come from the same village in England. They have two little girls, the same age as our girls. I thought that would keep them busy.' Roberts smiled ruefully. 'They don't know their mother is in the hospital.'

Kaveri nodded. Daphne had been taken to an asylum for the British in Chennai, Ismail had told them when he'd come to visit Kaveri the day after Daphne's arrest. She had gone completely over the edge, babbling and raving incoherently, trying to attack Roberts, claiming he had affairs with everyone in sight.

'I should tell you that this did not come as a complete surprise,' Roberts said quietly.

Ramu and Kaveri stared at him.

'I don't mean that I knew she had committed the murders,' he said, raising his hands ruefully. 'But she did always have an edge to her. Her mother was the same, you see. When we met, she was a moody, hysterical woman. Some years later, she went completely insane and was committed to a sanatorium. I was beginning to have my worries about Daphne too. Her mood swings were starting to become more violent. She went into rages at times where she would shout at me for hours. She even broke some of our crockery. I was mostly afraid for the girls. She had started to bring it up to them that they were orphans.'

Kaveri started at this.

'Yes,' Roberts said softly. 'Daphne could not bear children. When she was young, she was flung from a horse. Something was broken inside her. Perhaps it was a blessing, as they do not have her genes. We adopted our daughters as babies – friends of ours had passed away in an accident, and their children were left without parents. The girls are too young to remember, and I did not want them to feel unwanted, or different. I was beginning to get very worried about the effect that she was having on them – these past few months, she barely spoke to them, or played with them. They spent more time with their governess than their mother. I had spoken to my sister, and booked tickets on the boat to England next month from Chennai so I could send them to her for a few years. But I was worried about how to break the news to Daphne. In the end I didn't have to.' Roberts sighed. 'But it seems my intuition was correct. Something was deeply wrong with her.'

He stifled a sob, and turned away. Kaveri and Ramu sat in silence, giving him some privacy.

After a while, Roberts spoke up again. 'My sister has left from England. She is unmarried, and lives alone in a small house. She was lonely, and I had invited her over to visit us for a while, but Daphne refused. They did not get along, But now –' His voice trailed away again. 'She offered to come and stay with me for a few years,' he said. 'I think things will be different once she is here.'

Relieved that Roberts seemed to be recovering from the shock of finding that his wife was a murderer, Ramu and Kaveri relaxed, chatting about nothing in particular as they made their way home. Then Kaveri looked at Ramu.

'What?' he asked.

'I was just thinking of how fortunate we are,' she said.

'To have each other?' Ramu reached out and brought her hand to his lips, before putting it back on the wheel, turning into the gate of their home.

'Yes. I hope poor Dr Roberts can have a quieter, more comfortable life now, once his sister moves in. And the children too.'

'Speaking of a quieter life,' Ramu said, then cleared his throat portentously as they got out of the car.

'Yes?' Kaveri said coyly.

'Dare I expect that *my* life may get quieter and more comfortable now that my wife has solved the mystery of the murders? Or will you search for another case now, to keep yourself busy?'

He ducked, laughing, as Kaveri swatted him with her purse, running after him into the house.

Kaveri's Dictionary

ajji – grandmother

akka – older sister, honorific used to address an older woman

amavasya – day of the new moon

ammaavare – mother, honorific used to address an older woman

anna – older brother, honorific used to address an older man

annas – unit of currency – in British India, 16 annas equalled one rupee

appa – father

apsara – celestial Indian spirits famed for their beauty

athige – sister-in-law

ayya – Sir

baalekaayi bajji – deep fried fritters made from raw banana

bidi – hand rolled cigarette

Daakhtre – Doctor

dabba – small box

ekke gida – calatropis plant

firangi – foreigner

kadalebele – lentil

kutcha – unfinished

laddu – round sweet

lathi – large, heavy stick

lungi – loose piece of unstitched cloth worn around the waist by men

kurta – long, loose shirt

naan – flat bread

namaskara – respectful greeting

paan – betel nut leaf, with various additions, commonly eaten after meals

pakora – crisp, deep fried fritters

pallu – the loose end of a sari, usually draped over the shoulder

payasa – Indian sweet

pudi – powder

puja – Hindu rituals of worship

pujari – Hindu priest

raita – side dish of spiced 'yogurt' below in recipes mixed with vegetables

rangoli – a common household art, in which geometric patterns are drawn on the floor in front of a house every morning, using rice powder or chalk – considered auspicious, bringing good luck to the home

rava – semolina, coarsely ground wheat

salwar – traditional trousers, wide at the waist and narrowing at the bottom

sambhar – sour and spicy lentil dish with vegetables

samosa – deep fried pastry with a savoury filling

saaru – sour and spicy watery dish made with lentils

sondige – fried crisps made from sun-dried batter

tandava – divine dance performed by the Hindu God Shiva

tulasi – holy basil

tiffin – light meal of snacks

vada – savoury doughnut-shaped fried snack

Kaveri's Adventures
in the Kitchen

The recipes on the following pages are Kaveri and Ramu's favourites. You can make the five recipes together, for a complete south Indian feast, but they can also be made individually. The original recipes mentioned in *The Bangalore Detectives Club* are fairly complicated and time consuming, but these simplified versions are easy to make – and delicious!

DRINK: Majjige (Salt Lassi)

In the hot summers, Kaveri and Ramu like to catch up on the day's events over a glass of *majjige* in the evening instead of coffee. This is a refreshing drink that can be spiced up in many ways for contemporary tastes. Kaveri prefers her *majjige* plain, but Ramu adds cumin powder to his. Uma aunty, who likes her food spicy, always adds finely chopped green chillies to her glass.

If you're in the mood to celebrate, you can add in a splash of vodka – with some diced green chillies for an extra kick if you're so inclined. Make your *majjige* a bit thicker in that case (by reducing the amount of water, or adding more yogurt).

Ingredients (for four glasses)
1 cup plain yogurt (make sure you buy the unflavoured kind)
4 cups water
1 teaspoon salt (to taste)
1 inch piece of ginger, finely grated
2 tablespoons finely chopped coriander

Optional
1 teaspoon cumin powder
1 teaspoon lemon juice
1 tablespoon finely diced onions
1 tablespoon finely chopped curry leaves

Method
Mix one cup of yogurt with four cups of water in a blender, or using a whisk, till smooth. Add salt, ginger, chopped coriander, and any optional ingredients. Mix well, and pour into tall glasses. Serve chilled, or with ice cubes.

SALAD: Sweet Corn and Pomegranate *Kosambari*

Traditional *kosambari* is made with soaked lentils and grated cucumber or carrot. But this modern-day version, with sweet corn and pomegranate, is equally delicious, and far quicker to make.

Ingredients (feeds four people, if serving as a salad – or two, if eating with soaked lentils as a one-dish meal)
1 cup sweetcorn kernels (frozen or fresh)
1 cup pomegranate seeds
3-4 tablespoons fresh grated coconut (unsweetened)
2 tablespoons finely chopped coriander leaves
1-2 teaspoons salt (to taste)

Optional:
1 tablespoon vegetable oil (any kind except olive oil)
1 teaspoon whole black mustard
1 tablespoon curry leaves
½ cup split, yellow mung dal lentils (you can get this, and curry leaves, at any Indian store, and increasingly, at a number of large supermarkets too).
1-2 green chillies (or more, if you like it spicy!)

Method
Cook the sweetcorn kernels for a couple of minutes on the stove, or in the microwave, until tender. Drain away any excess water. Mix in the pomegranate seeds, coconut, chopped coriander, and salt.

If you want this spicy, mix in some chopped green chillies. If you'd like to add the seasoning, take a smaller pan, heat the vegetable oil for a minute till it begins to smoke, and then turn down the heat. Add the mustard seeds, and wait a minute or two for them to pop. Then add the curry leaves and lentils and roast for a minute or two till they crisp up a bit. Mix the seasoning into the bowl, and serve fresh.

If you want to convert this into a complete meal, add some protein in. Soak the split mung dal lentils for a couple of hours in cold water, then drain out the water, and add the soaked lentils to the *kosambari*.

Note: *You can make this a few hours ahead of time, and leave it in the fridge. But make sure you add the salt just before serving. Otherwise, the mix can become soggy and lose some of its fresh, delicious flavor.*

Main course: *Bisi bele huli anna* (spiced rice with lentils)

This traditional recipe from Karnataka is a sure-fire hit. Kaveri cooked this for the doctors and their families when they came over for lunch, and everyone loved it. The original version is rather complicated, and requires hours of cooking. Here is a contemporary, simpler InstaPot alternative. Traditionally, onions would not be used in this recipe, but they add a lovely flavour.

Ingredients (serves four)
One cup rice
One cup toor lentils, also known as pigeon peas
6 cups water
2 red onions, chopped into large pieces, about 1" size
2 tomatoes, each chopped into eight pieces
1 cup mixed vegetables, 1 inch in size (use any 2-3 of the
    following: green capsicum, potato, peas, beans, cauliflower or
    carrots. Avoid okra, broccoli, courgettes, squash, green leafy
    vegetables or any soft mushy vegetables).
4 tablespoons vegetable oil (any kind except olive oil)
3 tablespoons unsweetened grated or powdered coconut
1 teaspoon turmeric powder
2-3 tablespoons bisibele bath powder, or sambhar powder
    (MTR is a good brand to get – if it's not available, just get
    any other brand)
½ teaspoon tamarind concentrate
1 tablespoon finely chopped curry leaves
1 tablespoon ghee
2 teaspoons salt (to taste)
1 large bag of potato crisps

Method

Soak the rice and lentils in the instapot with six cups of water for about 30 minutes. Then add the oil, curry leaves, onions, tomatoes, vegetables, and all remaining ingredients, reserving the ghee. Set the InstaPot to Pressure Cook, keeping the timer set for 8 minutes. Once cooked, it may seem a little watery, but the mix will thicken over a couple of hours. Stir in a tablespoon of ghee just before serving.

Traditionally, this would be served with fried pappads or *sandige* (fried crisps made from sun-dried batter). But it tastes fabulous with potato crisps too. Get the regular, unflavoured kind – and make sure you buy a large bag or two. It's a good idea to double the recipe. *Bisi bele huli anna* is one of those dishes where leftovers are king (or queen!) – this tastes even better the next day

Side dish: Beans *paliya* (dry beans curry)

An easy side dish of vegetables, which can be eaten by itself, or (more typically) with rice or chapatti. This is Kaveri's go-to recipe when she's working on a mystery or a maths problem, and is rushed for time.

Ingredients (serves four as a side-dish)
Two cups green beans, chopped into 1 cm pieces
2 tablespoons fresh grated or dessicated coconut
  (make sure it's unsweetened!)
2 tablespoons vegetable oil (avoid olive oil)
1 teaspoon turmeric powder
1 teaspoon black mustard seeds
1 tablespoon coriander leaves
2 teaspoons salt (to taste)

Optional
Asafoetida powder (available in Indian stores, and many large
  supermarkets)
1 teaspoon chilli powder or a couple of green chillies – if you
  like it hot

Recipe
Heat the oil in a large pan on the stove for a minute, then and add a pinch of asafetida powder (if you have some). Add in the mustard seeds, and wait for them to pop. Then add the beans, and roast for about five minutes, stirring frequently. Add a splash of water, and cover the lid for about ten minutes till the beans

soften and cook through. Make sure you open the lid every few minutes and stir it, adding more water as needed to prevent the beans from sticking to the bottom of the pan. Once the beans are soft and cooked through, but not mushy, remove the lid. Add the turmeric powder, coconut, salt, and chilli powder/ green chillies (if using). Mix, and serve.

This is a very flexible recipe, which you can adapt to use with a number of different vegetables – including cabbage, carrots, beetroot, cauliflower, sweet potato, and okra.

Dry fruit *laddus*

These laddus are Ismail's favourite go-to snack. As a policeman frequently on the road, he misses a number of meals – and a man of his size needs regular feeding! His wife ensures he carries a small box of laddus in his pocket at all times. Ramu loves it too, and makes a batch on weekends, for Kaveri to carry with her when she goes swimming.

This is an incredibly tasty, nutritious, homemade alternative to trail mix and energy bars, and a favourite with most kids. Best of all, they are super quick to make.

Ingredients (for about twenty laddus)
¼ cup each of any four of your favourite nuts or seeds (you can safely use cashew, almond, walnut, pistachio, macadamia, pecan, sunflower seeds, or pumpkin seeds. I recommend against using flaxseeds or chia seeds, though).
½ cup soft deseeded dates
¼ cup figs
¼ cup raisins

Optional
½ teaspoon cardamom powder
1 teaspoon lightly toasted sesame seeds
2 tablespoons dessicated coconut flakes
2 tablespoons ghee or honey

Recipe
Lightly roast the nuts for a couple of minutes on the stove, or in a microwave, and set aside to cool. Separately roast the sunflower, pumpkin and sesame seeds. Chop the nuts, dates, figs and raisins

coarsely with a knife, or in a food processor. Mix in the seeds and add in any optional ingredients you'd like at this time. The mix should be soft, and you should be able to shape these into round balls – *laddus* – with your hand. If it's hard and difficult to shape (which can happen if the dates and raisins are hard), add a couple of tablespoons of ghee or honey to make it stick together.

These will last for at least a week outside, and a couple of weeks in the refrigerator. You'll probably find you eat them much faster, though!

A Note on the Setting

As a 'princely state', Mysore State was in the unusual position of having two rulers. It was ruled directly by the Maharaja, and indirectly by the British. With the Maharaja as a buffer between the British and the local population, the nationalist Indian independence movement was relatively slow to take off in Mysore State in the 1920s, gaining momentum in the 1930s. But rumbles of discontent and anger were evident in the 1920s, even if kept carefully hidden from those in power.

Bangalore was Mysore State's largest city. The local population of Indians lived in the old *pete*, and new areas like Basavanagudi, where Ramu and Kaveri made their home. Europeans lived in the part of Bangalore known as the Civil and Military Station, or the cantonment. The kings and queens of Mysore State were progressive. They encouraged education, and promoted women's rights. Child marriage was banned, child widows were educated and encouraged to remarry, and many girls went to primary school. Very few girls – less than 2 in every 1,000 – made it all the way to high school though.

Those who did complete high school, such as Kaveri, could go to 'girls' colleges' such as the Maharani's college in Mysore, and the Vani Vilas Institute in Bangalore. Young women were discouraged from taking courses in 'boys colleges' such as the Central College in Bangalore, because many disapproved of male teachers being allowed to teach women – a real catch-22 situation. Who would teach the first women, then?

Because of these notions, science remained the preserve of men in the early 1920s. Though the Maharaja and Maharani promoted women's education, they were heavily opposed by other influential men. Women were not allowed to enrol in BSc courses, to apply to the Mysore Civil Services, or even to vote. In 1922, one legislator said defiantly 'it will be one century before we can get one woman to vote in the villages and other places.'

Fortunately, it didn't take that long. But young women like Kaveri had an uphill task ahead of them.

Acknowledgements

Kaveri and Ramu first dropped into my head in the summer of 2007, when Kaveri insistently demanded that I write a book about her. It took me 13 years to get there! Venkatachalam Suri and Dhwani Nagendra Suri, my husband and daughter, brainstormed ideas with me, and patiently proofread multiple drafts. Dhwani was not yet born when I started writing *The Bangalore Detectives Club* – it has been so lovely to watch the book come to life as she grew, started to read and added her strong feminist perspective. And without Chalam, who has been my support, inspiration and bouncing board for ideas for close to 30 years, none of this would be possible. They propelled me along with their energy, enthusiasm and love.

Since Bangalore's history is an area of professional research for me (as part of my day job as an ecologist), I benefited from a treasure trove of information on colonial Bangalore. I am indebted to a number of archives, including the Karnataka State Archives, the Mythic Society, the Indian Institute of World Culture, and the British Library. Family stories, reminiscences and recipes shared by my mother Manjula gave me an intimate view into the lives of women and men who lived more than a century ago, impossible to get from books and maps alone.

Priya Doraswamy, childhood friend and incomparable agent, loved the idea of a book on Bangalore, our favourite city. She has helped me through half-written drafts, and been the best advocate for the book that I could ever wish for. And I truly lucked out with a dream team at Little, Brown, with brilliant editorial inputs from Sarah Murphy and Krystyna Green, and Tom Feltham's insightful copyedits.

Finally, this book is a tribute to all the remarkable women who lived in previous times, on whom Kaveri, Mala and Uma aunty are modelled. Defying societal restrictions to forge their own path, they blazed the way for generations to follow.

Harini Nagendra is a professor of ecology at Azim Premji University. Her previous books include *Nature in the City: Bengaluru in the Past, Present and Future*, and *Cities and Canopies: Trees in Indian Cities*, which won Book of the Year at the Publishing Next Awards in 2020. *The Bangalore Detectives Club* is her first crime fiction novel. She lives in Bangalore with her family, in a home filled with maps. She loves trees, mysteries, and traditional recipes.